NAUGHTY ON ICE

Also by Maia Chance

DISCREET RETRIEVAL AGENCY MYSTERIES

Gin and Panic
Teetotaled
Come Hell or Highball

FAIRY TALE FATAL MYSTERIES

Beauty, Beast, and Belladonna
Cinderella Six Feet Under
Snow White Red-Handed

AGNES AND EFFIE MYSTERIES

Bad Neighbors
Bad Housekeeping

NAUGHTY ON ICE

Maia Chance

MINOTAUR BOOKS
New York

This is a work of fiction. All of the characters, organizations, and events portrayed in this novel are either products of the author's imagination or are used fictitiously.

Printed in the United States of America. For information, address St. Martin's Press, 175 Fifth Avenue, New York, N.Y. 10010.

www.minotaurbooks.com

Library of Congress Cataloging-in-Publication Data

Names: Chance, Maia, author.
Title: Naughty on ice / Maia Chance.
Description: First edition. | New York: Minotaur Books, 2018.
Identifiers: LCCN 2018022775| ISBN 9781250109071 (hardcover) |
ISBN 9781250109088 (ebook)
Subjects: LCSH: Women private investigators—Fiction. |
Murder—Investigation—Fiction. | GSAFD: Mystery fiction.
Classification: LCC PS3603.H35593 N38 2018 | DDC 813/.6—dc23
LC record available at https://lccn.loc.gov/2018022775

Our books may be purchased in bulk for promotional, educational, or business use. Please contact your local bookseller or the Macmillan Corporate and Premium Sales Department at 1-800-221-7945, extension 5442, or by email at MacmillanSpecialMarkets@macmillan.com.

First Edition: November 2018

10 9 8 7 6 5 4 3 2 1

For Henry and Aesa

What normal healthy girl doesn't like to be both smart and naughty!

—Colleen Moore in

Chicago Daily News, 1922

NAUGHTY ON ICE

Prologue

It was a medium-size, rectangular envelope. Postmark: Burlington, Vermont. No return address. Patchy lines from a typewriter in need of a fresh ribbon read,

```
The Discreet Retrieval Agency
9 Longfellow Street, Apt. B
New York, New York
```

And inside, the most humdrum of Christmas cards. You know the sort: golden, scrolly script commanding *Have a Merry Christmas* across the background of a snug village, white-steepled church, frosty fir trees, and ice skaters.

The typewritten poem inside, however, was distinctly lacking in yuletide feeling.

```
When it comes to fetching stolen things
They say you ladies are rather grand.
```

So could you retrieve my stolen ring
From Aunt Daphne's thieving hand?

Auntie's boozy thirst she slakes—
Expect neither protest nor wail.
Leave ring in breadbox—piece of cake!
Expect payment in the mail.

Anonymous
requests the Honor of
the Discreet Retrieval Agency's Presence
Drinks and Dinner
Goddard Farm
Maple Hill, Vermont
December 19, 1923
Eight o'clock

1

Maple Hill, Vermont
December 19, 1923

The circumstances, I do realize, were ghastly. A chunk was missing from the molasses layer cake on the kitchen table. A corpse lay, probably still warmish, out on the living room carpet. And I was aware that, having been caught in the act of removing a ruby ring from an elderly lady's finger, my detecting partner, Berta Lundgren, and I looked as guilty as masked bandits in Tiffany's.

The policeman, who had announced himself as Sergeant Peletier, stood over the kitchen table, wearing an *Oho, what have we here?* expression. "You're the uninvited guests, I reckon," he said. "Mrs. Lundgren and Mrs. Woodby?"

"We were invited," Berta said coldly.

"That's not what I was told," Peletier said. He surveyed drunken Aunt Daphne, the ring, and the cake. "Having a bit of dessert with a side of jewel thieving, I see. Mighty funny thing to do right after your hostess has expired."

"Aghamee do eshplain," I said.

"I beg your pardon?" Peletier said.

I swallowed cake. "Allow me to explain," I repeated.

This wasn't the plan. The plan had been to retrieve the ring, pop it in the breadbox, slink out of the house, and skip town on the next train out.

"Yes," Peletier said. "Please explain. Mrs. Goddard lies dead in the other room, and you're here in the kitchen shimmying a ring off Mrs. Lyle's finger?"

At the mention of her name, Aunt Daphne raised her champagne glass. "Cheers," she crowed.

"I will explain," Berta butted in. She was a rosy, gray-bunned lady of sixty-odd years who spoke with a faint Swedish accent and resembled a garden gnome. "What you see before you is a tried-and-true method for removing stuck rings from fingers—fingers, you understand, that have . . . expanded."

We all regarded Aunt Daphne's fingers, which, short and plump and swollen, resembled a litter of Dachshund puppies. The too-small ring had been maneuvered to just below the knuckle with Berta's trick of looping embroidery thread under the ring, winding the thread tightly around the finger, and then unwinding the thread from the bottom. With each loop that was unwound, the ring edged up another millimeter. The downside was that it looked rather painful. However, Aunt Daphne, drinking champagne and shoveling cake with her free hand, had yet to complain. There really are no better painkillers than cake and booze.

"My mother always used butter to remove stuck rings," Peletier said.

"A pound of butter wouldn't get this thing off me," Aunt Daphne said. "Believe me, I've tried it! This darned thing's been stuck on my finger since the summer of 1919."

"When you stole it," I prompted.

"Stole it?" Aunt Daphne snickered, and with her free hand she lifted the glass of champagne to her lips and polished it off. "I never said that!"

"Yes, you did." Panic zinged through me. I turned to look up at Peletier. "She stole it. She told us she did. In the summer of 1919. We have merely been, um, asked to remove it."

"By Mrs. Lyle, here?"

"Well, no. . . ."

"Sounds like thievery to me. And now, coincidentally, Mrs. Goddard is dead."

My cheeks were growing hot. "As I said, Aunt Daphne stole the ring, and we are merely attempting to restore it to its rightful— Hold it. What are you suggesting? 'Coincidentally'? Mrs. Goddard died of a heart attack, didn't she? That's what it appeared to—"

"Oh, no, no, no," Peletier said. "It was poison."

"Poison!"

"I smelled it on her breath. Cyanide. Likely in the cocktail she'd been drinking at the time of her death."

"Are you certain?" I said. "I happened to notice she was drinking a Negroni. Those are made with Campari, you know, which itself is as bitter as poison—"

"'Happened to notice,' eh? Any chance you fixed it for her?"

"No!"

Phooey. It had been Berta's idea to carry on with the ring-retrieval job even after Judith Goddard had kicked the bucket about an hour earlier. Having nothing else to do while waiting for the authorities to turn up, we had conferred in the butler's pantry amid the family silver. I had whispered that it was unseemly to filch a ring under the circumstances. Berta had whispered, "Oh no, we did not come all the way up here to the snowy wilds of Vermont for nothing, we are finishing the job." I had conceded. Our train tickets had been costly.

Now I gave Berta a bug-eyed *I told you so* look.

She ignored it and busied herself with completing the ring removal.

"Oh, all right," I said to Peletier with a sigh. "The jig is up. We're private detectives—"

"Go along!" Peletier said.

"Truly."

"Ha-ha-ha!" Peletier slapped his thigh.

"Did you bring a card, Mrs. Woodby?" Berta asked.

"No. You?"

Berta flicked Peletier a frosty look. "I did not expect to be asked to provide my credentials this evening. Ah! There. The ring is—" She wiggled it from Aunt Daphne's fingertip. "—off."

"You're an angel of mercy," Aunt Daphne said to Berta. "Thank you. My! Just look at the divot it left behind." She massaged her finger, and then helped herself to more champagne.

"Buying that's against the law, you know," Peletier said, pointing to the champagne bottle.

"Oh, to Hell with your Eighteenth Amendment," Aunt Daphne said. "It's for the dogs. And politicians and church ladies."

"Would you mind if I placed the ring in the breadbox?" Berta asked Aunt Daphne.

"Not at all. I never want to see that thing again."

Berta went to put the ring in the metal breadbox on the counter—*plink*—and then sat back down.

Peletier pulled out one of the ladder-back chairs, sat, and extracted a notebook and pencil from inside his coat. He was small and wiry, with a flushed face, beady eyes, and tufting gray hair and eyebrows. He called to mind a disgruntled North Pole elf. His embroidered badge read MAPLE HILL, VT POLICE and featured a deer and a pine tree. Cute.

"Start at the beginning," he said.

In a tumbling back-and-forth, Berta and I explained to Peletier that we were private detectives with our own small agency in New York City. How, last week, we'd received an invitation from an anonymous sender asking us to dinner at Goddard Farm, requesting that we retrieve a stolen ring, place it in the breadbox, and to subsequently expect payment in the mail. That we'd only arrived in Maple Hill earlier that afternoon, having taken the night train, and that we had rooms at the Old Mill Inn only for that evening. How Anonymous had not revealed him- or herself to us upon our arrival at Goddard Farm (really a mansion on a ridge above the village).

How we'd been gobsmacked when Judith Goddard went toes-up only fifteen minutes after our arrival.

"I understand that this was a family gathering to celebrate Mrs. Goddard's recent engagement," Peletier said. "How did you explain your appearance at a family affair?"

"Well, at *first* it was a bit awkward," I said. Only Judith Goddard, her brother Roy, her aunt Daphne, Judith's three adult children, her brand-new fiancé, and two servant women had been present in the house. "*You* know how it i—"

"We had no choice but to fabricate an explanation," Berta interrupted. She was serenely sawing the molasses cake.

"They said that I invited them," Aunt Daphne said. "That we'd met at a ladies' poetry luncheon at the country club in Cleveland. I can't remember much anymore, of course, and poetry knocks me out cold, so I didn't realize that they were lying—"

"Mrs. Woodby and I are innocent of any wrongdoing," Berta said. "We were merely doing our job. Surely, Sergeant Peletier, you are able to understand that."

Peletier snorted and stood. "Come down to the station tomorrow morning, and if you can show me this anonymous invitation of yours, maybe I'll let you off the hook. Until then, don't even think about leaving town. Good evening." He left the kitchen, Aunt Daphne drifting after him with the champagne bottle.

Berta and I looked at each other across the collapsing cake.

"Would it be absolutely unconscionable to leave right now?" I whispered.

"There has been a death in the family, Mrs. Woodby, and we are strangers. We should leave them to their grief."

"Maybe there is something we could do to help—"

"There is nothing worse than having to speak with strangers when one's heart is breaking."

Honestly, I hadn't gotten the impression that Judith Goddard's demise was cracking anyone's heart in two. Not even the heart of her fiancé-to-be. "They aren't an especially happy family," I said, "but I suppose none are. Happy families are a myth."

"Nonsense. You must simply know one when you see it. They sometimes come in unusual forms. Now, come along. After we show the invitation to Sergeant Peletier in the morning, our hands will be washed clean of this terrible affair."

I felt like an absolute gink as we sneaked to the entry hall to fetch our coats, hats, scarves, and gloves. We didn't encounter any of the family or the servants, although voices rose and fell in distant rooms.

We stepped out the front door into the night. Our breath billowed in the icy air. Berta bent her head into the wind and toddled toward our rented pickup truck, an REO Speedwagon with a boxy cab and wooden rails around the bed. She winched herself up into the passenger seat.

I followed, mincing like Comet or Cupid through the crunchy snow in my high heels. I took the hand crank from the cab floor, resuscitated the engine, climbed behind the wheel, flicked on the headlamps, and we were off.

"Oh, it is so very cold," Berta said with a shiver. "As cold as I remember Sweden being when I was a girl, but I am no longer young."

I inched the truck down a steep, snow-packed road. Bristling black forest encroached from beyond the headlamp beams. I was accustomed to the glitter and hum of Manhattan. Nighttime in the countryside was giving me the jumps.

"I have a bad feeling about this," I said.

"If you slip, steer into the slide. That is the only way to avoid a tailspin."

"Not that. The *murder*."

"We will be on our way home tomorrow."

How I wished I could believe it.

2

The next morning, I awoke disoriented in my small room at the Old Mill Inn. Where was I, and why was the air so cold and quiet?

Then it all rushed back like a herd of Pamplona bulls: Vermont. The ring-retrieval job. That unpleasant Goddard family. *Murder.*

Ugh.

After bathing, I bundled up, stuffed my small Pomeranian dog, Cedric, into a red-and-white snowflake sweater, and took him outside to pay a call upon a picket fence. He had been a very good boy the previous evening when I'd been up at Goddard Farm. Left alone in my room, he'd disemboweled only one pillow.

Maple Hill, Vermont, was snuggled into a river valley amid low-lying farms and rolling mountains. It wasn't the blink-and-miss-it size of some New England villages, but it could barely be classified as a town. Though prosperous looking, it boasted only one commercial street—hardware store, general store, a few shops and cafés, attorney's office, two churches, and, in the middle of it all, the bulky, three-storied Old Mill Inn. From behind River Street stretched a straggling web of houses, town hall, library, a knitting factory, and a large building with a sign reading ROGERSON'S BRAND MAPLE SYRUP. On the other side of River Street, the frozen river wandered away down the valley, fringed with leafless thickets.

Inside once more, I packed my suitcase and set it beside the door in readiness to depart. There was one afternoon train out of Maple Hill, along an electric line running the ten miles to Waterbury. In Waterbury, one could board the train that ran daily between Montreal and New London, Connecticut. From New London, it was but a hop, skip, and a jump to Grand Central Station and home.

When I strolled into the inn's dining room and spotted Berta at a window table, I instantly knew that something was the matter. Her cheeks were ashen, her lips pinched. Hugging Cedric close, I weaved my way through the busy tables. Cedric tipped his nose to the air, which was warmly aromatic with maple and bacon.

"What is it?" I asked, sitting down across from Berta. "I haven't seen you look so upset since the Giants slathered the Yankees in the World Series last—wait—you aren't ill, are you?"

"No."

"Well?" I plopped Cedric at my feet.

"Disaster."

"Of what variety?"

"The dossier has gone missing."

"*No.*"

"Yes."

"When?"

"I am not certain. It was in my suitcase, in the inner pocket with my extra wool stockings."

Berta, always thorough, had taken to compiling dossiers for each of our cases. Some of her research was conducted in the periodicals room of the Main Branch of the New York Public Library. Some of it was done on the telephone, or while pretending to gossip at the laundry or the butcher. Berta knew people who knew people.

The ANON. INVITATION CASE 12-17-1923 dossier (as Berta had labeled it) contained the following:

- The invitation (a Christmas card with typed verse inside), with original envelope.
- A clipping from last Friday's *Cleveland Courier* society gossip page, depicting Judith Goddard and her soon-to-be fiancé, Maynard Coburn, in black-tie dress, on the steps of the Cleveland Museum of Art. (The caption made no mention of the impending engagement.)
- Notes Berta had taken on several other library-owned issues of *The Cleveland Courier.* Mentions of Rosemary Rogerson, Mrs. Goddard's daughter, and son-in-law, Wilfred Rogerson (a cash-and-carry grocery store tycoon). Mentions of George Goddard, Judith's elder son (a playboy bachelor). One mention of the presence of Daphne Lyle, a widowed aunt of Judith's, at the Cleveland country club poetry luncheon.
- An issue of *The Country Gentleman* magazine, dated December 1922, containing an advertisement for Chesterfield cigarettes featuring Maynard Coburn, the nearly famous ski jumper and alpine skier.
- An issue of *Physical Culture* magazine, dated January 1923, with Maynard Coburn's likeness on the cover, skiing handsomely.
- Brief notes on Rosemary Rogerson's two books, both put out by a prominent New York publisher in the last three years: *Mrs. Rogerson's Practical Guide to Housekeeping,* and

Mrs. Rogerson's Practical Guide to Childrearing. (Berta had written, *officious, rigid, and snobbish advice—and regrettably ill informed with regards to the health benefits of butter.*)

- Train schedule of the electric line between Waterbury and Maple Hill.

And now Berta was saying the whole kit and caboodle was missing.

"I did not think to check if the dossier was in my suitcase last night," Berta said. "How could I guess that a thief would break into my room and pilfer it? But I did check for it this morning, as I was packing. It is gone."

"When was the last time you saw it?"

"Not since I packed my suitcase in New York, the day before yesterday."

"Could it have slipped under the suitcase lining or something?"

"I checked."

"Could it have fallen out of your suitcase somewhere between New York and here?"

"I always keep my suitcase locked during train journeys."

"But who would steal the dossier? And why?"

"To keep us in Maple Hill, perhaps." Berta leaned forward. "You must recall that Sergeant Peletier said we could leave town only if we produce the invitation, and now that invitation has vanished."

"But *that* could mean—"

"This could be a frame-up job. Yes. As I said, it is a disaster." With shaking hands, Berta poured out steaming cups of coffee for us both from the pot on the table.

I doused my coffee with cream. I drank some. Then I took a stab at sounding plucky and levelheaded. "Perhaps Sergeant Peletier will see reason and allow us to go home anyway."

"That is unlikely."

"Well, we must try. We'll go straight to the police station after breakfast. I don't want to miss today's train out of here." I wasn't going to mention it, but I had a dinner and dancing date for the following evening with my gentleman caller and maddening distraction, Ralph Oliver, PI. He'd been away for weeks on a case in Chicago, and I was perishing to see him, ideally beneath a sprig of mistletoe.

"Oh! Our waitress is coming," Berta whispered. "When she brought the coffee earlier, I recognized her."

"Really? Where di—?"

"*Shush*, Mrs. Woodby."

A waitress appeared beside our table, a slim, golden-bobbed young woman with large, thick-lashed blue eyes, a storybook sort of beauty. "Could I take your orders, please?" she asked in a sweet voice.

I, too, had seen this young woman before.

"Good morning," I said. "I beg your pardon, but weren't you working at Goddard Farm last night?"

"Yes." The waitress gave Berta and me closer looks. "Oh yes, and you're the women who turned up uninvited. You fibbed and said Mrs. Lyle invited you, but Sergeant Peletier said that really, you're private detectives from New York City—"

"Please—" Berta's eyes darted around the dining room. "—we prefer to remain *discreet*."

"Sorry. I'm Patience. Patience Yarker. Mrs. Goddard hired me from time to time to help out up at the house when there were a lot of guests. Which wasn't very often, these past few years. Hester Albans manages by herself when it is—*was*—only Mrs. Goddard and Fenton staying. No one lives in that house year-round, you see."

"Hester Albans was the other woman working at the house last night?" I asked. I'd glimpsed a rangy, dour woman in an apron a few times. She had attended to Mrs. Goddard's hysterical daughter after the death.

"That's right. But I reckon you'll be leaving this afternoon, won't you?"

Golly, I hope so. "Perhaps," I said.

Patience's eyes widened. "Oh. And . . . have you . . . have you spoken to Hester about last night?"

"No," I said.

"Oh, well, good."

"Why is that?" Berta asked.

"It's nothing, only that Hester tends to be . . . superstitious, I suppose you'd call it. She said she saw a-a *thing* last night. Out the windows at Goddard Farm."

My scalp prickled. "What sort of thing?"

"She called it a—" Patience swallowed. "—a 'furry critter.'"

I racked my brain, trying to think what sort of creatures roamed northern Vermont. "A moose?"

"She said it was, well, 'walking upright'—"

"Upright!" Berta said, touching the locket she always wore at her throat.

"—but you ought to ask Hester about it, really. I only mentioned it because, well—" Patience bit her lip. "—I don't want you to suppose we're all backward hayseeds here in Maple Hill."

"Of course we don't," I said. "Mrs. Lundgren and I both grew up in rural places, you know." I had whiled away my formative years in Scragg Springs, Indiana, before Mother had decided a career change for Father was in order and we moved to be within pillaging distance of Wall Street.

Patience was fidgeting with her apron tie. "Isn't it just awful about Mrs. Goddard?"

"Shocking," I said.

"I'm awfully sorry for her children," Patience said. "I've known them my whole life, you see. They came to Maple Hill every summer growing up."

"Did you play with them?" I asked.

"Only a little, and on the sly, out in the fields or down by the river, when their nurserymaids and tutors lost track of them. Their mother didn't want them consorting with the rural folks." Patience sighed. "Poor Fenton. He was so attached to his mother, went everywhere with her . . . now I just don't know *what* he'll do."

Fenton was the younger of Judith's two sons, a wan, stringy young man of about twenty years.

Berta said, "But his mother was about to remarry. Surely Fenton would have set out on his own then? Or gone back to college?"

"Fenton doesn't attend college. He lives—lived—with his mother in Cleveland."

"Mrs. Goddard mentioned something about a long honeymoon in Europe," I said. "Was Fenton planning on tagging along for that?" I pictured Judith and Maynard Coburn at the Eiffel Tower, motoring along the cliffs of Capri, and yachting amid Greek isles, all with silent, heavily pomaded Fenton in tow. "That sounds . . . unusual."

"Fenton *is*. Unusual, I mean to say."

Berta cleared her throat. "Patience, a small, rather insignificant item has gone missing from my suitcase," she said in a grandmotherly tone. "I know that I locked the door to my room when I was out yesterday evening. Tell me, who has access to the room keys?"

Patience's eyes widened. "I'm terribly sorry to hear that, Mrs. Lundgren. We've never had anything stolen from any of our guests before. Dad takes pride in that."

"Your father is—?"

"Samuel Yarker. The innkeeper."

"He checked us in yesterday, yes," Berta said.

"This inn is our family's place." Patience lifted her chin a notch. "Always has been."

"Ah. And . . . the keys?"

"Well, there's only the numbered room keys, one of each—we keep those behind the front desk."

As in most hotels, at the Old Mill Inn one turned in one's room key before going out.

"There are no other keys?" Berta asked.

"No. The cleaning women use the room keys." Patience glanced over her shoulder. "Grandma will give me a stern word if I don't hurry up and take your orders. We're awfully busy this weekend on account of the Winter Carnival."

For the past ten years or so, winter carnivals had popped up all over the map in northern climes, from Winnipeg to Portland, Maine, offering festivities like skating, toboggan racing, sleigh rides, and ice-sculpture carving. Some local club usually sponsored the things. I'd been told that the final preparations for Maple Hill's annual Winter Carnival were under way, so merrymakers were arriving to fill every boardinghouse, inn, and spare room for miles around.

With any luck, I'd be missing the carnival.

Berta and I ordered sausage and johnnycakes with maple syrup, and I asked for extra sausage and a bowl of water for Cedric. Patience slipped away.

"Should we ask Patience, or her father the innkeeper, where the police station is?" I asked Berta.

"No, indeed. We cannot have them knowing we are mixed up in this bad business. After all, we could end up needing to stay an extra night. We should inquire elsewhere in the village."

I thought, but did not say aloud, that Patience Yarker herself was mixed up in this bad business, too, if only by happenstance. After all, she had been in the room when Mrs. Goddard's drink was poisoned.

3

After breakfast, Cedric and I bundled up to go outside again—Cedric in his sweater, I in my coat, hat, gloves, and the fur-lined, high-heeled boots I'd splurged on at Wright's Department Store on Fifth Avenue the previous week. I made certain I had several Discreet Retrieval Agency business cards inside my handbag, and as an afterthought, I tucked Cedric's favorite red rubber ball in my handbag, too. He did not always consent to walk in the snow, in which case I would need to throw his ball so he'd get a spot of exercise.

I encountered Berta in the upstairs corridor. She, in serviceable, flat-heeled, shin-high lace-up snow boots, clucked her tongue when she saw my choice of kicks.

"They're comfortable," I lied, "and anyway, I feel just like a motion picture star."

This was only a little bit true. Yes, I was blessed with a shiny brunet Dutch bob, large blue eyes, and a happy mouth. And given plenty of sleep, a minimum of bathtub gin, and a maximum of Guerlain lipstick, I was generally considered rather fetching. However, motion-picture stars were always lithesome paper dolls, whereas my own figure was unrelentingly three-dimensional. Not that Ralph Oliver, for one, had ever filed a complaint.

"You shall be singing a different tune shortly," Berta said to me. "A tune of blisters and twisted ankles."

"Hooey."

Downstairs in the lobby, we passed the innkeeper, Samuel Yarker (and, we now knew, Patience's father), reading the *Burlington Daily Free Press* behind the front desk.

"Morning," he said, and promptly coughed. He was perhaps fifty years old, gnarled by the elements, with the figure of a beer keg, and bushy blond hair. Even though the lobby was warmed by a coal fire, a green tartan scarf was bundled and knotted around his throat.

"Good morning," Berta and I chimed in unison.

I felt Samuel's eyes on us all the way out the door.

"There's the general store," I said, blinking in the sudden cold. Hopefully my Maybelline Cake Mascara was up to the challenge. I pointed across the street. "Someone in there will know where to find the police station. Let's buy something, and then ask in a casual, offhand fashion."

"I am not certain it is possible to be offhand when asking about the fuzz," Berta said, "but very well."

We picked around snowbanks and parked vehicles, crossed the street, and went inside. The store was dimly lit, heated by a potbellied stove, and fragrant with the mingled aromas of coffee grounds, yeast, and spices. Worn floorboards creaked underfoot.

A man in a wool jacket sat behind the counter, gnawing on an unlit pipe and sorting through his till. "Morning," he called without looking up.

Berta and I perused the shop, which sold everything from tinned smoked oysters and salt crackers (in a barrel—I hadn't seen a cracker barrel since I'd left Scragg Springs!) to garden shovels and chintz tablecloths. We lingered at a display of maple syrup and maple sugar candies. Cedric, tail swishing, sniffed the shelf displaying cloth-wrapped sausages.

I selected a box of maple sugar candies and carried them to the counter.

"In town for the Winter Carnival merriments, I reckon?" the shopkeeper said as he took my dollar bill.

"Actually," I said, "we wish to visit the, um—" I swallowed audibly. "—the police station?"

"That so?" The shopkeeper's eyebrows lifted. He slid my change across the countertop. "Well, then, go west along River Street, which turns into the Waterbury highway. It's, oh, a mile, mile and a quarter out of town. Can't miss it."

The bell on the door tinkled, and the shopkeeper glanced past Berta and me. "Morning, Titus," he called.

A big, lantern-jawed fellow loped inside. A greasy-looking red cap was pulled down over shaggy black hair. His coat and boots appeared to have been many-times mended.

The man—Titus—said nothing to the shopkeeper, but went straight to a large electric icebox against the rear wall. A handwritten sign affixed to the icebox's wooden door said *MILK BUTTER EGGS*. He unlatched the door, stooped, reached past the front two rows of milk bottles, and pulled one from the very back, causing all the bottles to shudder and clink. He shut the icebox, went to the counter with the milk tucked under his arm, and, shoving an outlandishly long arm between Berta and me, slapped a quarter on the counter. Then he was gone with a bang of the door and a jingle of the bell.

"Peculiar one, that Titus Staples," the shopkeeper said, plucking the coin off the counter. "Always takes the bottle of milk from the back corner."

"Perhaps he believes it will be fresher," Berta said.

"Not in my store. I get new milk every morning—one bottle is as fresh as all the others. Anything I don't sell I give away at the end of the day to Widow Arthur. She's got six children, you understand. No, Titus just isn't right in the head." The shopkeeper opened his cash register, dropped the quarter inside, and slammed it shut—*briiing-clang.*

I wedged the maple sugar candies into my handbag, next to Cedric's rubber ball. "Thank you for the directions," I said.

"Stolen, eh?" Sergeant Peletier said to Berta and me, once we'd told him our tale of woe. "Stolen right out of your suitcase, in a locked room? A likely story."

"I beg your pardon?" Berta drew herself up.

We both stood in front of Peletier's untidy desk. Cedric was slung over my arm. The police station was a tiny, squat brick building that smelled of wet socks. There was but one room, and only two policemen—Peletier and a pale, doughy fellow called Clarence, who was making coffee on a kerosene burner in the corner.

"I've been thinking it over." Peletier leaned back in his chair and crossed his arms. "I reckon you made up the story about that invitation. Oh, I know you've got yourself a silly little ladies' detective agency—I already telephoned down to the New York City police to confirm that—but I reckon finding lost cats and stolen umbrellas isn't really paying the bills, so you decided to do a little thieving to cover the rent. You came up here to Goddard Farm, cased the house, poisoned Judith Goddard, and then set about stealing the family jewels."

"That doesn't make a bit of sense," I said. "To begin with, we didn't steal Aunt Daphne's ring. We left it in the breadbox. You saw Mrs. Lundgren put it there!"

Berta asked, "Have any family jewels gone missing?"

"You tell me."

Berta opened her mouth as though she would tell Peletier something, all right.

I delicately trod upon her toe.

She shut her mouth.

"You two are up to no good, and we're going to figure out exactly what it is—isn't that right, Clarence?"

"Oh, sure," Clarence said. His coffee was coming to a boil.

Peletier gave Berta and me a stern look. "Don't you dare leave Maple Hill until this is sorted out."

"But—"

"What's more, if we catch that dog of yours doing his business where he shouldn't—" Peletier gave Cedric a loathing look. "—it's off to the pound in Waterbury for him. Lots of real big dogs in the pound. That clear?"

Clarence snickered.

I pressed Cedric so tightly to my chest, he paddled his paws in protest. "Quite."

Berta said nothing, but merely spun on her heel to go.

"Oh," Peletier shouted as we went out the door, "and Merry Christmas!"

Numb, I got behind the wheel of the Speedwagon—the engine was still warm, so it didn't require cranking—and shakily shifted into reverse.

"Drat," Berta said. "I have not mailed my Christmas cards yet."

"That's the least of our worries!" I cried. "That—that rotten *elf* thinks we're killers!"

"Calm yourself, Mrs. Woodby, and please do keep your eyes on the road."

I drove for a bit, half-blinded by sunlight bouncing off snow, snow everywhere. My thoughts spun just like the ice crystals flurrying behind the Speedwagon. "Obviously, we have to figure out who killed

Mrs. Goddard ourselves," I said, "because it doesn't appear that Sergeant Peletier is going to do it."

"It seems that we have no choice in the matter."

"Why is it that we never have any choice in the matter?"

"I wish I knew, Mrs. Woodby."

The first order of business was securing our rooms at the Old Mill Inn for another three nights. The very idea that Berta and I could crack a murder case in only a few days was utterly goofy, but it seemed bad for morale to book for a full week. Besides, next week was Christmas.

At the front desk, Samuel Yarker told us that, because of the Winter Carnival, the rooms we had stayed in the previous night were no longer available. "Every room in the county is sold out, I'd reckon," he said. "But one of you is in luck, because I've just had a cancellation for another room."

"Oh, good," I said. "We'll take it."

"Only one narrow bed in there, so you can't share. It's number three on the second floor, small but comfortable."

"*I* will take it," Berta said.

I shot her a glare, which she pretended not to notice. I turned to Samuel. "You don't have anything else? The trouble is, I can't leave town."

He scratched his head. "Well, I suppose you could sleep in the airing cupboard."

"Cupboard?" For Pete's sake, I wasn't a *hatbox*.

"It's more of a big closet," Samuel said. "It's real warm in there because it's next to the main chimney, see. It's where Mother dries the linens. I could put an old army cot in there—I've got one up in the attic—and fix you up nice and cozy. The third-floor shared bathroom is just next door, as a bonus."

Hearing the lav flushing through the night couldn't possibly be a bonus. "How much?"

"Two dollars a night."

The regular room-and-board rate was four. "Deal," I said. "Oh—and we'd like to continue renting the truck." Samuel had arranged our rental of the Speedwagon, which belonged to a local farmer who didn't use it during the winter.

"I'll fix it up."

I fetched my already-packed suitcase, and Samuel's mother, a wizened old woman in a black dress whom everyone called Grandma Yarker, showed me to the airing cupboard on the third floor.

Drying bedsheets and towels hung on long wooden racks. Feeble light shone from a bare lightbulb, and from a funny little window just above floor level. It was indeed warm, however, and it smelled pleasantly of Lux laundry soap.

I set down my suitcase.

"We'll put your cot up against the chimney—" Grandma Yarker gestured to the exposed brick. "—and you'll be snug as a hibernating critter in here. There is, however, one small matter."

"Oh?" I was thinking *mice*.

But Grandma Yarker said, "The door only locks from the outside."

"Oh." Now, of course, I was thinking of how the dossier had been filched from Berta's room.

"I'll make certain not to lock it, though," Grandma Yarker said, "and I'll tell Patience and the cleaning women not to, either."

I thanked her, then asked if there was a telephone that guests might use. She directed me to a coin-operated telephone on the main floor.

With Cedric, I went downstairs and, after a wrong turn into the kitchen, found a hallway with a curtained alcove containing a telephone. I slid my nickel into the slot and asked the operator to connect me to Ralph's number in New York. I needed to cancel our date. A few sweet nothings were also on the agenda.

The connection took a few minutes to go through. I imagined the long, long, snowy miles that separated me from New York. When the telephone finally rang, Ralph didn't pick up.

In my several months of being Ralph's girl, he'd taught me a thing or two. How to interrogate a suspect without twitching my left eyelid. That not *all* men were heartless ginks. And how not to get my hopes up when calling him on the telephone. He wasn't one to loaf at home.

I slung the earpiece in its cradle and went up to Berta's room. It was time to consult about the murder investigation that had thrust itself upon us.

Us. Suspects in a murder. *Absurd.*

4

Berta was ensconced in an armchair in her new room, with her detecting notebook on her lap and a freshly sharpened pencil in hand.

"We're making a list?" I sat in the other armchair and wrestled Cedric out of his snowflake sweater so he wouldn't bake.

"Indeed."

"Checking it twice?"

"I beg your pardon?"

"Never mind. Before we make a list, why don't we go over what we recall from last night?" I released Cedric to explore the room. Instead, he beached himself on a braided rug in front of the electric fire.

Berta was tapping her pencil on the paper, thinking. "Hester Albans answered the front door when we arrived at eight o'clock—the time specified on the anonymous invitation—and seemed surprised to see us."

"Yes." Hester had also seemed *annoyed* to see us. She had grumbled about extra place settings, and Mrs. Goddard's whimsies, and folks tracking snow into the house.

"She showed us to the living room," Berta said, "where everyone else was already assembled—and already drinking, if I recall correctly."

"And—do you remember?—they were all bickering. They fell silent when they saw us, and we stood there in the doorway—

"Realizing that we had not gate-crashed a large party, but an intimate family gathering."

"Ugh." I shuddered at the memory. "We were struck dumb with mortification."

"*You* were struck dumb, Mrs. Woodby. Not I. Judith Goddard immediately suggested that Aunt Daphne had invited us, to which I said, 'Oh yes, we met at the ladies' poetry luncheon at the country club in Cleveland.'"

"Mm. That was a ickle bit overembellished, don't you think?" I rifled in my handbag and pulled out the box of maple sugar candies I'd purchased at the general store.

"It was resourceful. If I had not compiled the dossier, we would not even have *known* Aunt Daphne belonged to the country club in Cleveland. And, as luck would have it, Aunt Daphne agreed that she had invited us."

"She was already tipsy."

"Indeed. And, it seems, inherently dotty."

"After that, they all lost interest in us." I held out the open box of candies to Berta. They were shaped like maple leaves.

"Not quite." Berta selected a candy. "Do you recall that Judith ordered her son Fenton to fix us drinks?"

"Oh yes, that's right. You had a gin and tonic, and I had a sidecar."

"We must think carefully about what occurred next."

We both chewed candy for a few ticks.

"The family was discussing a ski jumping contest that is to be part of the Winter Carnival," I said. "How Maynard Coburn was going to compete, and how George—"

"The older son—the playboy."

"Yes, how *he* had signed up to compete, too. And Judith was scolding George, saying he would break his neck, which angered him."

"He seemed rather drunk."

"Yes. A belligerent, nasty sort of drunk. Oh—and Rosemary, the daughter, was in on this argument, too, making snide little asides—what did she say?"

"That *she* would not attend the ski jump contest," Berta said. "On account of being embarrassed that her mother was marrying such an unsuitable man. No one appeared to care what Rosemary thought. As for Maynard Coburn being unsuitable—*well!* Maynard Coburn? He is one of the best ski jumpers in the world! He took third place at Chamonix-Mont-Blanc in 1921, and he *very* nearly broke a world record last winter at the Solbergbakken hill in Norway."

Okay-o. Berta was dazzled. I couldn't blame her. Maynard Coburn, with his wafting dark-gold hair, bronzed skin, flashing white smile, and athlete's physique, looked right at home on magazine covers. But the thing was, he wasn't the very best ski jumper in the world. He was simply the handsomest.

"He's quite a lot younger than Judith was," I said.

Judith, though she must have been at least fifty years old, had flaunted an intimidating, chilly beauty: shiny black bob (surely dyed), porcelain skin (courtesy of costly face powder), glossy cranberry lipstick, fashionably protruding collarbones. Her green taffeta dress had been a sculptural work of art. Ditto her Clara Bow eyebrows.

"Maynard Coburn must be about thirty," I said. "That's two decades younger than Judith Goddard."

"It is no wonder Rosemary was distressed. *She* seemed a very old-fashioned sort of woman, very unlike her mother."

"She didn't look at all like her mother, either," I said.

Rosemary Rogerson, to be blunt, was dowdy: thick figure, puddinglike face, eyeglasses, ill-fitting dress, and a brown pageboy bob that was somehow more soup kitchen director than flapper.

"Rosemary probably seemed middle-aged when she was twelve," Berta said. "Daughters of vain, aggressively glamorous women often compensate for their mothers thus."

"I got the impression that Judith was, I don't know, sort of pitting her son against her fiancé," I said. "Almost as though she enjoyed seeing them in conflict. And then she changed the subject, almost gloatingly, I thought, to the upcoming honeymoon in Europe, and *that* for some reason really annoyed the fellow they called Uncle Roy—Judith's brother."

"Judith Goddard was a selfish woman," Berta said. "The type whom everyone secretly wishes to bump off."

"She was about as maternal as Al Capone," I said.

"Indeed. What occurred next?"

I thought it over. "Well, the second I spotted the ruby ring on Aunt Daphne's finger, I was paying attention to her, not to the family. I mean, how were we to know a murder was in the works? I went to sit near her—she was lolling on that divan, remember, a little removed from the family group, near the Christmas tree—and we chatted aimlessly. I told her all sorts of tales about the fun we'd had at the country club in Cleveland, and she seemed to believe every word. She was around the bend, of course, swimming in French champagne—I wonder where she got that? The only thing I recall clearly was her saying that Fenton had taken to spending quantities of time down in the cellar."

"The *cellar*, Mrs. Woodby?"

"Yes."

"How odd."

"Oh—and of course, Aunt Daphne told me she'd stolen the ruby ring, in 1919, confirming what Anonymous's invitation had said."

"Now, here is the critical bit," Berta said. "A few minutes before Judith collapsed. What do you recall?"

"Well, Judith ordered Fenton to make her a fresh drink, and she insisted that he take her empty glass. I recall thinking that was needlessly demeaning to Fenton, because at that point Patience Yarker had come into the room, and she was going around with a tray collecting the empty glasses and putting out fresh ashtrays. There was no reason for Fenton to play the role of servant."

"Fenton took his mother's empty glass?"

"Yes. And he carried it over to the drinks cabinet." The drinks cabinet was on a far wall, a carved and mirrored Victorian beast.

"And he fixed the new drink—"

"Yes, another Negroni, and I watched him make it—absently, you know—but all the same, I watched."

"Out of a morbid fascination."

"Well, *yes*."

In my former life as a wealthy Society Matron, Berta had been my household cook. She was acquainted with my deathless hatred for any cocktail made with Campari, an orangey-red, toxically bitter Italian liqueur. Negronis are made with Campari, gin, and sweet red vermouth on ice.

And, in some cases, a pinch of cyanide.

I said, "I distinctly recall Fenton looking guiltily at his mother through the drinks cabinet mirror, and then proceeding to mix the new cocktail in the dirty glass."

"The dirty glass! Did he use a shaker?"

"Oh, no. He just dumped everything straight into the glass—ice, tipply—and stirred."

Berta was writing furiously in her notebook. "The . . . same . . . glass," she murmured, and underlined it twice. "That is exceedingly important, because it means that the poison could not have been in a new glass on the drinks cabinet. Now, think carefully, Mrs. Woodby. Could Fenton have slipped poison into the drink while you were observing him?"

"I think so, yes. I was observing him, but not with a great deal of interest, and I was speaking to Aunt Daphne. My eyes weren't glued upon him the entire time, you know. Then he carried the cocktail over to his mother. Less than a minute later, she was convulsing on the carpet and everyone was shrieking and shouting."

A minute after that, she'd been dead.

Berta and I took a moment of silence to eat maple sugar candy and reflect.

I got up, went to the window, and twitched the curtain aside. The window overlooked the rear of the inn: a small, snowy parking lot with two motorcars, and a two-storied garage. An open-sided shed along the garage held stacks of yellowish split wood. A stair, swept free of snow, led to the garage's upper level.

"It would seem logical that Fenton is the murderer," Berta said. "No one else touched the cocktail glass."

I turned, and leaned my rear bumper on the windowsill. "The other possibility is that the cyanide was somehow slipped into the drink *after* Fenton delivered it to his mother. If she set it down on a table, for instance."

"But then it could have been anyone," Berta said.

"Anyone except Aunt Daphne. She was right beside me the whole time. Well, then, the list of suspects is pretty simple: everyone who was near Judith just before she drank that cocktail. That was Judith's three children—"

"*Fenton . . . George . . . Rosemary*." Berta was scribbling in her notebook.

"Patience Yarker."

"Patience!" Berta looked up. "Truly, Mrs. Woodby? She is a mere slip of a girl."

"She was in the room. We must be objective. Oh—and Uncle Roy. He was right beside Judith on the sofa."

"Uncle . . . Roy."

"And Maynard Coburn, of course."

Berta pursed her lips, but I saw she wrote *Maynard Coburn.*

"What about Hester Albans, the servant woman?" I asked.

"She never came into the living room."

"All right, then, that's—let me see—" I counted on my fingers. "Six possible suspects."

"That is far too many. Where do we start?"

"We should go to Goddard Farm, I suppose. At least half our suspects will probably be up there. Of course, they'll wish to boot us out—"

"We will resist any such efforts."

"Aunt Daphne said something about Uncle Roy keeping a cottage in the village. We could begin with him. Warm ourselves up for the rest of the crowd. Say, why do you suppose the killer chose to poison Judith with so many people in the room? It was awfully risky."

"Risky indeed, yet assembling a family always means assembling several persons who would like to kill the victim. It certainly befuddled Sergeant Peletier."

"I'm afraid it has befuddled *us,* too."

Hearing a door slam, I turned to look out the window again. I saw a fair-haired woman in an unbuttoned, brown-and-cream checked coat—Patience Yarker—scurry across the rear yard and up the garage stairs. At the top, she rapped on a door. She waited, glancing furtively around, hugging her coat close.

"Patience Yarker is out there," I said to Berta. "I want to see what she does. She seems . . . jittery."

Patience recoiled slightly as the door opened, but I couldn't see who had opened it. She was speaking rapidly, her frozen breath ballooning into the air. Her brow was clouded, her shoulders hunched.

"She looks angry," I said to Berta. "She looks as though she's giving someone a piece of her mind— Oh. She's done." Patience was marching back down the stairs, cheeks flushed, eyebrows scrunched, hand to her belly—*that's odd*—coat flapping behind her. She went across the parking lot and disappeared. Moments later, a door slammed somewhere below.

"Whew," I said. "She was really throwing an ing-bing. I wonder with whom she was speaking."

"You are certain she did not see you?"

"She glanced up, but she gave no indication of having seen me."

"Well. It will be easy enough to discover who is staying above the garage."

"And . . . there's something else," I said. "Patience had her hand curved around . . . her belly."

Berta's pale eyebrows lifted. "A stomachache, perhaps?"

"Sure, it could be a stomachache. Or . . ."

Berta gasped. "Are you speaking of *peas*, Mrs. Woodby?"

"Yes. Peas. In pods."

"Surely not! Patience is unwed."

"We must keep our eyes and our minds open. Come on. Let's go find out who is staying above the garage, call upon Uncle Roy, and then motor up to Goddard Farm."

5

I packed Cedric back into his sweater. Berta and I put on our coats and hats. My coat was a scrumptious mink, left over from when I was flush, and my hat was a chic, low-brimmed black wool cloche. Berta wore a shapeless brown coat and a knitted blue hat with earflaps.

Down in the lobby, Berta passed her room key to Samuel Yarker (now perusing the *Weekly Caledonian*) and asked if he might tell her who lived above the garage at the rear of the inn.

He peered over the top of the newspaper. "Sleuthing, eh?" He gave a rattling cough into a handkerchief.

I wondered why, with such a lung ailment, Samuel Yarker was not abed.

"Patience told me you're lady detectives," he said, "and that's all well and good—even if it is downright silly—but I won't have you spying on my premises, you hear?"

"*Spying*?" Berta pressed a hand to her heart. "Heavens, no, Mr. Yarker. It is only that I happened to see, from my own window, that the occupant above the garage left *their* window open a crack, and in this weather surely they would wish to know, heating costs being what they are these days."

The suspicion drained from Samuel's face. "Maynard Coburn lets the rooms above the garage—"

Well, well, well.

"—and I reckon he's absentminded—distressed about Mrs. Goddard's death last night, you see. They were to be married."

"Yes, we know," I said.

"Does Mr. Coburn live above the garage the year around?" Berta asked.

"Has for years. Course, soon as he married Mrs. Goddard, he was to move away to her palace in Cleveland, but I guess that's not happening after all, is it?"

Berta and I thanked Samuel, and went out into the cold sunlight.

"Maynard Coburn?" I whispered once we were several paces along the icy sidewalk. "Patience Yarker had an impassioned, secretive argument with *Maynard Coburn*? After which she pressed a distressed hand to her belly—"

"You are embroidering, Mrs. Woodby. Precisely what does a 'distressed hand' look like? Besides, we have many people to interview before we draw any conclusions. Although it does strike me that Patience Yarker is a more natural fit, romantically speaking, for Maynard Coburn than Judith Goddard was. They are far closer in age, to begin with. And both with lovely golden hair—"

"Oh, sure," I said. "But while Judith Goddard was, by all appearances, rolling in lettuce, Patience Yarker is *not*."

"Mrs. Woodby! Are you suggesting Maynard Coburn is a fortune-hunter?"

"Isn't that the logical conclusion? I mean, how much dough does a second-rate professional skier make, anyway? He's living in rented rooms."

Berta *hmph*ed.

We stopped in at the hardware store and, finding a clerk sorting nails into wooden bins, asked for directions to Roy Goddard's house.

"You must mean Roy Ives," the clerk said. "He's on Judith Goddard's side of the family. That was her maiden name. Ives. Not from around here."

"Of course," I said. "Roy Ives."

The clerk gave us directions. It was no more than a five-minute walk, he said, down River Street and across a covered bridge.

Berta and I continued on River Street, now a sluggish stream of motorcars and trucks. People arriving for the Winter Carnival, I figured. The sidewalk bustled with families and couples, laughing and chatting, their breath billowing up into the cold, vibrant sky. Rosy children clustered around the general store's display windows, ogling the toy bears, wooden trains, tin whistles, and one glorious red-and-green National Steel coaster wagon on display.

Berta sighed as we passed. "Recalling the Christmases of my girlhood in Sweden used to fill me with joy, but now it is like a pain in my heart."

"But why?" I asked. In past years, Berta had regaled me with tales of special Swedish Advent treats—saffransbullar, pepparkakor, and glögg—luminous candles, and visits from Jultomten, the Swedish Santa Claus.

"I do not know. Perhaps it is the way the detecting profession requires one to be so very clear-eyed and without sentiment. Because truly, Mrs. Woodby, are our memories of Christmases past not embellished with a fictional golden glow?"

"Surely not!"

Berta sighed again. "Then perhaps it simply means I am growing old and sad."

My own heart wrenched. Berta couldn't grow old and sad. She was my business partner and, well, she'd become almost like family to me.

My feet grew heavy as we walked.

It wasn't long before little snowballs accumulated in Cedric's toe fluff and he mutely insisted that I pick him up.

My feet felt heavier still. Perhaps high-heeled snow boots hadn't been the most prudent choice.

Berta and I talked over our goals in interviewing the suspects.

"Number one," I said, "we must sniff out possible murder motives. I mean, they all had the opportunity to poison Judith and, as for means, well, cyanide isn't difficult to come by."

"Also, we must attempt to discern each suspect's feelings regarding Judith's death. Are they grieving? Or are they pleased, or relieved? Are they masking emotions of any kind? Recall that the great detective Thad Parker"—Thad was a fictional dime-novel detective—"says 'before a lie is uttered, a flicker of truth appears upon the countenance. Take heed of the flicker.'"

"Sure," I said, twiddling my fingers. Berta forgets that dime novels aren't meant to be instruction manuals.

We passed a skating pond edged with tall reeds. A dozen people glided or wobbled on the ice, everyone laughing. We crossed a covered bridge, our boots clopping hollow against the wood. On the other side only one house stood, backing onto a tree-covered slope. A packed snowy track led to the front gate. An open garage to one side contained a green Crossley motorcar.

"This must be Roy's house," I said. "Swish motorcar."

"And what a charming little home."

"That ridge up there—" I pointed. "—that's where Goddard Farm stands. I'd bet this was originally the caretaker's cottage—it looks like a miniature version of Goddard Farm." The cottage had the same yellow clapboard and white pillars and pilasters as the mansion. Shutters framed large, sparkling windows, and a picket fence ringed a small yard. Everything was covered in snow, but I assumed that the various lumps and bumps in the garden were ornamental shrubs. The front walk had been shoveled, and smoke curled from a brick chimney. "It looks as though he's home," I said.

We unlatched the gate and went to the front door. The brass knocker was shaped like a cow's head. I rapped, and we waited, but nobody came.

"Perhaps he is in the bath, or at the back of the house," Berta whispered.

"He might even still be asleep," I whispered back. "It isn't yet noon, and I happened to notice him twice refilling his glass with wine last night."

"The pathway around the house is clear. We could go to the back and knock at the kitchen door."

"All right."

We crunched along the snowy side path and found a small porch. I rapped upon the kitchen door, whose window was covered with a lace curtain.

Deep barking erupted somewhere inside.

Cedric vibrated in my arms, growling.

"That sounds like a rather large dog," Berta whispered.

The barking was just on the other side of the door now. The door shuddered—the dog must have jumped against it.

Cedric squirmed and yipped in my arms. Snowflake sweater or no, he imagined himself to be a roughie.

"Since no one seems to be at home, one is tempted to have a peek in the kitchen," Berta said over the sound of barking. She was peering around the porch railing to the side of the house. "That window is not *too* terribly far from the ground, is it, Mrs. Woodby?"

"Oh, no," I said. "No monkey business."

Berta adopted a logical tone. "But we are already here, and since no one seems to be at home, why, this would be a fine opportunity to take a peek at the domestic arrangements of one of our suspects."

"Oh, all right." I thrust Cedric at Berta, stomped down the kitchen steps, and went over to the windows at the side of the house. They were about five feet up, so in order to get a good look inside, I'd need a boost. Luckily, the house had a high foundation of uneven stones.

Inside, the barking grew fiercer.

I wedged a boot toe into a crack, gripped the windowsill, heaved myself up, and smushed my face against the icy window. "It's the kitchen."

"Why do you sound strangled, Mrs. Woodby?" Berta was standing below me with Cedric in her arms. "Is your scarf too tight?"

"This isn't easy, you know!"

"What do you see in there?"

"Big white cooking range—you'd adore it, looks like a Wedgewood. Table and chairs. No people. Bottles of wine and a glass on the table— *Oh!*" A big black dog's head had bounced up just on the other side of the window. A string of slobber swept across the glass.

"Good heavens!" someone cried behind us.

I started, lost my footing, and my gloved fingertips slipped. I clawed at the windowsill for a fraction of a second, and then thumped backward onto the ground with an "*oompf.*" Luckily, my fall was broken by about three feet of snow. Flakes puffed up.

Feeling like an overturned tortoise, I struggled to my feet. I turned to see a man standing on the other side of the picket fence, watching me with interest.

He wore a black overcoat and the sort of hat you only ever see on the clergy. Despite his austere garb, however, he had a pale, handsome face and intelligent hazel eyes.

"Is there any particular reason you are peering through Mr. Ives's window?" he asked. Inside, the dog was still bow-wowing. "I beg your pardon, but you very much give the impression of being, well, *burglars.*"

"Any particular reason you have just wandered down from the Goddard family's private woods?" I asked.

"That is quite simple." The man appeared to be amused. "I am Mr. Currier, the minister of Maple Hill Methodist Church, and I have just been up to Goddard Farm to counsel the bereaved family."

"Oh," I said, brushing snow from my coat to conceal my embarrassment. "And how are they, um, holding up?"

"As well as can be expected. Rosemary is seeking solace by going forward with her charitable work, George always keeps himself diverted, and Fenton, well . . ." A sigh. "I am worried about Fenton." Currier watched me brush snow off my hips with a distracted sort of interest. He caught me looking, and cleared his throat. "Terrible business—but wait. Who are you, and how do you know—?" Understanding glimmered in his eyes. "Ah. You must be the mysterious lady detectives who turned up uninvited at the family gathering last night. Mrs. Rogerson mentioned you."

Mrs. Rogerson? Oh yes—that was Judith's daughter Rosemary's married name. It also rang another bell. Phooey—what *was* it?

"We are indeed detectives," Berta said, "but we were invited."

"Yes," I said, "and it wasn't our fault that whoever *invited* us didn't cop to it."

"Either way, your appearance here in Maple Hill has—*ahem*—has aroused some interest." Currier's cheeks flushed, and his eyes strayed once again to my hips.

Berta smirked. I pretended not to notice.

"You've roused the beast," Currier said.

"I beg your pardon?"

"The dog." Currier gestured to the window, where a furry black blob was bouncing in and out of sight. "Ammut."

"He didn't look like a mutt," I said.

"No, no. Mr. Ives named his dog after the ancient Egyptian devourer of souls, Ammut."

"Eek."

"Quite. The dog is enormous—a Newfoundland—but really quite harmless. It is only that he takes his duties as guard dog seriously—like a sentry to the ancient Egyptian underworld." Currier's lips twitched at his little joke.

There was a rattle behind me, and a window sash rumbled upward. Roy Ives's face appeared sideways in the gap. He seemed to have just gotten out of bed, with red-rimmed eyes and tufting hair. "Goodness me," he said with a yawn. "Has a village meeting been called in my yard? *Quiet*, Ammut!"

At last, the dog fell silent.

"Good morning, Mr. Ives," Currier called up to Roy. "These ladies took a wrong turn and ended up on the wrong side of your picket fence. I have set them to rights." He lifted his hat in farewell, shoved his hands in the pockets of his coat, and crunched away in the direction of the village, a black silhouette against the glittering snow.

"Now that we're here," Berta said to Roy, "do you suppose we could come inside and speak to you for a moment?"

"It's about my sister Judy kicking the bucket, I suppose?"

"Yes."

"Oh, all right. Come around to the front door. I was just about to make some coffee." The window clacked shut.

6

A few minutes later, Berta and I were sitting in Roy's tiny dining room while Roy rattled around in his kitchen making coffee. A bright fire crackled in a small, ornate corner fireplace. Art prints in gilt frames cluttered the walls, nearly obscuring the yellow chinoiserie wallpaper beneath. An arrangement of pine boughs and red roses decorated the table. I felt as though we were crammed inside a very costly dollhouse.

Ammut, having sniffed Berta and me and found us boring, curled up on the hearth. He was a mountain of wafting black fur, huge tufty paws, and jumbo jowls streaked with drool. He was sweet, actually, although Cedric, rigid on my lap, was not inclined to agree. He kept growling in warning. Ammut ignored him.

"Almost ready!" Roy called from the kitchen.

"Splendid!" Berta called back.

I was in the midst of my second round of visually inspecting the room, and my gaze fell upon a few charred curls of paper—paper with handwritten letters—underneath the fireplace hob.

Roy had been burning documents of some kind? Interesting. And I had a few moments, surely, before he returned.

I went over to the fireplace, bent, and carefully plucked up one of the charred paper curls. Ash billowed. A few fragmented lines were visible:

ocery store tycoo
ayboy bachelor.
y club poetry luncheo

"Berta!" I whispered. "This is your handwriting—this is from the stolen dossier!"

"He is coming," Berta whispered back.

I dropped the charred paper into the fireplace and threw myself back into my chair a split second before Roy came in with a tray of coffee things.

"Now then, what's this visit all about?" Roy asked, placing the tray on the table. He sat. "I can't imagine you would be so foolish as to intrude upon the police investigation." He was somewhere around fifty years of age, with rough, florid skin through which gray whiskers sprouted. Maroon veins threaded his nose. His melon-shaped body was belted inside an olive green brocade robe. "Not to mention spying through my window," he said in an accusing tone, even as he poured out coffees.

Berta unbuckled her handbag, extracted one of our cards, and slid it across the tablecloth.

Roy glanced at it without picking it up. "Mm, yes. Sergeant Peletier mentioned that the two of you claim to be gumshoes. What a bizarre occupation for women. Well, well. Detectives on the scene from the get-go. Why, it's almost as though somebody knew in advance that Judy would be killed." His tone was wry, but I noted his coffee cup shook as he lifted it again to his parched lips.

Anxious? Or merely hungover?

"Who hired you to investigate?" he asked.

"No one, actually," I said. "I mean to say, someone anonymously hired us to retrieve a ring from Aunt Daphne—"

"I recall Sergeant Peletier mentioning that last night, too."

"And now he is most unfairly suspicious of us," Berta said, "so we must clear our names."

"Otherwise, we're stuck in Maple Hill indefinitely," I said.

"Oh, it's not so bad," Roy said. "Being stuck in Maple Hill, I mean. *I* have been for more than five years."

"Stuck?" Berta said.

"In a manner of speaking. Once you settle in here, something comes over you. It's like you're always half asleep, and you watch the seasons go by, one after the other, in a trance. Of course, it's a wonderful place to do my work in peace, and the scenery here is wonderful inspiration."

"What is your work?" I asked.

"I am an artist. Oil painting and poetry."

"And your house—did you decorate it yourself?"

"You're trying to get at whether or not I own this house, aren't you?" Roy said, his voice barbed. "Everyone wants to know."

"I—"

"It's a logical question—why on earth is rich, beautiful Mrs. Goddard's pudgy, dreary older brother living in the caretaker's cottage on her country estate? What's the catch? Pity? *Blackmail?*"

Berta and I sipped our coffees, all ears.

"Alas, it's not that interesting," Roy said. "Sorry to puncture your tire. It came about by happenstance. I was up here for the summer five years ago—this was the summer before her husband Elmer died—and I fell off a horse and broke my leg, and since the main house was absolutely overrun with noisy brats and raucous guests—Judy ran with a, shall we say, *fun-loving* set in Cleveland—I requested to convalesce here in the caretaker's cottage. No one was using it—all the servants lived up at the main house—and I took the library on the main floor as a bedroom, since stairs were unmanageable."

"Then, after your leg healed, you felt at home," Berta said, "and you did not wish to go."

"And of course it must be a financial boon to have such accommodations," I said.

"Aren't you the cheeky one," Roy snapped.

Bulls-eye. Roy was living here for free. Starving artist (metaphorically speaking, I mean) and poor relation? The one thing that didn't tally up was the richness of the décor. As undersized as the cottage was, the furnishings must've cost a mint. French wine doesn't come cheap, either, and Roy's robe had the sheen of the costliest silk. Then there was that gorgeous green Crossley out in the garage.

"What happened to Elmer Goddard?" Berta asked.

"Motorcar accident. In Cleveland, not here. Tragic, et cetera, although Judy weathered widowhood quite nicely. I'm surprised it took her five years to become engaged again, to be honest, but she then, she *did* enjoy her freedom." Roy's bloodshot eyes glinted with malice.

"You'll forgive me for asking," I said, "but what will become of your living arrangement, now that your sister is gone?"

"Ah, well, there's the rub. Depending on which one of Judy's wee darlings inherits the estate, I could be out on my ear—ah, I see you two exchanging looks. No, no, don't deny it—it's quite all right. Although surely you do see that, if you're trying to deduce who poisoned Judy, I of all the family have quite the *opposite* of a murder motive. Her death could leave me without a home. You're exchanging another look—you two really are very transparent—I know the real reason you've come today. To try to figure whether I knocked off old Judy. No, I'm not in mourning, and I *won't* apologize. Judy was an insufferable cow, and although it never crossed my mind to hope she would *die*, I am not at all sad that she has." Roy stopped, panting slightly, and regarded Berta and me with a lift of his chin.

"You're afraid that whoever inherits the estate will turn you out of this house?" I asked.

"Of course I'm afraid! Those children might simply sell off the estate—it's worth a fortune, thousands of acres of forest stretching to the north and east. Rosemary is the only one with any sentimental attachment to it—you've seen that drivel she pens in those books of hers, all about heritage and traditions? George has no sentimental attachment to anything, animal, vegetable, or mineral, and Fenton, well, *you* met Fenton."

"He spends a fair amount of time in the cellar, I understand," I said.

"How odd that you say that. I happened to see him coming out of the cellar door—it's in the kitchen—only yesterday."

"Have you any notion what he does down there?" I asked.

"No. Although I can very easily picture him hanging upside down from the ceiling like a bat."

At that moment, my eyes happened to rest on one of the small, gilt-framed prints on the wall. My impression of the prints had been vague, but now I saw, first, that they depicted picturesque New England villages and landscapes, and second, that one print in particular looked awfully familiar, right down to the golden, curlicued font reading *Have a Merry Christmas*.

"Mr. Ives," I said, "are these prints your work?"

"Yes."

"They are lovely," Berta said, "but why are they all so very small?"

"Because they're greeting cards," I said. I turned to Roy. "You're a greeting card artist—"

"I thought every frumpy middle-aged woman under the sun had heard of LeRoy Ives."

"LeRoy Ives!" Berta exclaimed. "Why, I have seen boxes of your Christmas cards at the stationery shop in New York City. Selling like hotcakes, I might add."

I frowned. Did this mean Roy wasn't a starving artist and poor relation, after all?

I said, "You mentioned that you're a poet, Mr. Ives, so I suppose that means you write the verse inside the cards, too?"

"You mean the nauseatingly sentimental treacle?" Roy poured himself more coffee. "Mm. I have frequent nightmares about finding words that rhyme with 'stockings' and 'mincemeat pie.'"

"It's not nauseating," I said with an inexplicable sense of dismay. "It's nice."

Roy snorted. "Pandering to moist-eyed nostalgic patsies who long for a sort of Christmas that never, in fact, existed?"

Berta was nodding, as though she agreed with Roy.

"No," he said. "That's not at *all* nice."

"Yes, it is," I said with a funny wobble in my voice.

"You aren't very hard-boiled at all, are you?" Roy said with a nasty chuckle. "If it weren't so pathetic, it would almost be winsome. I suppose you lead the dreary life of an unmarried career woman in the city—walk-up apartment, stuffy subway rides, endless meals at the Automat—but you long for a simpler, more wholesome life in the country?"

"Sentiment doesn't make a person stupid," I said.

Berta glared at me. "Mrs. Woodby, please do not stray from the point." She turned to Roy. "It is an unfortunate habit of hers. As Mrs. Woodby noted earlier, we came to Goddard Farm yesterday evening because we had received an anonymous invitation some ten days ago, requesting that we retrieve a stolen ring from Aunt Daphne's hand and place it in the breadbox. As you may already be aware, that invitation was identical to this one—" She pointed to the print on the wall. "—with the badly rhymed and somewhat sinister invitation typed inside."

Roy went blotchy with anger. "What do you mean, *as I may already be aware*? Are you suggesting that *I*—?"

"I suggest nothing, Mr. Ives," Berta said, "but I cannot help but wonder, why was the invitation one of your greeting cards?"

"I think the answer is quite simple," Roy said. "Clearly, one of my own family sent that invitation, and they evidently thought it would be clever to implicate me in their vile little scheme."

That made sense. More sense than Roy implicating himself. On the other hand, his fireplace held the charred remains of the dossier—including that original invitation.

Two heavy thuds made us all jump. Cedric yipped and sproinged in my lap. Ammut lifted his head and woofed.

"Oh dear," Roy murmured. "That's Titus at the kitchen door."

Titus? Weird Titus of the milk bottles in the general store?

"I plumb forgot that he was coming today. I'm sorry, ladies, but I've got a fellow here to help with a bit of heavy lifting in the cellar."

"Of course," I said, swallowing. "The cellar. We must be off, at any rate. Thank you for the coffee. We can see ourselves out the front door."

7

First, Fenton is reported as having been whiling away the time in the cellar," I whispered to Berta as we walked down Roy's snowy front walk. "And now Roy is fiddling around with heavy things in *his* cellar. What is going on with this family and their cellars? It's downright ghoulish."

"The laboratory of Doctor Moreau springs to mind," Berta said softly, unlatching the picket gate.

We hesitated outside the gate. In one direction lay the covered bridge and the village. In the other direction, a snowy path disappeared into a steep slope of maples. "Let's walk up to Goddard Farm this way," I said. "It'll be quicker. That minister, Mr. Currier, seemed to have come down from this path here. It can't be more than, oh, half a mile."

"Half a mile *uphill*," Berta said. "And with you in those silly boots with heels like ice picks."

"Ice picks? Sounds handy. Come on. The exercise will clear our heads."

"Oh, very well."

We set off on the snowy footpath, ascending the slope on a gentle incline. The path had been well traveled since the last snowfall. It was packed down, and icy in spots. As we went, we softly talked over what we had learned from Roy Ives.

"If he's LeRoy Ives the successful greeting card artist, then he isn't the starving artist and poor relation I took him to be," I said. "And if he isn't poor, why does he depend upon having a gratis home in which to live?"

"Perhaps it is not the 'gratis' part that is important to him with regard to the cottage. Perhaps he has an attachment to the place. It is, after all, his home, and it is decorated in a cozy and charming—if perhaps somewhat pretentious—manner."

We trudged uphill in silence for a spell. Chickadees flitted on twigs. Icicles dripped in the sun.

"Should we have asked Roy about the burnt dossier?" I said, trying not to sound as wheezy as Berta did.

"No. That would only have put him even more on his guard."

"Do you think he went into your room at the inn to steal it?"

"That is difficult to picture. Perhaps he paid someone—a cleaning woman, for instance—to look through my suitcase."

"But when? While you were sleeping last night?"

"Ugh. I do hope not. If Roy sent the invitation, he would have known we were coming to Maple Hill, so he could have had my suitcase—and yours—searched yesterday after our arrival at the inn. While we were having our afternoon coffee, for instance."

"Any one of the family members mentioned in the dossier could have some reason to want it destroyed," I said.

"Yet it was in *Roy's* fireplace."

"Anyone could have stolen it and then taken it to Roy's house to burn it."

The matter of the burnt dossier was baffling, but we agreed to try not to formulate any firm conclusions until we had spoken to all the suspects on our list.

"I observed red wine stains on Roy's robe," Berta said.

"And I saw wine bottles in the kitchen," I said. "However, difficulties with tipply are neither here nor there when it comes to murder."

"But it is interesting that it is always *wine* with Roy, is it not? French wine last night. Red wine on his robe. Wine in his kitchen. Wine is not nearly so easy to come by as gin or even whiskey these days."

"He must have a special supplier."

We trudged up and up. Cedric romped, joyfully free of his leash, chasing a squirrel here, a finch there. He seemed to have forgotten his distaste for snow. My feet grew sore and numb in my fur-lined boots, but I would admit that when pigs followed in the footsteps of the Wright brothers.

"I believe these are sugar maple trees," Berta said, panting.

"Are they? For some reason they seem to have a distinctly Transylvanian flair this morning."

"Do not be silly. I have never understood people who are frightened of forests. They are places of beauty and shelter."

"Then you haven't read your fairy tales."

"When I was a girl, I traipsed about endlessly in the forests near my village, picking mushrooms and wildflowers."

"Okay, maybe you lived *inside* a fairy tale."

The footpath was now following a tight ravine full of saplings. Down at the bottom, a small stream gurgled beneath a layer of ice. Across the way, the slope rose sharply, with a bristly dark undergrowth of some kind of evergreen shrub.

The shrubs rustled.

I froze. Fear zapped down my limbs.

Berta, ahead of me, went a few paces before noticing I'd stopped.

She turned. "Mrs. Woodby, what is the matter? You look as though you have been struck by a baseball ba—"

"*Shh.*" I was peering hard at the shrubs across the ravine.

Berta followed my gaze.

We watched, spellbound, as the shrubs quivered, exactly as though someone—or some*thing*—quite large were pushing through them.

Cedric, who had been sniffing a fallen log up ahead on the path, began to growl, his ears pricked in the direction of the shrubs.

My heart, already thumping from the hike, kicked into a frantic tempo.

And then—the shrubs stopped quivering. Whoever or whatever had been over there was gone.

"We are quite safe," Berta whispered. "It could have been any number of creatures, but whatever it was, it cannot easily reach us with this ravine in the way."

"It could've been a person," I whispered back. "They could've been eavesdropping on our conversation. They could've heard us speculating about Roy's drinking, and the possibility of him being a murderer—"

"A *person*, Mrs. Woodby? With black fur?"

"You saw black fur?" I yelped.

"Yes. You did not?"

"No!"

"It was only the briefest glimpse."

"Could it have been a hat? Or a coat?"

"Perhaps." A long pause. Then Berta whispered, "Patience Yarker said—"

"Yes." I swallowed.

Patience had told us that Hester Albans claimed to have seen a furry critter walking upright in the darkness outside Goddard Farm last night.

"But what kind of furry creature walks upright?" I said. "And I'm not talking about within the pages of *Lurid Tales* magazine."

"One sometimes *sees things* in the forest," Berta said darkly. "Uncanny things."

I chose not to request further details. I already had the jimmies.

As we continued up the slope, I *tried* to be rational and serene, to be hard-boiled and scoffing and calm. Yet I kept thinking I glimpsed dark fur slipping just past the edges of my vision. When I'd snap my head to the side, though, I'd see nothing but swaying pine boughs or fidgeting birds.

At last, we emerged on the open hilltop upon which Goddard Farm sprawled.

"How beautiful!" I exclaimed. It *was* beautiful, although mostly I was relieved to be out from under the trees. There was nowhere for furry monsters to hide up *here*.

Snowy mountains rolled away in all directions from the house's splendid seat. Down below in the valley, Maple Hill's rooftops and church steeples peeked over a froth of gray tree boughs.

"You can practically see to Canada," I said, turning my overheated face to the cold breeze coming from the north.

"Let us proceed to the house before my feet freeze solid."

"But Canada is where Jimmy the Ant is hiding out," I said.

"I do not enjoy being teased, Mrs. Woodby."

Jimmy was Berta's on-again, off-again gangster beau, a lizardlike little fellow with one glass eye, spats, and a taste for crime. He'd recently peeved his boss, Lem Fitzpatrick, and fled to Canada. I knew he sent Berta lovey-dovey postcards, but they never had a return address. I wondered if Berta's melancholy had something to do with missing Jimmy. Of course, I would never ask her this. She was as impervious as a battleship.

Goddard Farm stood in all its glory, a yellow Colonial-style mansion with tall white pillars. A large garage stood at a distance behind the house, and beyond that, stables and fenced snowy pastures that eventually gave way to more forest.

Three motorcars were parked near the house: a Rolls-Royce beneath the porte cochere, a sporty Vauxhall, and a saggy Model T. Smoke puffed from both the massive brick chimneys.

Hester Albans answered the door. "Oh. Hello." She did not appear to be tickled pink to see us.

"Hello, Miss Albans," Berta said. "Good gracious, you work long hours!"

"Someone must see to the family," Hester said flatly. She was a rangy woman of middle years with a work-ravaged air: flyaway salt-and-pepper bun, red knuckles, creased forehead.

"Speaking of the family," I said, "we would like to see Aunt Daphne—Mrs. Lyle, that is—"

"She's still abed." Hester's nostrils flared. "*Hungover.*"

"What of Mrs. Rogerson?" I asked. I meant Rosemary.

"She's gone down to the village."

"All right, then George—"

"George is at ski jumping practice."

Whew. Funny thing to do the day after your mother was bopped off.

"And Fenton?" Berta asked.

"Fenton's up in his room, I believe, but I don't think he'll wish to speak to anyone." Hester's eyes went flinty. "What business is it of yours to be pestering the family, anyway? Folks have been wondering just what *your* hand was in all this, you know. Big-city detectives showing up unannounced like that, trying to pinch a helpless old lady's ring?"

"We are letting cold air into the house," Berta said, trundling past Hester into the entry hall, "so we are happy to wait inside for

Fenton or Mrs. Lyle to come downstairs." She plunked herself onto a bench.

I followed, and Hester, clearly flabbergasted, shut the door.

I sat down beside Berta with Cedric on my lap.

"Suit yourself," Hester said with a shrug. "You could be waiting an age. *I* must get back to work, boxing up all the Christmas decorations and covering all the mirrors. This is a house of death now." This was spoken with certain morbid relish. She began to walk away.

"Before you go," I said, "I wonder if I could ask you a question or two."

Hester's bony shoulders hitched. She turned. "What is it?"

"Patience Yarker told us you saw something out the window last night," I said. "A critter."

Hester touched a hand to her throat. "She spoke to you about that?"

"Only in passing," I said. "What was it?"

"It was . . ." Hester swallowed thickly. "You city folk won't understand."

Berta leaned forward. "Oh, but we are not truly city folk, Miss Albans. I myself was raised in a small Swedish village, and Mrs. Woodby comes from the bleakest of farm towns in the Midwestern United States—"

"It wasn't really *bleak*," I said.

"—so we understand country ways."

"It was Slipperyback," Hester said.

"Slipperyback?" I blinked. "Who's that?"

"Folks say he's only a silly legend," Hester said, "but is it silly when Slipperyback knocks over woodpiles? Is it silly when he breaks into cellars and steals everyone's cured hams? Eh?"

My heart was squeezing. "What is he? A—a monster?"

Hester's eyes flared. "A bear."

"A bear?" Berta said. "But bears hibernate in winter."

"Slipperyback doesn't. He's no ordinary bear. He's enormous. He's wily. He's at least one hundred years old—some say twice that—he always walks on two legs, and no man's traps or bullets can harm him. That's why he's called Slipperyback, you see. He causes a ruckus, plays tricks, steals and breaks and frightens, and then—" Hester spread her big hands. "—slips away into the woods."

Berta and I exchanged sidelong glances: Had *we* just encountered Slipperyback on our way up here?

"I see you don't believe me." Hester sounded angry and hurt.

"No! We do," I said. "We *do*. Tell me, Miss Albans, what precisely was Slipperyback doing outside the house last night?"

"Peeking in at us, of course."

My skin crawled. "Weren't the curtains shut?"

"The living room curtains never close properly. There's always a little crack. Something's the matter with the curtain rod. And I saw his footprints last night, too."

"Where?"

"Just outside the kitchen door. I burned a batch of bread rolls, you see, and I had to open the door to let out the smoke, and that's when I saw them. Paw prints, going right past the kitchen porch. Then I knew for certain it was Slipperyback and not some other critter, because it was just the two paws. Not four."

"Because he walks upright," I said.

"That's right."

"Do you suppose he had anything to do with Mrs. Goddard's death?" I asked.

"Certainly not!"

"Miss Albans," Berta said, "who do you believe poisoned Mrs. Goddard last night?"

"One of her children, of course. For the inheritance."

That was the obvious answer, of course. But then, which child?

"Or perhaps—" Hester lowered her voice. "—it was Maynard Coburn. It was as clear as day he pursued Mrs. Goddard for her money. Why, she was more than twenty years older than he."

"Still, Mrs. Goddard was very beautiful," I said.

"Beauty is as beauty does. Mark my words, Maynard is a fortune-hunter—we don't know if he was in her will or not, do we? He's not from around here, you know. He's from Maine. Son of a poor Skowhegan timberman. Grew up half-starved and half-frozen, with his eyes on bigger prizes. The worst of it is, he attended college with George—down in Hanover at Dartmouth, you know. Maynard had a scholarship, of course, and he'd come up here to Goddard Farm for the summer and Christmas holidays. Poor Elmer, well, Elmer got to thinking of Maynard almost like a son. Not that *Mrs.* Goddard thought of him as a son, oh no—when she was here at all, because even when her children were small, she'd be off gallivanting in distant places half the year—"

"I beg your pardon," I said. "Are you suggesting that when Maynard was in college, he and Mrs. Goddard—?"

"Oh no, not back then. She didn't give him the time of day till about a year ago. Once he'd gotten almost famous, on magazine covers and such. Then she started parading him down in Cleveland like a show pony."

Ugh. I'm no prude, but taking up with one's son's college pal really was the limit.

"I must get back to work," Hester said. "I'll tell Mr. Goddard"—she meant Fenton—"that you're here." She had thawed toward Berta and me, I could tell. Sharing gossip has that effect. "I've got my other jobs to tend to today, too, and then more of my Christmas fruitcakes to bake. I'll be selling them at the carnival, if you happen to like fruitcake. We are raising money to give the Methodist church a new coat of paint."

"Fruitcake? Scrumptious," I lied. I would not deign to use a fruitcake for a doorstop, for fear of offending the door. "What are your other jobs, Hester?"

"Well, there's my work at the maple syrup factory—that's just a day or two each week except in sugaring season—and I do a sweater here or there at the knitting factory, and of course there's the inn every afternoon, and I look after the Reverend Mr. Currier's house—"

"The inn?" Berta said.

"The Old Mill Inn. Didn't you know? I clean the rooms. Now. I must get to boxing the decorations." Hester went away.

8

Hester Albans is a cleaning lady at the Old Mill Inn," I whispered to Berta once Hester's footfalls had receded. "That means she has access to all the room keys! She could have stolen the dossier from your suitcase!"

"Do calm yourself, Mrs. Woodby," Berta whispered back. "You resemble a pink balloon on the verge of bursting. Hester is not one of our murder suspects, so why would she have stolen the dossier?"

"Maybe she stole it for Roy. She certainly seems gullible enough to be taken in by a murderer—I mean, what of that Slipperyback nonsense?"

I wouldn't mention how spooked *I* still was about Slipperyback. Berta would scoff.

"We must speak with Maynard Coburn," Berta said. "He is far more enmeshed with the Goddard family than we previously supposed."

"That makes his little argument with Patience Yarker at the inn all the more suspect, doesn't it?" *Not to mention the possible pea-in-pod.*

We waited for a few minutes more, straining our ears to hear voices or footsteps upstairs.

Nothing.

A grandfather clock ticked the seconds. Cedric drifted off to sleep in my lap.

"Perhaps we could just pop upstairs and have a word with Aunt Daphne," I whispered.

"She is abed, and hungover."

"I could mix up a hangover cure—do you suppose there's any Worcestershire sauce in the pantry?"

"Ugh. Mrs. Woodby, such cures do not work. Nothing is better for a hangover than a strong cup of coffee and the hair of the dog."

I looked at Berta's capacious black handbag, sitting primly on her lap. "I don't suppose you have your flask in there?"

"Of course I do, Mrs. Woodby. It is wintertime. Come along. Let us make some coffee."

We stole to the kitchen, which was scrubbed clean of all traces of last night's dinner party. By some miracle, I found a little lukewarm coffee in the stovetop percolator. Berta and I quickly put together a tray—cup of coffee, pitcher of cream, sugar bowl, spoon, napkin ("What a lot of nice silver they have in this house," Berta said, admiring the spoon)—and, keeping our ears pricked for Hester's footfalls, tiptoed upstairs via a back staircase.

"Now what?" I whispered, readjusting the tray in my hands. Berta was carrying Cedric.

"Now you must begin knocking," Berta said.

"*I* must? I'm carrying the tray!" The upstairs hallway was broad, richly wallpapered, and lined with a demoralizing number of doors.

"My hands are full. Use an elbow. Use your boot."

I knocked on the first door with my elbow. My feet were too sore for kicking.

No answer. I knocked on another door, and another. The coffee cup rattled against the cream pitcher.

"What if *Fenton* answers one of these doors?" I whispered with a sinking belly.

"He is merely a frail youth, Mrs. Woodby."

"But he hangs around in the cellar!" I bonked my elbow on a fourth door. Ouch.

Rustles within. Then, the fluting voice of Aunt Daphne. "Enter!"

"You go in," Berta whispered. "I will stand guard. Oh—I very nearly forgot." She set Cedric on the floor, unbuckled her handbag, pulled out her flask, and placed it on the tray.

I entered Aunt Daphne's room. Berta shut the door.

The room was dim and overly warm, and smelled of talcum powder, rose perfume, and cigarette smoke. On the bed lay a small, meat loaf–shaped figure beneath a quilted pink eiderdown.

"Oh," Aunt Daphne said. "My pretty friend from the country club. Good morning."

"Good morning, Mrs. Lyle," I said, carrying the tray over. "I've brought you some coffee."

"Oh! Wonderful. I have the most wretched headache, you know." She struggled upright against a mound of pillows. "Too much champagne. Now, where are my cigarettes? Ah. Be a darling and pass those over."

I settled the tray on the bed beside Aunt Daphne and found a cigarette case, a holder, and a lighter on the bedside table.

"Something horrid occurred last night." She blinked blearily as she corked a cigarette into the holder and lit it. "What was it?"

"Your niece Judith died," I said gently.

"Ah, yes. Someone finally worked up the nerve to do it." She cackled, smoke spurting from her nostrils.

"Would you like cream in your coffee?" I asked. "Sugar? Something stronger?"

"All three, please."

I was bursting with questions for her, but I first doctored her coffee—cream, sugar, a glug from Berta's flask (smelled like gin)—and passed the cup over.

Aunt Daphne slurped greedily.

"I wonder if you could tell me from whom you stole that ruby ring in the summer of 1919," I said, attempting to strike a light tone.

"Did I say that?"

"Yes," I said. "You did."

Aunt Daphne took another slurp of coffee, and then a long pull from her cigarette holder. "Now I recall. Yes. I stole it from Judith."

My breath caught. "Are you certain?"

"Helped myself to it, right out of her jewelry box, to spite her, you see, for cheating at bridge. She was always such a cheat. I didn't even *desire* the ring, you know, but it was the most valuable bauble in the box, so on my finger it went! Alas, it was too small. I don't know how I ever got it on."

Judith Goddard had been Anonymous. She had invited us here to steal the ruby ring. Perhaps she had wanted to wear it as her engagement ring, since Maynard Coburn probably couldn't afford to put a lima bean on her finger. It had nothing to do with her murder. Yet here Berta and I were embroiled in her death, all the same.

Aunt Daphne said, "Judith and I didn't mingle, you know. I have my own circle in Cleveland, and she had hers. She *was* from my side of the family—she was my late sister Diana's daughter—but when she married Elmer Goddard, she made her bed. He was *new money*, you know."

"Why did you come here to the family gathering, if you didn't mingle with Judith?"

"Rosemary telephoned and begged me to. Blithered on about

family traditions and all that sort of garbage. My friend Lydia invited me to her place on Lake Champlain for Christmas, so I thought I may as well swing by Maple Hill on the way and see what my hideous family had been up to lately. I'll be on my way to Lydia's this afternoon. I won't stay for the funeral—it is to be here in Maple Hill, Rosemary tells me, the day after tomorrow. Funerals are *so* dispiriting."

"And Judith's will is to be read the day after tomorrow, too?"

"I believe so."

Mental note: Be a fly on the wall when that will is read.

"Who do you suppose poisoned Judith?"

"Roy," Aunt Daphne said without hesitation.

"Roy! Her own brother? But why?"

"Because he did not wish to baby-mind Fenton for several months while Judith and that swaggering Maynard Coburn went away on their honeymoon."

That did not sound at all like a good motive for murder to me, and I said as much.

Aunt Daphne's cigarette end crackled. "Ah, but Roy is a selfish slug, and he has already spent every penny he inherited from his parents."

"But his greeting cards—he is rather successful, and he surely has an income from those."

"Oh, he has an income from those, but it is a *moderate* income, dear, and Roy's tastes are not at all moderate."

I thought of his richly appointed cottage, his sumptuous brocade robe, his plushy motorcar.

Aunt Daphne continued, "His style of living entirely depends upon living in that caretaker's cottage, free of charge. That allows him to spend all his income on the little luxuries—eau de cologne, French wine, antique furniture, foppish clothing—that he cannot seem to do without."

"But to *kill* to preserve his style of living . . . ?"

"Ah, well, Roy is, as I said, hoggishly self-centered, and—just between you and me—he drinks too much. It'll all come clear when the will is read, but to my mind, Roy must have been sure that Judith left him that cottage in her will. It all adds up, doesn't it?"

It did, actually.

"Do you know what Roy might keep down in his cellar?" I asked.

"His cellar? Didn't even know he had one. Top me up, won't you?" Aunt Daphne held out her coffee cup.

I unscrewed the flask and splashed more gin into the cup.

"Ah, thank you," she murmured, sinking back upon her pillows. "Oh, my poor head." Her crepey eyelids sank shut as she sipped.

"Could I fetch you some aspirin?"

"No, dear. I'll just rest." She sipped again without opening her eyes.

I crept out.

Berta and Cedric were waiting, bright-eyed, in the corridor.

"Judith was Anonymous," I whispered excitedly. "*She* sent that invitation! I suspect she wanted the ring back to wear as her engagement ring. Judith invited Aunt Daphne up here to Goddard Farm simply to get that ring—and Aunt Daphne is leaving this afternoon."

"If Judith was Anonymous, then the ring should still be in the breadbox," Berta said.

"It should, shouldn't it?" I looked up and down the corridor. Empty. "Let's go and check."

I picked up Cedric, and we hurried down the back stairs into the kitchen. I went straight to the green metal breadbox on the counter. I lifted the lid.

No ring inside. Only crumbs.

"It's gone!" I whispered. "I don't believe it!"

"Perhaps one of the family moved it to a more secure place. We made no secret that we placed it in there."

I swung the breadbox lid back down. "And since we know that the ring isn't related to Judith's death, it's a closed book." I hesitated. "Before we go . . ."

"You wish to speak with Fenton?"

"I suppose we *should*, but also . . ."

"Surely you are not thinking of the *cellar*, Mrs. Woodby?"

"Why not?" Yes, a foray to the cellar sounded creepy as billyo. On the other hand, I was itching to see what was down there. "The door to the cellar is in the kitchen, Roy said."

"That must be it." Berta was already toddling toward a mysterious door.

I joined her.

Hinges creaked as she pulled it open. Darkness yawned, and a moldy smell wafted up on a breath of cold air.

"On second thought—" I said.

"This was your idea, Mrs. Woodby," Berta whispered back. "We do not have all day." She pressed a switch on the stairwell wall, and a feeble electric light flashed on. "Come on." She went down the steps.

I took one last look over my shoulder—the coast was clear—snuggled Cedric more securely in my arms, and followed her downward.

9

Shuddery wooden steps led down to a wide-open space with a stone floor and a low, raftered ceiling. Barrels, crates, and boxes cast dense shadows. The lone lightbulb was too weak to illuminate the margins of the cellar.

A mouse streaked past my feet. Cedric growled and lurched in my arms, but I restrained him. The mouse vanished.

"I see no evidence of anyone doing much of anything down here," I whispered. "Except for the spiders." Cobwebs netted the ceiling and the high-up windows. "The spiders have been awfully busy."

"But we have heard from more than one person that Fenton spends time down here," Berta said. "Let us search a bit."

We walked slowly between wooden support pillars. We came upon a door standing ajar, but when we peeked through, it proved to contain nothing but dusty shelves of pickles and fruit preserves.

We came to another door.

"Padlocked," I whispered. "This could be Fenton's lair!"

"It is a good thing it is padlocked, so we may be certain he is not inside." Berta removed her hat and pulled a hairpin out of her bun. "I do not think my nerves could bear—"

Somewhere upstairs, there was a gentle thud.

"Get a wiggle on," I whispered.

"Do not hurry me, Mrs. Woodby." Berta bent, took the padlock in her hand, and poked around in the keyhole with the hairpin.

"How come you're so good at picking locks?" I whispered.

"*Shush.* I must focus."

"Did Jimmy the Ant teach you?"

"One must have something to talk about besides tommy guns and peach orchards." *Click.* "There." The padlock fell open. Berta slid the hairpin back in her bun and replaced her hat.

I removed the padlock gently, took a deep breath, and pushed open the door.

Shadows inside. And that *smell*—a weird, tangy, nostril-shriveling potpourri.

"Is there a light?" I patted the walls with my free hand.

"I do not know. Oh, what is that awful odor?"

"Here." I felt a dangling string, and I gave it a yank.

Dim red light washed a room barely bigger than a closet, with shelves cluttered with bottles, a porcelain sink, tables arrayed with trays, and—clothespinned to lines strung from end to end—photographs.

"It's a darkroom," I whispered. "Fenton must be a photographer." I stepped forward to study the string of photographs closest to me.

One photograph showed Mrs. Goddard on the telephone, her face turned away. Another photograph showed Rosemary in an apron with a wooden spoon stuck in a mixing bowl, scowling at the camera. Yet another captured what I was sure was Titus (you know, of the milk bottles and the heavy lifting in Roy's cellar). Titus was shown skiing past a smudge of trees and boulders with what appeared to be a bulky knapsack on his back.

Berta was peering at photographs on another line. "Oh my," she breathed. "Oh my, my, my, my, *my*."

"What is it?" I whispered, going over to her side.

"It seems that Fenton is a photographic Peeping Tom. And his brother, George . . . oh, goodness."

A grainy photograph depicted a man and a woman, wearing coats and hats and standing in a snowy forest, locked in a passionate kiss.

"That's certainly George Goddard," I said.

Berta nodded. "His eyebrows and forehead are clear. And the woman—something about her is familiar . . ."

"It's Patience Yarker."

"Patience! Truly?"

"She was wearing the same checked coat today when I saw her through the window." I shook my head. "Patience Yarker canoodling with George Goddard? Although, I suppose it isn't truly surprising to see the dashing young scion of the local moneybags clan smooching the prettiest girl in the village. But in the light of Patience's apparent argument with Maynard Coburn—"

"Spies!" someone shrieked.

Berta and I spun around to see Fenton lurching into the darkroom. His hair was lank, his eyes wild in the red light, and a camera swung from a leather strap around his neck. His outstretched hands clawed the air.

Cedric paddled his paws so hard, I lost my grip on him, and he catapulted himself to the floor. Yapping shrilly, he bounded forward.

"Get out!" Fenton screamed. "Get out of here! How dare y— *Ow!*"

Cedric had sunk his teeth into Fenton's ankle.

"Get off me, you vicious cur!" Fenton kicked his foot—with Cedric attached—in the air.

Cedric held on for a few kicks, and then flew off, hit the bottom of the shelves, and sprawled.

I screamed.

Glass bottles rattled, and one toppled onto the floor beside Cedric. Somehow, it didn't shatter.

"You monster!" I shouted at Fenton. I dived to my knees and gathered Cedric up in my arms. "Poor little peanut. Mommy's here. Are you hurt?"

"Get out of here before I telephone the police. Your dog bit me!" Fenton, panting through his teeth, bent to massage his ankle. "Look! He drew blood! He's vicious! He ought to be taken out behind the stables and shot."

My eyes fell on the bottle that had hit the floor. The light wasn't good, but I easily read the label:

KODAK

POTASSIUM FERRICYANIDE

POISON

And a skull and crossbones.

I floundered to my feet, hugging Cedric close. "I'm sorry about the bite. He thought you were attacking me." I dodged past Fenton to the door through which Berta was just going. "Anyway," I said over my shoulder, "I've been bitten by him before while playing. It's like being bitten by a hamster."

Fenton gave a garbled howl of outrage.

Berta and I half ran across the expanse of basement, up the stairs, across the kitchen, and out the door into the blinding white, blessedly pure air.

"To the village?" I said, clattering down the porch steps.

"Unquestionably."

The door crashed open behind us.

Without stopping, I looked over my shoulder to see Hester Albans on the porch, waving a copper dustpan.

"I'll telephone the police!" she shouted. "You're upsetting the peace in this village!"

"I suppose this means Hester doesn't like us anymore," I said breathlessly as Berta and I kept going.

"I suppose not," Berta replied, equally breathless.

"Have you ever noticed we always get blamed for upsetting the domestic peace when there's a murder?"

"People must have *someone* to blame, or their self-delusions will be shattered. And if *that* occurs . . . one may as well play about with gasoline and a box of matches."

We didn't speak again until we were out of sight of Goddard Farm, hoofing it down the steep, tree-edged road upon which we had driven last night. Cedric trotted along beside us, looking immensely proud of himself. His hackles still fanned up from under the collar of his sweater.

"Did you see the bottle?" I asked Berta.

"What bottle? There were dozens of bottles."

"Well, sure, but the one that fell on the floor was potassium ferricyanide. Potassium cyanide."

Berta gasped. "Are you certain?"

"Labeled clear as day."

"But why—?"

"The bottle also said 'Kodak.' We should make certain, but I suspect cyanide is one of the chemicals used to develop photographic film."

"I shall telephone dear Myrtle. She will be able to research that quite easily." Myrtle was a librarian at the Main Branch of the New York Public Library. She pawed through the card catalogs and periodical indices as deftly as a concert pianist on a Steinway. She had proved to be an indispensable fact-checker for our agency.

"Good," I said. "That police sergeant said Judith was poisoned with cyanide, and now we know there was a big bottle of cyanide sitting in the cellar—under lock and key. What if Fenton is the only one with a key to his darkroom?"

"Someone else could have picked the padlock, as I did."

"True."

"What do you make of Fenton's photographs?"

"I'm not quite certain what to make of them, except that they're awfully creepy—I mean, he had to be *spying* upon people to take the snaps that he did. And did you happen to see his trousers?"

"Not in the melee, no."

"They were wet and muddy about the cuffs."

"Oh?"

"As though he'd just been outside in the snow."

"You are not suggesting it was *Fenton* in the thicket? In a fur coat, perhaps?"

"If that was him—oh golly. He could've been taking photographs of *us*."

"We have nothing to hide."

"Not yet."

When we reached the bottom of the hill and crossed a red covered bridge (a different bridge from the one we'd traversed to reach Roy Ives's cottage), we came upon an Esso filling station. It was originally a T-shaped farmhouse, and a large roof had been built to cover the gasoline pumps. A sign announced that Green's Coffee Shop lay within.

"Oh, let's stop here," I said, practically teary with relief. "I'm so thirsty, and my feet are—"

"Yes? Is it your impractical boots, Mrs. Woodby? Bunions and blisters?"

"Nope," I said quickly. "My toes are just a little . . . cold."

We crossed the icy highway—there was only a little traffic—and went into the coffee shop. It was warm and cramped, with a lot of old-timers drinking coffee. They looked curiously at Berta and me, smirked at Cedric, and then proceeded to ignore us. They must have thought we were tourists in town for the Winter Carnival.

I sank into a chair, limp with thirst and foot discomfort.

"Of our six murder suspects," I said softly to Berta once we had been served large helpings of shepherd's pie, "we have already spoken to three. Not bad for a morning's work. I'd like to get to the bottom of Patience Yarker's relations with Maynard Coburn. Something was funny about their argument. It was so . . . intimate. And if she's been kissing George Goddard . . ."

"We must speak with Maynard, yes, as well as George and Rosemary. Miss Albans said that George was practicing at the ski jump."

"Funny that he's going ahead with the contest in the light of his mother's death." I spooned up steaming mashed potato and meat. "I wonder if Maynard will go ahead with it as well."

"We ought to ask him."

"The sixth suspect on our list is Rosemary. The minister Mr. Currier said something about her doing charitable work. I wish I had pressed him for more facts."

After lunch, Berta and I set forth once more, now in the direction of the ski jump hill. Our waitress at the coffee shop had given us directions. ("Yonder, past the school and Emmeline's boardinghouse. Village thins out, trees begin, but don't let those trees frighten you. Just go right on through, and you'll find a cleared-out slope with the ski runs. There'll be plenty of boys up there, I reckon. They're all mad for ski jumping and tobogganing and whatnot. Break their necks, I wouldn't wonder. Mad.")

Berta had declared that we should go on foot, since the jump was only a little outside the village. Pride kept me from objecting, despite a pulsating big-toe blister.

It was early afternoon, yet the pale sun was already low in the sky, sending long blue shadows across the snow. A smattering of tiny, dry snowflakes floated through the air.

"How short the winter days are in the country," Berta said with a shiver as we walked. "In the city, with all the lights and noise everywhere, it is easy to forget."

"Look." I slowed. "Isn't that Rosemary Rogerson getting out of a motorcar up the street?"

"Indeed it is."

Berta and I slowed to a snail's pace, watching as Rosemary mounted a porch and knocked on the door of a rust-red clapboard house. The door opened. A woman greeted Rosemary and stepped aside for her to enter.

Just before the door fell shut, Rosemary cast a furtive look over her shoulder.

Her gaze fell upon Berta and me. Her expression clouded.

"*Rats,*" I muttered. Smiling, I made a twiddly wave. "Hello, Mrs. Rogerson!" I called.

The woman said something to Rosemary, and Rosemary shook her head. They both disappeared inside the house, and the door fell shut.

"How do you like that?" I said. "She's avoiding us! What do you suppose she's up to?"

"Paying a call upon a friend, or else attending to her charitable work," Berta said.

"And yet . . . she looked guilty."

"As guilty as a fox in a henhouse."

"Let's take a peek through the windows," I said.

"In broad daylight?"

"We don't have time to waste, Berta. See?" I swept a hand around the street. "No one's around except that cat in the window there."

"Oh, very well," Berta grumbled.

We walked to the rust-red house. It had a tiny, snow-covered yard with no fence, so it was a cinch to creep up to one of the side windows.

Slowly, we raised our eyes to windowsill level and peeked in.

We were looking at an unoccupied dining room.

"I see people moving about through that doorway," I whispered.

We crept to the next window. Again, we raised our eyes and peeked through.

Two women—Rosemary and the woman who had opened the door—stood at a kitchen table. The woman was rolling dough. Rosemary was watching, holding a tin pie pan and talking, but we couldn't hear what she said.

Berta and I ducked down and hurried away from the house.

"Piecrust and gossip," I said. "If that's all she's doing, why the guilty look over the shoulder before she went inside?"

"Perhaps it is because they are using lard, not butter, in the crust," Berta said. "It is *disgraceful*."

10

Berta and I walked on. The village was alive with activity. Parked vehicles cluttered the narrow streets that had been built before the era of motorcars. People in snow boots and colorful scarves strolled along sidewalks. In the village green—which was in fact white with trodden snow—ice sculptors chipped away at blocks of ice with hammers and chisels. Men were constructing an igloo, and children, shouting and rosy cheeked, were building a snowman under a bare oak tree.

The houses thinned, and the village merged into snowy forest.

We followed a well-beaten snowy track through a stand of fir trees (I peered hard at every rustling branch), and several yards along, we found ourselves in a clearing with a few more haphazardly parked vehicles. Bundled-up men loitered. Behind them, a mountain reared up.

"Ah." I stopped. "There's the ski jump, then." This was uttered in an ironic tone, since the ski jump was impossible to miss. It sat halfway up the mountainside, which had been shorn of trees. With its wooden scaffolding that reached high into the air at least one hundred feet, it resembled a portion of a Coney Island roller coaster. Its swooping length was covered in packed snow.

An engine had rumbled to life, and now a new, black Rolls-Royce Tourer was edging toward us, its elegant lines out of place amid the other rusty, ice-caked vehicles.

"Berta!" I whispered. "It's George Goddard." I called out, "Mr. Goddard! Oh, Mr. Goddard!" He was rolling just past us now, no more than two yards away. "Mr. Goddard! George!"

He kept his eyes forward, revealing his matinee-idol profile. I could tell by the set of his jaw that he was deliberately ignoring me. With a spurt of slush, he accelerated away toward the village.

"I don't believe it!" I cried to Berta. "First Rosemary and now George, giving us the blow-off!"

"It is no wonder," Berta said. "They do not wish to be interrogated by detectives. I cannot blame them—"

"Detectives?" a man said behind us.

Berta and I turned to see a wiry, bowlegged, white-mustached man approaching.

"You must be the lady detectives everyone's abuzz about," he said with a friendly smile. His bright green eyes lit keenly upon Berta.

Berta drew herself up. "I beg your pardon—you are—?"

"Daniel Pickard. President of the Maple Hill Alpine Club." He stuck out a wool-gloved hand and gave first Berta and then me a sprightly handshake.

"Mrs. Lundgren," Berta said.

"Pleased to meet you, Mr. Pickard," I said. "We came here hoping to speak with George Goddard, but I'm afraid he's just left—"

"Eh? What?" Pickard tore his eyes from Berta to regard me blearily.

Holy smokes. An instant conquest for Berta. How *did* she do it? Because this wasn't the first time she had bowled over a gray-templed fellow. Oh, no. Fellows, perhaps intuiting her baking prowess and spirit of adventure, buzzed around her like worker bees around their queen.

"We wished to speak with George Goddard," I repeated. "Do you know if he plans to return today?"

"Nah, not until tomorrow morning at ten o'clock." Pickard saw Berta gazing up at the ski jump. "It's a new jump this year—the tallest in North America. The club spent all summer building it. Took every dime we made on the last four Winter Carnivals combined."

"Is the jump . . . dangerous?" I asked.

"Takes a smidge of extra finesse, I guess you'd say."

A few people were milling around on the platform at the jump's summit.

"Is anyone going to jump now?" I asked.

"Nah, we're shutting it down for the day. Wind's too nasty up there."

"It looks rickety," I said. "And the railings are so *low*—why, just one little push and you'd simply topple over the side—"

"Oh, the fellers are experienced," Pickard said. "And we skiers have good balance, of course." He wore a green wool ski costume, I noticed, and oiled snow boots. Pinned to his breast was a badge that read MAPLE HILL ALPINE CLUB, with two crossed skis over a snow-peaked mountain. He noticed me eyeing the badge. "The Alpine Club started the Winter Carnival here in Maple Hill," he said with obvious pride. "Twelve years ago, now—took years off during the war, of course. Every year it's a little bit bigger—getting too big for its britches, really. There's not enough places for folks to stay. But the inns and shops and restaurants, why, they've come to depend on the carnival. Brings dollars to our out-of-the-way little village. Not that we started the carnival for the sake of money, of course." This last utterance was directed at Berta.

"Oh?" Berta said. "For what sake did you start it, then?"

"Why, for the love of snow sports, Mrs. Lundgren. Ski jumping, snowshoeing, toboggan racing, and alpine skiing, too—we've got plans to install a rope tow on this slope here." Pickard's eyes twinkled at Berta. "I'd enjoy giving you a skiing lesson before you leave town—if, that is, you don't suppose Mr. Lundgren would mind."

It was an effort not to roll my eyes.

"There is no Mr. Lundgren," Berta said, "and as for skiing, I am already proficient, but thank you."

"You? *Ski?*"

"Of course."

I wasn't sure if this was a whopper or not. Berta cannot abide officious persons, and sometimes she fibs in order to keep them in check.

Berta went on, "I was born and raised in Sweden, Mr. Pickard. We invented skiing."

Another man pulled up beside us, this one tall and lanky, with frizzled white eyebrows peeking out from a blue wool hat. He, too, wore oiled snow boots, a worn ski costume, and a MAPLE HILL ALPINE CLUB badge. "Hello, Pickard," he said. "Ladies. I could not help but overhear your discussion about the origins of skiing."

"Mr. Strom is the *other* president of the Maple Hill Alpine Club," Pickard said in a grudging voice.

We did another round of introductions and handshakes, with Strom clasping Berta's mitten tight in his own and not letting go. "I overheard you say you are from Sweden, and that the Swedes invented skiing. I myself was born in Norway, and I beg your pardon, but in fact the *Norwegians* invented skiing."

"Indeed not!" Berta tugged her hand away.

"Dear lady, you are mistaken." Strom's blue eyes sparkled.

"Don't antagonize her," Pickard said out of the corner of his mouth. To Berta he said, "Please forgive my friend. He isn't accustomed to speaking with ladies."

"Alas, that's true," Strom said, edging in front of Pickard. "Mrs. Lundgren, if I may be so bold—and if, of course, there is no Mr. Lundgren who might voice an objection—"

"Nope," I said, to help speed things along. With gloved fingers, I was clumsily fishing two of our agency cards from my handbag.

"Ah, good—then, Mrs. Lundgren, would you care to join me at the Alpine Club Lodge this evening for a drink? It's nice and cozy up there."

Berta's eyes glittered. "Only if you concede that the Swedes invented skiing."

"Ah, but I cannot tell a lie."

"Then I am afraid that I cannot accept your invitation."

Strom's shoulders sagged. Pickard, however, was smiling again.

"Mr. Pickard, Mr. Strom," I said, passing them the agency cards. "As you have heard, we are private detectives, now investigating the unfortunate death of Judith Goddard. If you don't mind, I have a few questions that perhaps you could answer."

"Glad to help," Pickard said, inspecting the card.

Strom said, "Certainly."

"Well, to begin with," I said, "why do you suppose George Goddard is going ahead with the ski jumping contest in the light of his mother's demise?"

"Oh, that's on account of Maynard Coburn," Pickard said.

"What do you mean?"

"Well, Maynard's going ahead with the contest, too."

"With his fiancée not yet buried?"

"Not much respect for the dead there, I'll grant you that," Pickard said. "But Maynard and George, well, they're just like two mountain goats with their horns locked. Neither is willing to back down. It's been like that for years, and it's a sad thing, too, seeing as what good friends they used to be."

"It all began with Patience Yarker," Pickard said.

Now we were getting somewhere. "What occurred with Patience Yarker?" I asked.

"She's a sweet girl," Strom said.

"I know, I know," Pickard said irritably. "It wasn't *her* fault what happened."

"What happened?" Berta asked.

"George Goddard and Maynard Coburn both fell in love with her at the same time, that's what," Strom said. "About a year back."

"It's terrible when two men fall for the same girl," I said, lifting a knowing eyebrow at Berta.

She gave me a stony look in return.

"Did Patience return either of the men's affections?" I asked.

"Didn't seem to," Strom said, "but that wasn't for lack of them trying. It was a wooing contest for months on end. George, what with his wealth, why, he showered the girl with flowers and chocolates and gosh knows what else. Maynard doesn't have much to his name, but he'd give Patience little attentions—pick her apples, write her little notes and leave 'em at the inn. Poor Patience, well, she seemed more embarrassed than anything else—she's a quiet, well-mannered girl, and from a good family, too—and it all died down late last summer. George went off somewhere for the fall—Europe, I think—and the next thing you know, Maynard's engaged to marry George's own mother! *Well.* I reckon George thinks Maynard's out to take everything that's his, if you know what I mean. And *that* brings us back to the ski jumping contest on Sunday. It's not really about the jump. It's about two young bucks' self-esteem. And *that,* ladies, is a dangerous thing."

"Will Maynard be practicing on the jump today?" I asked.

"He's already come and gone," Strom said. He turned to Berta. "How long will you be in Maple Hill, Mrs. Lundgren?"

"I am not yet certain." Berta patted her earflapped hat with a mitten.

"But surely you won't leave until you've solved your case?" Pickard said.

"No, we certainly won't," I said. "You fellows are in luck."

Berta shot me a dark look.

Strom grinned. "Then perhaps I shall see you at the coronation tomorrow evening, Mrs. Lundgren—if not before."

Berta frowned. "Coronation?"

"Of the Winter Carnival King and Queen. That's George Goddard and Patience Yarker, matter of fact. Funny, I didn't think how awkward that might be for 'em until just now."

11

Berta and I took our leave of the Alpine Club co-presidents and set forth for the village. Cedric was like a furry anvil in my arms and my feet were screaming with pain, but each time I set Cedric on his own four paws, he'd plop to a seated position and refuse to budge.

"He must have a little more exercise before we go in for the rest of the day," I said, lugging him along, "or he'll whittle the chair legs. Oh—I've just remembered. I have his rubber ball in my handbag. I'll look for a nice, open spot to give it a throw."

"Very well," Berta said, "but not for *too* long. I must return to the inn and rest. All this trooping about through forest and dell! It is wearisome."

"On the positive end, it's kept us nice and warm. And," I added slyly, "I suppose you'll want to look your freshest for the Winter Carnival tomorrow?"

"*Please,* Mrs. Woodby." Berta compressed her lips.

"Here's a theory," I said. "Despite what Mr. Pickard and Mr. Strom told us, what if Patience really *did* return Maynard Coburn's regard—

perhaps secretly? Then Maynard jilts her and becomes quickly engaged to Judith Goddard, and so Patience turns around and poisons Judith."

"Out of jealousy, you mean."

"Yes, and perhaps also desperation—if, you know, there's a pea in the pod."

"It makes some sense, I suppose. But then, why would Roy Ives have stolen the dossier from my room and burned it? And does he have a darkroom in *his* cellar?"

"Perhaps there is some connection between Patience and Roy that we haven't uncovered yet." I tried—and failed—to snap my gloved fingers. "I've got it—what about going to Roy's cottage to have a look in his cellar?"

"You mean *break in* to his cellar?"

"You make it sound criminal."

"It *is* criminal. I suppose we could do it . . . if Roy is not at home."

"You're reluctant."

"Of course I am reluctant, Mrs. Woodby! I am more than sixty years of age. My very bones ache from all this cold and higgledy-piggledying about, and it seems that every time I turn around, someone is killed!"

"That's only happened to us a few times," I said.

"One quick look in the cellar, and then I am afraid I must stay in for the remainder of the day and rest. I do not wish to be feverish in bed on Christmas Day."

We made our way through the bustling village to the covered bridge.

"Dandy—no one appears to be home," I said to Berta as we walked up the track to Roy Ives's cottage. "His motorcar is gone, and there's no smoke coming from the chimney. Let's try the kitchen door, so we'll be out of sight if anyone shows up."

We went through the picket gate and circled around the cottage.

"There is nothing to do about our footprints, I suppose," I said.

"No. But there are already lots of other footprints here, including our own from this morning."

From inside the cottage came the booming barks of Ammut. At least I now knew that he was harmless, if alarmingly large.

We were mounting the kitchen porch when I said, "Look. There's the cellar door." I pointed to a ground-level entrance, a wooden bulkhead door set at an angle against the foundation of the house.

The kitchen door shuddered against Ammut's weight.

Berta and I went down the porch steps and over to the cellar door.

"Rats," I said. "It's padlocked. Could you do your hairpin trick again, Berta?"

In silence, Berta removed her hat, extracted a hairpin, replaced her hat, and then bent over the padlock. She fiddled with it for a minute. Then two.

Ammut kept on barking, lending a sense of panic to an otherwise pastoral setting. The maple-treed slope rose up behind the cottage. I couldn't help wondering if I'd see a stealthy flash of dark fur—

"Presto," Berta said as the padlock made a tiny click.

I privately didn't think *presto* was quite accurate for a lock-picking that took three minutes to execute, but I would say that to Berta at my own peril.

Berta was opening the cellar door. The hinges squawked, and a stale odor puffed out. "Are you ready, Mrs. Woodby?"

I gulped. "Champing at the bit."

For the second time that day, I followed Berta into the dank unknown.

The cellar was dirt floored, and it smelled earthwormy. Instinctively, I hugged Cedric and tucked my nose into my scarf to filter the unwholesome air. The only light came in a pale shaft from the stairwell behind us. It wasn't a large space. We saw everything.

"Well," Berta said. "I believe *this* explains quite a bit."

"Does it?" I said. "Because I have questions."

About a dozen wooden crates sat in a low, untidy stack. One crate was open, revealing grime-filmed wine bottles. I picked up one—it was full, cork intact—and scrubbed grime from the label with my glove. "Château Margaux 1901," I read aloud. "Golly, this is a fine bottle of booze, Berta. Where did Roy get it?"

"Where does anyone get wine in this country? From a smuggler's middleman. It hardly means he is a killer."

"No. But it does confirm his impossibly luxurious tastes. If he wants to keep up this style of living, maybe he really does need to inherit—wait. Did you hear that?"

"Motorcar engine."

Berta and I scrambled out of the cellar, snapped the padlock back on, and dashed around the cottage. We were squashing ourselves simultaneously through the picket gate when a green motorcar rolled out of the covered bridge.

"*Rats*," I said under my breath as I waved to Roy, who was behind the wheel. "What's our story?"

"We were merely knocking upon the kitchen door, hoping to find him," Berta whispered back. She was waving, too.

"But why?"

"Ahh . . ."

Roy parked his motorcar and waddled over in a capacious camel coat and a cashmere scarf. "Good afternoon," he called, his eyes beady with suspicion.

"*Think of something!*" Berta whispered from the corner of her mouth.

"Hello, Mr. Ives," I said. "We were in the neighborhood, and we thought we'd ask if you'd, um, like to join us for dinner at the inn tonight."

Roy stopped. "Don't you think that's pushing things a bit far?" he asked coldly. "I mean, aren't I one of your murder suspects?"

"No?" I said cheerfully. "Oh well, it was worth a try. Come along, Berta." I tugged her sleeve, and we walked at a clip toward the covered bridge. "Have a lovely evening, Mr. Ives."

I didn't look back, but I knew Roy watched us until we vanished into the shadows of the bridge.

After a few minutes of walking, we were passing a flat, snowy field stretching alongside the frozen river, just on the edge of River Street. On the opposite side of the road stood the white clapboard Methodist church and, beside it, a trim green house with a picket fence and lace curtains in which, I suspected, the Reverend Mr. Currier resided.

"This field looks like a nice place to throw Cedric's ball," I said, setting Cedric down.

He looked up at me with accusing button eyes.

I took his red rubber ball from my handbag and threw it across the snow.

He perked his ears, skittered after it, and brought it back.

I threw it twice more, and he retrieved it. For a Pomeranian, he is an uncommonly enthusiastic retriever. On the third throw, however, the ball went too far and bounced into a heavy thicket close to the river.

"Phooey," I said. "I'll just go and get that." I stepped off the road and into the deeper snow of the field. Tiny Cedric had been bounding around on the icy top crust of snow, but with each step, *I* sank knee deep.

"Be careful at the edge of the river," Berta called after me. "You never know which parts are not frozen for one reason or another."

"I won't go anywhere near the river," I called back over my shoulder. Actually, it wasn't clear exactly where the field ended and the river began, although I assumed it was somewhere near those dry brown reeds spiking up from the snow.

I crunched laboriously toward the thicket, Cedric prancing along beside me on the crust. Freezing wind whipped down the valley and rattled the branches.

Then—a tiny blur of red sailed out of the thicket and landed near the river—no, *on* the river.

Cedric's ball. Some unseen person had thrown it—

And Cedric was running flat out after it.

"No!" I cried. "Cedric! Stop!"

Cedric ignored me.

I slogged after him, knee-deep in snow. He was crashing through the reeds, out onto the river ice—

"Come!" I screamed. If he were to fall through—

The red ball rolled across the river's flatness.

Cedric kept going, four yards, six, toward the middle of the river.

I reached the reeds and shoved through them. This was certainly frozen river here, although the crusted snow made it not so slippery as it could've been. "Peanut!" I cried. "Come! Come on, boy."

Cedric's nose touched the ball, sending it shooting even farther across the ice.

"No!" came Berta's windswept wail behind me. "Mrs. Woodby, it is not safe!"

"Cedric!" I croaked.

He pranced after his ball.

Horror clawed at my heart. Cedric was the only real family I had, and if he were to fall through and get swept away in a freezing dark current . . .

I minced and slipped after him across the marbleized ice.

A cracking sound cut the air. The ice beneath me shifted incrementally.

I managed to stay upright. I kept going.

"Cedric!" I cried. "Come!"

Cedric finally caught up to his ball and snatched it in his jaws. He turned, tail swishing, to look at me.

I should have turned back. He probably would have followed me to the riverbank. But I was so panicked at seeing my little peanut out there on the ice—a toy-size, bright-eyed marmalade puff—that I took the last few steps and swept him into my arms.

More cracking. The ice beneath me dropped an inch or two. Water oozed up from a long, dark seam.

"Mrs. Woodby!" Berta was calling behind me, closer now. "Turn back!"

"Mrs. Woodby!" came a man's voice. "Stay there! Don't move! I'm coming for you!"

Verrrrrry slowly, my pulse throbbing in my throat, I turned.

Mr. Currier was striding across the snow-covered field in shirtsleeves, carrying a ladder over his shoulder. "Don't move an inch!" he shouted. Berta was hovering amid the scrim of dry reeds.

Cedric squirmed in my arms. From the corner of my eye I saw the long, dark crack in the ice travel, as though alive, farther out.

I sank another inch. Water—so cold, it was almost jellylike—submerged my boots.

A whimper rolled out of my lungs.

"I'm going to slide this ladder across the ice," Currier called. He walked carefully onto the ice—his trousers were covered with snow—and, a few yards out, he crouched and lay the ladder flat. Slowly, he pushed it toward me. It made a scraping sound.

My feet were numb and soaked. Cedric wouldn't stop squirming. The crack was growing—and there was another crack now, too, stretching at another angle.

I spoke, trying to sound rational, but in fact sounding mousy. "I don't want Cedric to get wet," I said.

"Keep hold of him," Currier called. "Now. The ladder is only a yard away. Lean down—slowly—and catch the end rung."

I leaned.

The ice below me sagged and tipped. Water rushed up to my shins. I slipped, and fell to my knees. Cedric leapt neatly out of my arms and skittered toward the bank.

"Grab on!" Currier shouted.

I half fell, half dived for the end of the ladder just as the ice below me gave way, pitching at a sickening, RMS *Titanic* angle into a dark, swirling current. But I caught the last rung of the ladder, first with one hand and then—with a grunt—the other. Currier was dragging the ladder—and dragging *me*, like an enormous furry-wet seal.

I was in the reeds on the bank. Alive. Panting. Trying not to burst into tears.

"You're safe, Mrs. Woodby," Currier said. "*Safe*. Come along, before you catch your death of cold. My house is just on the other side of the road. You must warm yourself immediately."

I nodded. My teeth chattered, and the muscles in my back were tremoring in waves.

Berta had Cedric, and we made it across the field, over the road, through the gate, and into the minister's house.

12

Several minutes later, I was sitting in front of the wood fire in Mr. Currier's small, book-filled parlor with my snow boots (ruined!) and stockings off, a thick quilt laid over my lap, and Cedric on top of that. He wasn't even wet, except for a few melted snowflakes on his whiskers. He had lost his red rubber ball somewhere in the commotion, but I wouldn't mind never seeing that thing again.

And I was still shivering, with the odd tooth-chatter every thirty seconds or so. My feet felt cold to their very bones. I kept blinking away the image of the river's dark swirl whooshing under the ice. . . .

Currier could be heard in his kitchen at the rear of the small house, rattling china. Berta sat beside me.

"Someone was spying on us from that thicket," I whispered to her. "They might've even been following us."

"Spying?" Berta clucked her tongue. "The ball merely bounced off a tree trunk, causing it to ricochet onto the river—"

"No. Someone threw that ball. I'm sure of it. I saw the way it just shot out of the thicket. It was too . . . too *forceful.*"

"All right, and who do you suppose threw it? The fabled bear prankster, Slipperyback?"

"No," I said, although honestly, the idea *had* popped into my head. Blame it on shock. "I think it was Fenton Goddard."

"Fenton!"

"Think about it. We found his darkroom and his Peeping Tom photographs. We found *cyanide* in there. Besides, he didn't exactly hit it off with Cedric, you may recall. Fenton has every reason to wish to frighten us off, as well as to harm my dog." I stroked Cedric's fuzzy domed head. "We saw him today at Goddard Farm, after which he could easily have followed us—maybe even with his camera."

"Could not it have just as easily been Rosemary, or George, or Roy? We saw all of them, as well."

"Don't forget, Berta, that Fenton *kicked* Cedric. He's violent, and he's angry at us."

Mr. Currier entered, carrying a tray of tea things, which he set on a table. "Feeling all right?" he asked me. "Are you warm now?"

"Yes. Just a little nervy."

Currier poured cups of tea and passed them around. "Would you care for a slice of fruitcake?" he asked. "My housekeeper brought me one just yesterday. It looks rather delicious."

"No, thank you," I said quickly.

"Yes, please," Berta said.

We spent a pleasant hour drinking tea. Berta and Currier ate slices of dark, nutty fruitcake. I ate bread that Mr. Currier toasted on the fire, one slice at a time, and then slathered liberally with butter from a dairy that he said was only a few miles distant. Berta oversaw the butter slathering with silent approval. Currier told us about life in Maple Hill, where he had been minister for only two years, fresh out of Harvard Divinity School.

"That explains your library, then," I said, pointing to the book-lined walls.

"Yes."

"I believe reading is terribly important," Berta said, forking up her last bite of fruitcake. "Without it, one's mind is crippled. Mrs. Woodby and I are, of course, voracious readers."

Neither Berta nor I mentioned that our literary diet consisted mainly of pulp. One doesn't admit such things to graduates of Harvard Divinity School.

"You haven't lived in Maple Hill terribly long," I said to Currier, "but you must be acquainted with the Goddard family."

"Oh yes, of course. They aren't churchgoers—except for Mr. Ives. He is a regular attendee."

I tried to picture Roy Ives sitting in a church pew. It was a strain on the noodle. On the other hand, it wasn't as though *I* was a churchgoer. My mother was secretly an Irish Catholic, but she kept this fact hidden like a patch of ringworm. She never spoke of church once we moved to Park Avenue except in the context of society weddings, which were strictly Episcopalian.

"Still," Currier was saying, "one learns all about one's neighbors in a town as small as this. Of course, the Goddards are not year-round inhabitants—again, except for Mr. Ives. They have always kept themselves aloof, and, I am told, this aloofness only intensified after the death of Judith's husband, Elmer. He was a child of this place, but she was from a prominent Cleveland family."

"Elmer Goddard was born in Maple Hill?" Berta asked.

"Yes. He was a farmer's son, but he went away to Cleveland to make his fortune, rose through the ranks of the hotel business—he started as a bellhop, I believe—and eventually became the owner and manager of a rather luxurious hotel in Cleveland. Having made his fortune, he built a lavish country house near the Vermont village of his birth."

"Goddard Farm."

"Yes. Even with his newfound wealth from the hotel, Elmer still had old friends from childhood. Not many family, however. I believe there are no more native Goddards in this valley."

"Are the Cleveland Goddards friendly with the villagers?" Berta asked.

"Not really, no. Although Mrs. Rogerson—Rosemary—has lately become friendly with the woman who comes in to clean and cook for me every morning, Hester Albans."

"Hester Albans?" I said, feeling a lift of excitement.

"Do you know her?"

"We have met her briefly a few times at Goddard Farm."

"Oh yes, of course. Well, ever since Rosemary arrived in Maple Hill for her visit two weeks ago, she has been paying lengthy calls upon Miss Albans in my kitchen to enjoy a cup of tea and a cozy chat—by the by, Miss Albans baked this fruitcake."

"It is exceptionally flavorful," Berta said.

"Miss Albans and Mrs. Rogerson are an unlikely pair of friends," Currier said, "but then, that is so very often the nature of friendships."

"That reminds me of another friendship about which we learned today," I said. "Well, a rivalry that was once a friendship."

"Ah. You must be speaking of George Goddard and Maynard Coburn."

"Yes."

"I do not know George well at all. He is not a churchgoer, nor is he a regular resident of Maple Hill—although he was here for a several-month stretch last spring and summer, apparently wooing Patience Yarker, but nothing seemed to come of that and he went away, only to turn up again last week. I know Maynard slightly better, although he is not a churchgoer, either. He is a good fellow, keeps very busy, you know, with his sport. Skiing in winter—here and abroad—and in the summers, it is mountaineering. I encountered him once, high on a ridge above the village, which was rather amusing, since we both imagined ourselves quite alone—I am something of a mountaineering enthusiast myself. It is a tremendous help in writing sermons.

"Forgive me—I'm rambling. With regards to the rivalry between George and Maynard, I am not clear as to its nature. But I'm told the late Elmer Goddard saw something of himself in young Maynard—the deprived background and so forth—you know that Maynard's father was a Maine timberman, yes? When it was announced that Maynard was to marry Judith Goddard, I was equally as surprised as everyone else and, I confess, relieved that they intended to marry at an Episcopal cathedral in Cleveland rather than here. Alas, now I shall perform her funeral service the day after tomorrow at ten o'clock. How mysterious are the workings of God. At any rate, it is no wonder that her children were upset about the match—although, of course, no one should ever be upset enough to commit *murder.* More fruitcake, Mrs. Lundgren?"

After my boots and stockings were more or less dry, Currier and Berta left me alone in the parlor to pull them back on. Through the open curtains I saw deep shadows and fading streaks of light in the sky.

A sick horror washed over me when I realized that whoever had thrown Cedric's ball out onto the ice *could be watching me still.*

I yanked the curtains shut.

"Thank you for the tea," I said to Currier on his front porch. "And for rescuing me. I hope there is some way I can repay you."

"There is no need for that," he said. "My only hope is that you do not suffer any ill health as a consequence of exposure to that dreadful cold water."

Berta and I set off toward the inn. Snowy River Street looked blue in the twilight. The buildings along the way glowed with yellow light, and a few straggling merrymakers crisscrossed here and there, voices sharp in the cold air. We passed a lopsided snowman with a top hat and a carrot nose.

I couldn't shake the feeling that someone could be watching us, *following* us. . . .

Berta said, "It is a shame you did not sample a slice of Miss Albans's fruitcake."

"Ugh. No, thanks."

"It was most peculiarly soaked in alcohol."

"Really!"

"Whiskey, I think."

"Do you suppose Mr. Currier knows it?"

"I do not see how it could be avoided, Mrs. Woodby. Why, I feel rather zotzed after two slices."

That was the absurd thing about Prohibition. Giggle juice might have been illegal, but everyone and their granny was still drinking. Heck, we were all drinking more than before the amendment passed, because things are always more fun when they're naughty.

At the Old Mill Inn, a young man was sitting behind the front desk reading the funny papers. He fetched Berta's key. The airing cupboard in which I was to sleep, of course, did not have a key.

Which, come to think of it, wasn't a pleasant thought in the light of my possibly-being-watched-and-followed feeling.

"Where is Mr. Yarker?" I asked.

"*I'm* Mr. Yarker," Funny Papers said. He was plump and yellow-haired, with a stippling of pimples across his forehead.

"Samuel, I mean."

"Oh. Uncle Samuel. Abed."

"Is it his cough?"

"Gee whiz, you're nosy," Funny Papers replied. "You're the detectives, I guess."

"Is Mr. Yarker's illness serious?" I asked.

"It comes and goes. Dr. Best says it's chronic, whatever *that* is."

Next, Berta and I went to the coin-operated telephone in the remote hallway. We meant to ask Berta's friend Myrtle about potassium ferricyanide, and I meant to try to get hold of Ralph again.

Berta got on the telephone first, rattling off the number of the shared telephone in Myrtle's apartment building.

"Ah, Myrtle, dear, how are you?" Berta said when Myrtle at length picked up. "Goodness, what a crackly connection—please do speak up, dear—yes, far away. Vermont. I am so very glad to have caught you at home." They exchanged pleasantries about a great-nephew's birthday party, a crocheted cardigan, and an upcoming New Year's Eve party at the apartment of someone named, inexplicably, Zephyr the Magnificent, and then Berta got to the good stuff. "Myrtle, I wonder if you could check a fact for me. Potassium ferricyanide—yes, dear, do get a pencil—you do not require a pencil? You are well acquainted with—? Yes. Potassium ferricyanide—what was that? Oh yes, I *had* very nearly forgotten that your sister Olive is a photography hobbyist. . . . Yes, we do have our own camera, Myrtle, dear, the Eastman Kodak Brownie, but we always take our film to the camera shop to be developed so we do not . . . Yes. Thank you, Myrtle, and I do hope to be back in the city by Christmas. Yes. Goodbye, dear." Berta hung up the telephone and said to me, "Potassium ferricyanide is a fixative for gelatin prints, and it is every bit as toxic as other sorts of cyanide."

"Holy cow."

Berta and I agreed to meet for dinner in the dining room in an hour and a half. After she had toddled off, I pulled the alcove curtain shut, slid another nickel into the slot, and asked the operator to put me through to Ralph's number in the city.

Lots of rings, but no answer.

13

Carrying Cedric, I started wearily up to the inn's third floor with the intention of having a hot bath and a lie-down before dinner. I heard happy chatter from the dining room, and in the inn's sitting room, someone was playing "Deck the Halls" on a badly tuned piano.

All around me, other people were wallowing in Christmas joy. And here I was with nothing but wet stockings, a naughty little dog, a missing beau, and one pair of shockingly expensive, ruined boots.

It was time to face facts: Christmastime doesn't matter much when you don't have a family to share it with. And I no longer had a family.

Actually, my late husband Alfie's idea of a rollicking good time at Christmas had been hoofing it after hours with an assortment of gum-cracking chorus girls and gin-drenched profligates. Leaving me at home, of course, alone with the baked goods and the Victrola. So perhaps I was no worse off than before.

And Ralph, well, Ralph *never* had been bound by domestic rituals.

Homeless, we had found each other, but since we had failed to make a home together, we were doomed to drift in and out of each other's paths.

I couldn't blame Ralph or myself, really. It was simply a symptom of our mad, whirling, modern world.

Berta and I didn't talk much at dinner, but tucked into our pot roast and biscuits in a businesslike way. Grandma Yarker served us, saying that Patience was under the weather—and no, that did not go unnoticed. Although I would have supposed Patience's particular (theoretical) affliction would have made her feel under the weather in the *morning*.

Berta and I were both ravenous, and loopy with exhaustion, and my feet throbbed. I would have to do something about getting new boots in the morning. For the time being, I was wearing the frivolous black velvet T-straps that I'd worn at the ill-fated party at Goddard Farm last night. My feet had swollen so much, putting them on felt like stuffing baked potatoes back into their peels.

"Let's meet at eight o'clock for breakfast," I said as we were polishing off slices of pecan pie. "That will allow us plenty of sleep, and we know for certain that we wish to catch George Goddard at the ski jump at ten o—"

"*Shhh*." Berta placed a warning finger to her lips and tipped her head.

A man I hadn't fully noticed was hunkered over a nearby table, shoveling up bites of pie. He wasn't looking at us, but he wore the too-blank expression of an eavesdropper. He was squat and florid, with a threadbare three-piece suit and a disreputable air.

Walking upstairs, I asked Berta who the man was.

"I do not know, but he was most certainly eager to hear our conversation."

"Could he be another detective?"

"It is quite possible."

On the second floor, we bade each other good night, and I continued up to the third.

When I stepped into the airing cupboard, the bare dangling lightbulb glowed.

I'm in the habit of turning the lights off whenever I leave a room. I was certain I had yanked off the light before I went down to dinner.

And—what was *that*?

My nerves dithered as I stepped closer to my suitcase, which lay open on the floor as I'd left it.

Nestled inside the open blue satin pouch that held my cosmetics was a red rubber ball.

Cedric lost his ball somewhere out by the river. Someone brought it back.

This could be interpreted in only one way: it was a threat.

In the lavatory, I brushed my teeth and cold-creamed my face quickly. Back in the airing cupboard, I piled my suitcase, my handbag, my snow boots, and my coat against the unlockable door. That wouldn't prevent anyone from getting in, of course, but hopefully it would slow an intruder down.

I snuggled with Cedric on the army cot. It took me a good long while to fall asleep.

I bolted awake with a gasp. I did not know the time or where I was, but Cedric was somewhere—not in the cot—growling.

"Cedric?" I whispered. My mouth was dry.

More growling.

I peered into the darkness. I saw Cedric's fluffy silhouette against that peculiar floor-level window.

I stumbled over, sweeping hanging sheets from my path. I knelt beside Cedric and peered out.

The window faced the side of the inn, with a view up River Street to the east. While other windows in the inn had fans of frost at their corners, this one was clear, presumably because the airing cupboard was as warm as a Siberian sweat lodge.

I instantly saw what was causing Cedric to growl: a man was coming down the snowy, deserted street. He appeared to be intoxicated—he was weaving ever so slightly, and he wasn't wearing a hat. When he passed under one of the few streetlamps, I saw that it was Maynard Coburn.

Cedric and I watched until Maynard passed from view behind a store. He'd be circling around to his apartment above the inn's garage, probably.

"Come on, peanut. Showtime's over." I switched on the overhead lightbulb and checked my wristwatch, which I'd laid upon the *Christmas Romance* magazine next to my cot. It was 3:25 in the morning.

Where had Maynard been? Carousing at the Alpine Club Lodge, perhaps? Yes, that must have been it.

I went back to sleep.

I found Berta in the inn's dining room the next morning at eight o'clock.

"I'm afraid my poor boots are done for," I said, sitting down and placing Cedric at my feet. "Did you happen to notice a shoe store in town?"

"Certainly not. This is Maple Hill, not Madison Avenue. I did notice that the general store had a stock of sturdy-looking boots, however."

"Fine," I said, picturing the medium-heeled lace-up kind that the farmer's daughters always wear in theatrical productions. Those are actually rather cute, if not particularly warm. I'd wear two pairs of stockings. "Oh—I saw something odd last night—or, rather, in the wee hours of the morning—but allow me to drink some coffee first. I slept badly."

Berta poured me some coffee and nudged the cream pitcher across the tablecloth. She said, "Grandma Yarker and the cheeky young man from the front desk last night—"

"Oh, you mean Funny Papers?" I asked, pouring cream.

"If you insist. The two of them appear to be run off their feet this morning with the breakfast service. I do believe they are both cooking *and* serving."

"No sign of Patience, then?"

"No."

I drank some coffee. Then I told Berta about the red rubber ball I had found in my suitcase.

"Ah," she said knowingly. "A threat."

"Exactly," I said. "It was a reminder of how Cedric and I had very nearly fallen through the ice—likely to our deaths."

"Then the *murderer* must have placed the ball there."

"Yes."

"Perhaps to scare you off the investigation." Berta's voice spiraled upward with indignation. "Or perhaps as a sort of taunt. We cannot cave to threats or taunts, Mrs. Woodby."

"I wasn't planning on it," I said, sounding much braver than I felt. "And I have more to tell you." Between sips of coffee, I told Berta about seeing Maynard Coburn staggering home, apparently drunk, at three thirty in the morning.

"Say! Now, that's real inneresting," someone said. A newspaper, two tables away, lowered to reveal the florid face of the fellow we'd noticed eavesdropping last night. "*Real* inneresting," he repeated, rustling his newspaper for emphasis.

"I beg your pardon?" Berta said. "Have you been listening to our conversation?"

"Come on, gals, no need for the vinegary faces. I know your game—"

Berta went rigid with fury.

"—you're detectives. Everyone in town knows it. Why, when I checked in yesterday, the young pup at the front desk talked like you two were one of the local attractions. Aside from the murder, that is." The man's piggish little eyes sparkled. "Pretty juicy stuff, huh? *Pri-tee joo-seee.*"

I loathed him already.

"Now it's all coming clear," I said, pouring myself more coffee. "You're a reporter, aren't you?"

His eyebrows shot up. "How'd you know?"

"Threadbare three-piece, ink-stained fingertips, well-worn shoes—you walk a fair amount, don't you, sniffing down leads?"

"You're kinda swellheaded, aren't ya?" the man said.

"Not especially, no." Swollen-*footed*, yes.

"The name's Persons. Clive Persons. I'm a sportswriter for the *Cleveland Daily News*. Up here to cover the big ski jumping contest the day after tomorrow."

"Ah," I said.

Berta said, "Precisely why, Mr. Persons, did you remark that an early-morning sighting of Maynard Coburn was interesting?"

"Whaddaya mean? Coburn's the big draw. 'Cause now he's not just America's golden-boy skier—not that he's a world champ or anything, but folks are sure gaga about his hair." Person snickered, revealing a discolored snaggletooth. "What was I saying? Oh yeah. Now, his rich fiancée's gone and gotten *murdered.*" He was rubbing his hands together, as though sitting down to a feast. "And that was just the *first* stroke of luck for me."

What a creep. I said, "Why's that? Because now your story is about ski jumping *and* murder?"

"Egg-*zactly*."

"I'm not sure I wish to know about your second stroke of luck," I said.

"Well, that gets me back around to how come it was real inneresting hearing about Coburn coming home in the wee hours. Because I guess you haven't heard. . . ." Persons paused for dramatic effect, simultaneously licking his underlip and smiling.

Berta sighed heavily. "Please proceed, Mr. Persons."

"Whelp, it just so happens that there was a motorcar crash early this morning, only a few miles outsida Maple Hill."

My breath caught. "Was anyone hurt?"

"That's the funny thing about it, actually. The motorcar crashed into a stone wall alongside the road, see—next to some kinda farm—and the folks in the farmhouse heard the collision, woke 'em up, see, but when they ran outside—no one was there. Just the smashed, steaming motorcar. And the *real* funny thing is that the police said that car belonged to a pair of old folks down the valley. Turns out the motorcar was stolen recently and they never noticed, on account of them not having left the house for a week." Persons sat back in his chair. "Say, for a couple of detectives, you sure aren't catching on too quick, are ya?"

"Are you suggesting—" I did a quick scan of the dining room to make sure no one else was listening. "—are you saying you suppose *Maynard Coburn* was driving the motorcar? And that I saw him walking home afterwards?"

"Thatta girl."

Maynard's slight staggering *could* have been not drunkenness, but the woozy aftermath of a motorcar accident.

"Who told you all of this?" Berta asked Persons.

"Feller behind the counter at the general store. Went in to buy the papers before breakfast. I've got one word for you, ladies." Persons leaned in. "*Bootleggers.*"

"Bootleggers?" I said.

"Ya know. Daredevils who get paid to pick up a cargo of hooch at one of those line houses on the Canadian border and drive it down to a drop location in the United States? Quick and easy cash, but not exactly for the faint of heart."

Oh, I knew about bootleggers. The only catch was, the federal government was onto the game, and agents from the Bureau of Prohibition and the Customs Service were lurking behind every knoll in the border counties, on the lookout. I had read somewhere that a dead giveaway was the bootleggers' bad driving. They were usually nervy young men, and what's more, they would often drink to boost their courage before a run.

Persons was brushing crumbs off his waistcoated paunch. "I'll tell ya one thing, if I prove Maynard Coburn's a bootlegger, there'll be no more sportswriting for me. They'll hafta promote me to the big stories."

In silence, Berta and I watched Mr. Persons leave the dining room.

"We *must* speak with Maynard, pronto," I whispered.

"We cannot be distracted like kittens by every shiny thing that is dangled in our paths, Mrs. Woodby. Besides, I simply cannot believe Maynard Coburn would undertake such a foolish enterprise. He is famous."

"Sure, he's famous—*somewhat* famous—but he isn't wealthy. And what with his ski jumping and mountaineering and whatnot, why, he's probably got nerves of steel. Bootlegging would be a cinch."

"Would a person with nerves of steel crash a motorcar into a stone wall, Mrs. Woodby?"

"Maybe the Feds were on his tail. Maybe the motorcar slipped on the ice. Or maybe he simply lost his nerve because, oh, I don't know, his fiancée is dead?"

Berta sniffed. "Sheer speculation."

Funny Papers, the Yarker cousin with the pimply forehead, arrived beside our table in a ruffled chintz apron. "May I take your orders, ma'ams?" He was flushed with the exertion of waiting on several tables.

We ordered more coffee and cream, johnnycakes with maple syrup, sausages, and a bowl of water for Cedric.

"Where is your cousin Patience?" I asked him.

"Still abed. Won't get up. She told Grandma she's queasy and to leave her alone."

Geewhillikins.

"I beg your pardon," Berta said to Funny Papers, "but where does Patience live?"

"In the house right next door. Uncle Samuel, Patience, and Grandma, all under one roof. I live with my parents." Funny Papers' mouth pinched. "Patience doesn't care that we're booked solid and there's twice the usual amount of work to do. Hester Albans came in to help in the kitchen, thank goodness, but I'm still stuck wearing this apron."

"Perhaps someone should send for the doctor," Berta said.

"Nah, Patience'll recover, all right," Funny Papers said with a smirk. "She's got the Winter Carnival Queen coronation this evening, and she wouldn't miss wearing that crown for the world—even if it *is* only made of glass beads. She thinks of herself as a cut above, if you know what I mean. And . . . funny thing is—" He glanced over his shoulder and leaned in close. "—Maynard Coburn usually comes and has his breakfast in the kitchen—he doesn't have anything but an electric burner for coffee up in his apartment, see—but this morning *he's* still abed, too." He lifted a pale eyebrow. "You know, Patience isn't as innocent as she makes herself out to be."

Then, brisk again: "Okay, I'll go and put your orders in." Funny Papers left.

Berta and I looked at each other.

"I know what you're thinking," I said.

"And I know what *you* are thinking," Berta said.

"Of course, Funny Papers was dropping hints—these are the sorts of things he *wants* us to think. He feels resentful toward Patience, he wants to get her in trouble, and he knows we're detectives—"

"Still," Berta said, "what if there is some truth in the matter? What if Patience and Maynard are at this very moment . . . *together*?"

"A shocking notion." I sipped my coffee. "But surely not impossible. You packed the camera?"

"The Brownie, yes."

"It's all set with a spool of film?"

"Yes."

"Then I may have thought of an elegant solution to our problem of being stuck in Maple Hill. All we've got to do is snap a photograph of Patience and Maynard, you know, *together*, develop the film, and take the photograph to the police—"

"That does not sound elegant at *all*."

"—and surely that will be enough proof for anyone that Maynard had secrets from Judith Goddard, secrets big enough for which to kill. Or that Patience could have poisoned her rival, Judith. Or that Patience and Coburn were in cahoots."

"This is utter madness."

"Don't you want to be home for Christmas?"

Berta sighed. "Very much, yes."

14

It was a stab in the dark. I suppose Berta and I were growing desperate, but we didn't discuss desperation, only whether we should look for Patience and Maynard in the Yarker house next door or in Maynard's apartment above the inn's garage.

Having decided to try Maynard's apartment first (bonus: we knew where it was), we went to Berta's room and fetched our Eastman Kodak Brownie. This was a boxy little hobbyist's affair with a retractable lens. Not glamorous, but in the past it had delivered the goods.

"What shall we do if his door is locked?" Berta said.

"I've got a skeleton key in my handbag—I'll put it in my coat pocket."

"A skeleton key?"

"Sure. Ralph gave it to me for a present. So much more useful than flowers."

We put on our coats and, leaving Cedric on Berta's rug with a

Milk-Bone, went outside through a rear door and mounted the steps leading to Coburn's apartment.

At the top of the stairs, we put our ears close to the keyhole and listened. Absolutely anyone could've seen us if they happened to be looking out one of the inn's rear windows. This was a risk that I was willing to take if it meant I could catch the afternoon train out of town.

"I hear something," I whispered.

Berta checked the spooled film for the third time.

"No voices," I whispered. "Only a sort of rustling."

"There are no words in the language of love."

"Didn't I read that in *Christmas Romance* magazine?"

"We must act swiftly. If one of them jumps out of bed, I might not be able to get them both in the picture. It is important that they are in the same picture. Are you ready?"

I held up my skeleton key. "Ready." My pulse whooshed. This was nuts.

I fit the key into the lock. It made only a ghost of a rattle. I turned the key. I twisted the doorknob, shoved the door open, and stepped aside for Berta.

The next bit was a blur.

Berta thrust herself into the open doorway, camera to her chest. *Click* went the Brownie.

But she had not photographed Patience and Maynard cuddled in bed together. No, she had photographed Maynard standing at a mirror, lowering a toupee onto his patchily bald head.

He'd seen Berta through the mirror, seen her take the photograph.

He swung around, his face purple with fury, the toupee sagging over one ear. "What in the hell are you doing?"

"Oh dear," Berta said. "I beg your pardon. We seem to have come to the wrong place."

We spun around and stampeded down the stairs—"You two are off the tracks!" Maynard shouted after us—across the rear parking lot, through the inn's back door, and up the back stairs to Berta's room. We slammed ourselves inside.

I doubled over, laughing. "A toupee?" I gasped. "Not a lover, but a *toupee*?"

"I do not find it so very humorous, Mrs. Woodby. This is a dangerous development."

"What do you mean?" My laughter tapered off. I wiped a tear of mirth from my eye.

"When a man is seen with a lover, well, even if he ought not be in bed with her, his male pride has not been damaged. If anything, it is a *boon* to his pride. But a man whose use of a hairpiece has been not only discovered, but photographed?" Berta shook her head. "There is nothing so dangerous as a vain man whose pride has been hurt." She lowered herself into a chair. "That beautiful golden hair . . . a hoax. Maynard is famous for that hair, Mrs. Woodby. The way it wafts on the ski slopes . . . None of those magazine covers and cigarette advertisements he has appeared in would have been possible if it were publicly known that he is *bald*. I had only the briefest glimpse, but it did not appear to be the distinguished sort of baldness, either."

"No," I said. "It was the mangy sort."

"Mark my words, this is very dangerous."

"Then why don't we go back and, I don't know, hand over the film as a show of good faith?"

"It is too late. We have seen the unspeakable. What is more . . ." A long pause ensued, during which Berta's pale blue eyes gleamed.

"Why are your eyes gleaming like that?" I asked. "Have you detected a hot lead?"

"Better. I have just realized that having that photograph of Maynard's toupee application gives us leverage over him, should we need it in the future."

"Berta! *Blackmail?*"

"You need not pretend to be shocked, Mrs. Woodby. We must use every means at our disposal to swiftly solve this case. Perhaps, for instance, our possession of the photograph will prompt Maynard to be forthcoming when we finally have an opportunity to interview him."

A few minutes later, we set forth once more from Berta's room (this time with Cedric in his green turtleneck sweater), armed with a to-do list I'd jotted in my detecting notebook. It looked like this:

Speak with George Goddard (10:00 at ski jump)
Speak with Rosemary Rogerson and Fenton Goddard
Ask Hester Albans about her kitchen visits with Rosemary
Interview Maynard Coburn

"I've just remembered that Funny Papers said Hester Albans is helping in the kitchen this morning," I said as we went down the stairs. "Let's try to have a word."

Hester was indeed in the large, untidy kitchen, up to her elbows in suds at a zinc sink. Grandma Yarker and Funny Papers must've been out in the dining room. When I said "Good morning, Miss Albans," Hester's shoulders tensed.

She turned her head only halfway, so she was looking at Berta and me from the corner of her eye. "Oh. It's you." She kept scrubbing at something underneath the suds.

I said, "Miss Albans, the Reverend Mr. Currier told us that you keep house for him—"

"You leave Mr. Currier be!" Hester said, flushing.

Oh dear. Was it one of *those* dreary scenarios, then—the Reverend Mr. Too Handsome, secretly adored by his spinster parishioner?

"—and he mentioned in passing that you and Rosemary—Mrs. Rogerson, I mean—have struck up a friendship."

"So?"

"Do you . . . bake with Mrs. Rogerson?" I asked.

Hester's breath caught—almost inaudibly, but I heard it. "Get. Out," she snarled.

Gee. What could be so terrible about baking?

The door leading to the dining room swung open, and Funny Papers came in with a tray piled with dirty dishes. He went to Hester's side at the sink and placed the tray on the draining board. "Whew," he said, smearing his forearm across his brow. "The dining room is crackers this morning. I never saw so much bacon being eaten in such a short time. It's hair-raising. Say—" His eyes fixed on Berta and me. "—what're you two doing back here in the kitchen, anyway? Did you . . . find Patience?" Another eyebrow waggle.

"No, we did not," Berta said.

"Too bad," Funny Papers said. He was reaching for something on the open shelf above the sink—a small glass jug of maple syrup—then unscrewing the cap. He tipped the bottle to his lips and took a long swallow. "Ahhh," he said, coming up for air. "Nothing like Vermont's finest maple syrup to get a feller through the workday."

Berta and I traded a glance.

"Miss Albans," Berta said, "is that by any chance the same kind of *maple syrup* you use in your fruitcake recipe?"

"Maybe," Hester said on a grunt.

"Want some?" Funny Papers asked, holding out the jug.

"No, thank you," I said. "I can smell it from here. Whiskey, I think?"

"You got it."

"Thank you for your help," Berta said to Hester, even though she'd been as helpful as a kick in the caboose.

Berta and I hurried out the way we'd come.

"Whiskey in the maple syrup jug?" I whispered as we went along the back hallway. "Is *everyone* bending the elbow *all the time* in this town? Good grief!"

"It is the wintertime, Mrs. Woodby. It is cold outside. People do require the occasional warming nip."

The next order of business was purchasing a new pair of boots for my poor blistered feet. We went across the street to the general store.

To my horror, there were no cute, farmer's daughter medium-heeled lace-up boots to be had. There were only three pairs of men's work boots, brown, stiff, and clunky-soled.

"These?" I said to Berta in disbelief. "*These* are the boots you spoke of?"

"What did you expect? The latest frivolities from Paris? We are in Vermont, for pity's sake. Please do hurry up." Berta was peeling back her coat sleeve to look at her wristwatch. "I wish to reach the ski jump hill before George Goddard begins his practice, and it is already ten past nine."

"Then we've got gobs of time."

The smallest of the three pairs of men's work boots would still be a few sizes too large. Worse, I'd lose two inches of height. It wasn't that I was *short*, but those two inches were essential to my feeling not-dowdy. On the other hand, it *would* be scrumptious to walk without pain, and my velvet T-straps were out of the question in the snow.

With a sigh, I selected the smallest pair of boots, a pair of thick wool socks, a fresh box of maple sugar candies, and carried it all to the cash register.

After a trip back to the inn so I could change into my boots (Berta was practically bursting with impatience by then, but she was mollified by a maple sugar candy), we were going through the village toward the ski hill. Sunlight glinted off icicles. Children were out in force, shouting merrily, building snow forts, and sledding down any available slope. The mountains rose gently all around us, lacy with bare brown trees.

I stopped in my tracks. "Berta! Is that—? Yes, it's Rosemary Rogerson, and look, she's coming out of that house. She's at it again! Quick. *Hide*."

Berta and I scurried behind a snow-bogged hedge and crouched down. I created a peephole by burrowing my gloved hand through the hedge, causing some of the snow to cascade away.

Berta and I peeked through. Rosemary said goodbye to a woman in the doorway, went down the steps, and, after a furtive glance to the left and right, hurried up the street.

"Caught red-handed again," I whispered.

"Yes, but caught red-handed doing what?"

"Let's go and ask her."

"But the *time*, Mrs. Woodby—"

"We've got ages until ten o'clock."

Berta and I got up, brushed snow off our knees, and hurried after Rosemary.

15

Mrs. Rogerson!" I called as Berta and I followed Rosemary down the snow-clotted street. "Oh, Mrs. *Rogersooon*!"

Rosemary's shoulders stiffened, but she didn't stop or turn around. She was carrying a handbag, and some sort of book pressed tight to her bosom.

"I can't believe it!" I said. "She's speeding up!"

"Oh dear, we are destined to be out of breath again," Berta said with a light moan.

"Have two slices of pie at lunch and you'll recover." I had already picked up the pace, feeling unusually athletic in my new man-boots.

Rosemary was hiding something, and the fact that she couldn't face Berta and me suggested it was something important.

Something, perhaps, to do with murder.

Rosemary hurried through the streets, Berta and I huffing and puffing half a block behind.

"Do you believe it?" I said. "Rosemary's quicker on her feet than we are."

"She has guilt on her side. It works wonders on one's stamina, or so I am told."

Having traversed the busy length of River Street, Rosemary was headed for the red-painted covered bridge that, I knew, connected to the road to Goddard Farm.

"She must have walked to the village this morning," I said.

A motorcar was rumbling down the road on the other side of the river. It entered the bridge, and Rosemary had no choice but to stand aside and wait outside the bridge for it to pass.

This was just the amount of time Berta and I needed to catch up to her.

"Mrs. Rogerson," I said breathlessly.

Rosemary spun around. Her eyeglasses were fogged up. "Oh, what is it? You women are mad, do you know that? Mad! Chasing me down the street? Why, I have half a mind to go straight to the police station and report you!" She adjusted her grip on the book clasped to her bosom. It was a plain, brown book with no lettering, like a journal. "Well? Out with it."

Berta, gasping for breath, said, "To put it simply, we would like to know why you pay secretive calls upon women in the village."

Rosemary made a derisive noise. "*Truly*. Do you realize how absurd you sound? Why shouldn't I pay calls upon the village women? I've known most of them my entire life. Why don't you attend to the really dangerous people and leave me alone?"

"Who do you suppose the really dangerous people are?" I asked. "You must realize that it was likely someone in your own family who poisoned your mother. One of your brothers. Or your uncle."

"You're forgetting Maynard Coburn," Rosemary said. "*You* know, the fortune-hunter? Oh, I knew no good would come of it when Mother started taking him around to all her glitzy dos in Cleveland as though he were some sort of expensive lapdog." She turned her foggy eyeglasses in Cedric's direction.

"Am I to understand that you dislike dogs?" I asked in a cool tone.

"I *adore* animals," Rosemary said unconvincingly.

"I don't believe it," I said. "Your brother Fenton doesn't like dogs, either. He kicked Cedric yesterday—"

"Because you were intruding in his darkroom! He told me all about it. You *upset* him. But as I said, Maynard Coburn should be your chief suspect."

"Why is that?" Berta asked.

"Because he was more than twenty years younger than Mother, that's why! It was positively humiliating for me, you know, having everyone I knew asking me about their relations—and then, lately, their *engagement,* ugh!—not to mention keeping it from my little children, Mabel and Oliver, that their grandmother was bent on being the most decadent, most outrageous woman possible."

"Perhaps she was in love," Berta said.

"Love? Mother? Ha! She was incapable of love. She only wanted to prove to the world that she was still beautiful and desirable. As for Maynard, well, he only wished to marry her for her money."

"Then why would Maynard poison her?" I said. "Wouldn't that be a case of biting the hand that feeds you?"

"Heaven knows. Something to do with another woman, probably. He couldn't stick to only one, you realize."

"Do you refer to Patience Yarker?" Berta asked.

"Oh, he was done with Patience. Because, you see, the thing about Maynard is, he lives for thrills. Making a conquest gives him a thrill, but once that's done, he's got to move on to the next. There is something voraciously hungry about him. Insatiable. I suppose it's because of the way he grew up. Poor, you know, a filthy little hillbilly from the backwoods of Maine."

This was uttered with such venom, I wondered if Rosemary could herself have once been jilted by Maynard. No. Surely not. They appeared to be about the same age—around thirty—but while he was an Adonis (albeit a secretly bald one), she was the stodgiest of Society Matrons.

"It's just like Mother to get herself murdered, you know," Rosemary said. It wasn't that she had warmed to Berta and me, but that she had found a vent for her spite. It was coming hard and fast now. "She couldn't simply die quietly of pneumonia or something like that, oh, no. She must die in a sensational way that made it into the national newspapers. I only hope that the scandal dies down quickly, and without any harm done to my husband's business."

"Why did your family not accompany you here to Vermont?" Berta asked.

Rosemary sniffed. "I keep my children away from the noxious influence of their relations. I must do my familial duty and visit when required, but I'll leave my poor little darlings at home, thank you very much. And my husband, of course, is terribly busy with his work."

"I recall that your husband owns a cash-and-carry self-service store chain in Ohio," Berta said. This was a tidbit from her stolen dossier.

"Yes. Rogerson's Stores."

Rogerson's Stores. *Rogerson's Stores!*

At last, I realized why my mind had been pinging at every mention of Rosemary's married name.

"The maple syrup factory in the village is called Rogerson's Brand Maple Syrup," I said. "Is there any connection to you or your husband?"

"My husband owns the factory, yes." Rosemary pruned her lips. "He owns dozens of factories. I *do* hope I have satisfied your vulgar curiosity, and I'm afraid that I really must be going. Good morning." She spun around, clearly with the intent to hurry onto the covered bridge. But at that precise moment, a snowball arced through the air, hit her in the side of the head, and skewed her hat. She lost her footing, and as she flailed to regain her balance, the book spun out of her hand and thumped into the roadside snowbank.

Rosemary dived for the book, snatched it up.

I had only the briefest glimpse of scribbly penciled pages before she smacked it shut. "I wish you two would go away," Rosemary snarled, shoving her slipped glasses back up her nose. "You're nuisances."

"Who threw that snowball?" I said. "I didn't see anyone." I peered into a stand of icy brush on the other side of the road. Was that flicker in its depths a bird, or . . . something else?

"Some ill-behaved child," Rosemary said.

"If I were a superstitious woman," I said, "I'd blame Slipperyback." I said this only—all right, *mostly*—to see Rosemary's reaction to the mention of the legendary bear.

She scoffed. "The local fools blame every little prank and mishap on their monster. If you ask me, it only gives the local children an excuse to be naughty."

Rosemary marched onto the covered bridge, her footfalls thunking on the boards.

"Whoever threw that snowball could've gotten an earful," I whispered to Berta as we walked once more in the direction of the ski hill. "Her husband owns the maple syrup factory! And what do you suppose was in her notebook?"

"Addresses, perhaps, or reminders, or, well, it really could be many things. Did you make out any of the words?"

"No." The handwriting had been slanted and frail. Finishing school handwriting.

"Nor I."

"But . . ."

"If this entails more chasing, Mrs. Woodby, I am afraid I must decline. What is more, it is now approaching ten o'clock, and we risk missing George Goddard at the ski hill again."

"No chasing. We'll walk as slowly as molasses if you wish, all the way back to the house from which we saw Rosemary emerge, and ask what Rosemary was doing there. It's on the way to the ski hill."

Berta answered with a put-upon sigh.

However, when we spoke to the woman of that house, she was not inclined to answer.

She was a plump, pretty woman with hair tinseled with silver, in a well-made dress and apron. She looked at us suspiciously through a half-opened door. Delicious buttery, nutmeggy aromas wafted from behind her.

"Mrs. Rogerson? What business is it of yours why she's paying me calls? Who are you? Here for the Winter Carnival, I suppose? How I wish Mr. Pickard never got it into his head to start that everlasting thing! Our peaceful town overrun with noisy, rude city folk, and for what? A few extra dollars for the inn and the general store?"

"Mrs. Rogerson carried a notebook," I said.

"Aha, you're newspaper reporters, is that it? That explains why you're wearing men's shoes, then. Prying into poor Mrs. Goddard's death?"

"Um—" I said.

"Yes," Berta said. "Tell me, who do you suppose poisoned Mrs. Goddard?"

"I reckon it was only a terrible accident."

"And yet . . . ," Berta prompted.

"No, no more questions. I must say good morning to you. I've got pies in the oven." The door slammed shut.

We crunched along through the snow.

"Do you know what I think?" I said. "I think Rosemary has some way of preventing that woman from speaking with us—and Hester Albans, too."

"Blackmail?" Berta sounded excited.

"Not necessarily. Maybe she simply pays them not to disclose what she's up to. Whatever that could be . . . What *could* it be?"

"She could be planning something. A church function, perhaps. Or something to do with her husband's maple syrup factory."

"Why the secrecy, then?"

"Perhaps she is planning, oh, a surprise birthday party for someone."

"But she's so shifty and angry about it."

"Not every person to plan a birthday party is pleasant, Mrs. Woodby."

We were walking past the village green, bustling once more with carnival preparations, and then passing the knitting factory, then the long, white clapboard building with the sign reading ROGERSON'S BRAND MAPLE SYRUP.

"Shall we have a peek?" I whispered to Berta. "See if Rosemary's got any skeletons hidden in there? The windows are dark and there aren't any footprints in the snow leading to the door. Maybe it's no longer in business and Rosemary's broke—"

"Please. *Focus*. We must get to the ski hill!"

"Oh, all right."

"I do not know what has come over you, Mrs. Woodby."

"It's these boots. They make me feel invincible." Actually, they made me feel dumpy. Not, of course, that that was an important consideration.

16

We reached the bottom of the ski hill where, just like yesterday, a few vehicles were parked. I recognized the luxurious motorcar George had been driving when he evaded us. I released Cedric, and Berta and I looked up, up—shading our eyes from the bright sunlight with our hands—to see three men on the tippy-top of the scaffold.

"George is up there," I said. "We'll have to wait till he comes down."

"Oh, he *must* come down," Berta said.

Up on the scaffold, the men's voices grew more animated, and then George was positioning himself at the top of the jump, aligning his skis, bending his knees, leaning forward—finally he launched himself—

Down he went, picking up speed, then—UP! the swoop and into the air—and he was flying.

Forward and down George went over the mountainside, waving his arms a little for some mysterious sporty reason I couldn't fathom, and then—*wumph*—with a wobble he landed, steadied himself, and zipped along the silky snow to the bottom of the slope.

"Wowie," I said to Berta, "he isn't half-bad at this."

"No, although not nearly at the level of Maynard Coburn. Unless Maynard is in poor form during the competition tomorrow, I cannot imagine that George will stand a chance at besting him."

George caught sight of Berta and me gawking, and he did a fancy sideways swoosh on his skis and pulled up beside us. His handsome face was flushed with cold, and his brown eyes danced with what must've been elation from the jump.

"If it isn't the Detective Twins," he said, breathing hard. "How'd you like that?"

"It was marvelous," I said.

Berta said, "I suspect you would get farther if you leaned forward toward the tips of your skis once you are in the air."

George looked confused.

"Mrs. Lundgren is from Sweden," I said.

"Recent innovations in the sport suggest that leaning forward gets you farther," Berta said.

"You don't mean to say *you* ski," George said, looking Berta's sugar bowl figure down and up.

"Indeed I do," Berta snapped.

"Mr. Goddard," I said, wedging myself in front of Berta, "I wonder if we could have a few words."

"About my mother's death."

"Yes."

"Which you're investigating because the police forbade you to leave town."

I swallowed. "Yes."

"You can't be very good detectives if you go and get yourselves implicated in murders at every turn," George said. "And what kind of business are you operating, anyway, pinching jewelry for your clients? I'm sorry to break it to you, but that's not detecting. That's run-of-the-mill crime."

Pink spots had appeared on Berta's cheeks. "We have learned that your mother hired us to retrieve a ring that rightfully belonged to her. Your great-aunt Daphne has confirmed as much."

"Sounds like something Mother would do. She liked to pull the strings."

"It has come to our attention that your brother, Fenton, keeps potassium ferricyanide in his photographic darkroom in the cellar," Berta said.

"Potassium what?" George said, scratching his head beneath his wool hat.

"In short, cyanide," I said. "According to Sergeant Peletier, that was the poison that caused your mother's death. I do not mean to be overly blunt, but—"

"*I* will be blunt," Berta said. "Mr. Goddard, is it possible that Fenton poisoned your mother?"

George's eyebrows lifted. Then he squinted past Berta and me, as though pondering the possibility. Finally, he shook his head. "I don't buy it. It was an accident. It had to be."

Funny. George was the first person to suggest this.

"Perhaps it *was* an accident," I said. "Either way, we must get to the bottom of the matter."

"The police are investigating it."

"The more heads, the better."

"As my sister, Rosemary, said, too many cooks spoil the soup."

"That reminds me," I said. "We noticed Rosemary helping a village woman make a pie in a rather furtive manner."

George gave a bark of laughter. "Rosemary can't bake to save her life! She *wishes* she could—just like she wishes she kept a spotless house single-handedly and raised angelic children, as she lets on in those pompous books she writes—but she can't."

Mrs. Rogerson's Practical Guide to Housekeeping and *Mrs. Rogerson's Practical Guide to Childrearing* were a bunch of baloney, then?

"Mr. Currier, the Methodist minister, suggested that Rosemary is on quite friendly terms with Hester Albans, as well," Berta said.

"No! Hester? The *servant*? Haven't you two figured out that Rosemary is a snob? She only consorts with the peasants when she's at her charitable work."

"What is her charitable work?" I asked.

"Something about temperance—or was it orphans? I can't remember. She dabbles in it whenever she's here in Maple Hill—which isn't very often, actually. I think she wishes to keep up the Grand Benevolent Lady act for the villagers. Feeds the sense of her own nobility."

"Rosemary has been known to stop in Mr. Currier's kitchen when Hester is working there, simply for a cup of tea and a cozy chat."

"Oh? That's difficult to picture. Perhaps it's something to do with her charitable work as well. She's got to have *something* to do to kill the hours until the will is read."

"And when might that be?" I asked.

"After the funeral tomorrow."

"At the house?"

"Yes. The family lawyer is on his way from Cleveland now."

"Any notion who your mother's heirs will be?"

"Trying to figure out whether one of us bumped her off for the estate, is that it?"

"There are worse motives." I was thinking of what Aunt Daphne had said about Uncle Roy killing to preserve his style of living.

"I'll have you know that my siblings and I are comfortably off," George said. "Father set up trusts for us long ago, and they're more than adequate."

"What about Mr. Ives?" Berta said.

"Uncle Roy?" George scowled. "Well, of course, *he* doesn't have a trust fund. He's only Mother's lazy brother. Squandered his own inheritance years ago. He's a great, fat leech."

That's more or less what Aunt Daphne had said.

"But I understand he is a rather successful greeting card artist," I said.

"You call that a job?"

That was rather rich, coming from a young man who seemed to subsist entirely on a trust fund as he traveled the globe in pursuit of expensive pleasures. But I had known more than my share of good-for-nothing fellows with hereditary bucks. (I'd been married to one, after all.) They often felt that *they* were entitled to leisure, but that the riffraff must humbly toil.

"And Aunt Daphne?" I said. "Is she financially independent?"

"Don't tell me *she's* one of your murder suspects," George said.

"No, she isn't. She was sitting near Mrs. Lundgren and me during the critical moments."

"Aunt Daphne is Mother's aunt—she's really my great-aunt—and, yes, she's extremely well off. She and Mother didn't travel in precisely the same circles in Cleveland—I was surprised that Mother invited her up for the engagement party, actually, and surprised that she came. I suppose Aunt Daphne steers clear so she doesn't get saddled with baby-minding Fenton."

"Fenton does not attend college, I understand?" Berta said.

"You met him. He's a child, and always shall be. Can you imagine setting him loose on a campus? And then there was Fenton's jealousy of"—George swallowed thickly—"of Maynard. Mother wanted a long honeymoon with that scoundrel, and she meant to leave Fenton behind with Uncle Roy. Well, Fenton *and* Uncle Roy were raising a ruckus about that. Fenton was making Mother miserable, moping and skulking and complaining—even more than usual, I mean. Between you and me, I wouldn't be surprised if Mother poisoned herself just to be rid of Fenton." A pause. "That was a joke."

"Ah."

"Pardon me," Berta said, "but what was that you said about Fenton being jealous of Maynard Coburn?"

George rolled his eyes. "Well, of course he was. Fenton was in an absolute panic over the engagement. He's always been hideously jealous, and he's always sort of, well, *latched on* to women. Always *one* particular woman, you know, over whom he obsesses. When we were children, he was in love with our nurserymaid—a beautiful girl called Colette. Well, Colette preferred me over Fenton and Rosemary. Rosemary didn't care, of course—all she wanted was to be left in peace to play with her dollhouse—but Fenton, well, he couldn't stand it. This was when he was, oh, seven years old. He took it out on me, and then he took it out on Colette. First, it was only little things. Making an awful mess with his food so that she'd have to clean it all up. Pricking her with a pin. But then, one warm summer day when all the nursery windows were open—and the Cleveland nursery was up on the top floor, four stories up, you understand—Fenton tried to push Colette out the window."

Berta and I exchanged alarmed glances.

"It was a good thing Fenton has always been a weakling," George said, "because she would've died if she had fallen. She gave her notice that very day. After that, it was Mrs. Helmstein, who was a drill sergeant." George looked between Berta and me, and burst out laughing. "If you could only see the expressions on your faces! I know what you're thinking, but it can't be true. Fenton was too tied up in the apron strings to kill Mother. Someone else he could've poisoned, easily. But never darling Mother. As I said, I'm sure her death must've been an accident. But if you're bent on proving it's murder, why, if I were you, I'd take a good, hard look at Maynard Coburn."

"Why?" I asked.

"Isn't it obvious? He's a fortune-hunter."

"But fortune-hunters generally attempt to marry money," I said, "not commit murder before they get their hands on the boodle."

"Not if Mother already wrote him into her will."

Oh.

Berta said, "I was told that you and Maynard Coburn were once good friends, but that relations have cooled over the years."

"You certainly have been busy little bumblebees, haven't you?" George said. He was growing angry, now that the lens was trained upon him. "Yes, we were friends for a time at Dartmouth. We both enjoyed skiing and having a good time. We lost touch after college—the war began only a month after we graduated, and Maynard took himself off to be a hero." This was spoken with a sarcastic curl of the lip.

"Did you go to war, Mr. Goddard?" Berta asked.

"Oh, no. Not me." George scratched his nose. "Flat feet. Desperately frustrating for me, of course, that I couldn't do my bit."

We all regarded George's feet, shod in snow boots and strapped and buckled onto skis.

"How nice that you are still able to enjoy sport with your flat feet," Berta said in an innocent tone.

George flushed. "Mark my words, if murder's the game, then Maynard's your man. He's a—well, I guess you could say he's an innate thief. He's hungry for money, and it gives him a thrill to swipe things out from other men's noses."

"You mean, to swipe *women*," I said. "Such as . . . Patience Yarker?"

George's eyes flared.

Up on the ski jump platform, a man shouted George's name.

"Listen, I've got to go up and do a few more runs." George bent and unbuckled his skis, hefted them, and tucked them under his arm. "See you round." He started the trek up the mountainside.

"It is ever so narcissistic for George to believe that Maynard wished to marry his mother simply to goad *him*," Berta said once George was out of earshot.

"Forget about that," I said. "If that story about Fenton nearly killing the nurserymaid is to be believed—!"

"We must ask Rosemary to confirm the incident."

"She won't be pleased to see us again."

"No."

Golly, I didn't wish to go up to Goddard Farm once more. That place gave me the heebie-jeebies. "*Fenton* will likely be there," I said.

"Then we will stay away from the windows—and keep your canine restrained."

17

The Rogerson's Brand Maple Syrup factory sign called out to me as Berta and I walked back through the village to fetch the Speedwagon. We meant to drive up to Goddard Farm.

Berta noticed me eyeing the factory. "No," she said. "That place has nothing whatever to do with the murder."

"How can you be sure?" I said. "We may as well have a peek through the windows. Isn't the idea of huge vats of maple syrup at all intriguing?"

"You find it intriguing only because you are growing hungry for lunch, Mrs. Woo—"

"Look! Footprints. Berta, there are footprints leading to the syrup factory door—there weren't any when we passed by earlier. I'm sure of it. Someone is in there."

"Why should there not be someone in there?"

"I'm . . . I'm not certain. Something about the factory is bugging me, that's all. Perhaps because Funny Papers was drinking whiskey out of that maple syrup bottle."

"That was merely his decoy, so he could suckle with impunity."

"Let's go and ask a few questions of whoever's in there."

"You are stalling because you do not wish to go to Goddard Farm."

"Quite possibly."

We followed the single pair of footprints in the snow, up to the door under the syrup factory's sign. I knocked.

We waited. And waited. I tried to put Cedric down, but he wouldn't allow it. Down on the village green, partially visible from where we stood, ice sculptors were putting the finishing touches on angels, Santa Clauses, and an ice castle the size of two motorcars. The igloo appeared to be complete, and awning-covered tables had been set up under the trees.

I was just reaching for the door's handle when it swung open.

The worn face of Hester Albans appeared. "You again!" she said.

"Goodness, Miss Albans," Berta said cheerfully, "I did not expect to find *you* here. Why, you work in ever so many places, your poor thing."

Hester softened a little. "Yes, well, I never did marry and I've got to keep a roof over my head, haven't I?"

"We sympathize completely," Berta said. "Mrs. Woodby and I make our own livings as well—do you mind if we come in? Mrs. Woodby is most curious about the maple syrup operation—sweet tooth, you understand."

Hester shifted her weight from one foot to the other. "Well, maybe for a minute or two."

"Oh, good," Berta said, squeezing past Hester into the factory.

I followed, and Hester—after a worried glance out into the village—shut the door.

The factory was one enormous, freezing-cold room with a wooden floor. The only light came from high, square windows. One end of the space was taken up by stacks of wooden crates, half-lit by a ray of light. The middle of the room had two long, empty tables, and the other end was cluttered with mysterious metal equipment.

"The factory only runs during sugaring time," Hester said.

"When is that?" I asked.

"At the end of the winter."

That explained the shut-up look of the factory, then.

"During sugaring time," Hester said, sweeping her arm, "there's hustle and bustle in here. The factory employs a dozen village women—Mrs. Apple, Miss Yarker from the inn, Mrs. Allen and her daughter Astrid, and more besides. We're all happy for the extra income. Farmers bring in their sap and we boil it down, bottle it up, and slap on Rogerson's labels."

"Pardon me," I said. "Boil it down?"

Hester sniffed. "You city folk. I reckon you thought maple syrup came out of a faucet stuck in a tree, didn't you? Thought you could put your plate of flapjacks under the spigot and go to town?"

"Certainly not," I lied. "Although that does sound delightful."

"I beg your pardon, Miss Albans," Berta said, "but I confess to being surprised that Rosemary's husband owns this factory. I understand he is the owner of a large grocery store chain in Cleveland."

"Well, the factory fell upon hard times a few years back, so Mr. Rogerson snapped it up for a steal. It's now the chief supplier of syrup for his Cleveland stores. That's why I'm here today. I'm the factory's only year-round employee. The syrup is not only made and bottled here, but stored—see all those crates over there?" Hester pointed to the wooden crates. "I'm responsible for shipping crates down to the stores in Cleveland when they need them. They send me orders by telegram one, two times a week. Today I'm sending two crates down on the afternoon train. I label them with the store addresses and take them to the train depot. Doesn't pay much, but then again, it doesn't take much of my time, either."

That was it, then. Boring old commerce. A dead end that had nothing whatsoever to do with Judith Goddard's death.

I studiously avoided Berta's *I told you so* look as we thanked Hester and took our leave.

After that, we retrieved the Speedwagon from River Street and motored up to Goddard Farm. Rosemary answered the door. When she saw it was Berta and me, she yanked the door so it was open only a few inches.

"Have you no shame?" she said. Her eyeglasses were sliding down her nose.

"Mrs. Rogerson," Berta said, "did your brother Fenton attempt to push a nurserymaid out of a window when he was a little boy?"

Rosemary shoved her glasses into place. "You suppose that a boyhood indiscretion is somehow proof that Fenton killed Mother?"

I privately thought that attempted murder was not a mere *indiscretion*, but I kept my lips zipped.

"What of a motive?" Rosemary asked, her tone victorious. "Fenton was devoted to Mother."

I said, "We came across some of Fenton's unsettling photographs—"

"'Came across'? Hah! You were intruding!"

"—including one of Patience Yarker and George." I cleared my throat. "Canoodling."

Rosemary's cheeks went pasty. "That doesn't mean Fenton *killed* anyone. He's been creeping about, photographing people since Father gave him a camera on his tenth birthday. It's harmless."

"He spies," I said.

"So do you."

"Fair enough."

"*Someone* murdered your mother," Berta said. "If not Fenton, then who?"

"Maynard," Rosemary said. "Or Patience Yarker. Someone from outside the family."

Slam went the door.

"Lunch, Mrs. Woodby?" Berta said.

I had oodles of questions piling up in my mind, but Berta was quite right. Lunch was, as it so often is, the first order of business.

"Okeydoke," I said.

Back in the village, someone had taken my parking spot in front of the Old Mill Inn, so I had no choice but to leave it two blocks down River Street. The new spot, however, was just in front of Peggy's Restaurant, which looked bright and cheerful and warm, so we went in. The hostess didn't blink an eye at Cedric, luckily, and seated us at a table near a blissfully radiating woodstove.

Over hot, creamy potato chowder, Berta and I discussed what we'd learned (quite a bit) and what we could make of any of it (zip).

"I require rest after lunch," Berta said with a sigh. "I want nothing more than a hot-water bottle, a cup of tea, a footstool, and a book."

"All right," I said, feeding Cedric a last nibble of the steak I'd ordered for him. I wouldn't say it aloud—after all, Berta was three decades my senior—but I wouldn't have minded a rest myself. My spirit sagged under the knowledge that we weren't going to be leaving Maple Hill on the afternoon train. We were stuck for at least another day.

We needed a breakthrough like anything.

"This evening, the Winter Carnival officially begins," I said, wrapping the rest of Cedric's steak in a piece of notebook paper so he could have it for his dinner. "Perhaps we can glean more information there." I shoved the wrapped steak in my handbag. The things I do for love.

....

We set off walking toward the inn.

"This dreadful wind," Berta said, clutching her scarf against a cold burst from the valley. "I feel as though I do not have the fortitude to fend it off."

"You always say Nature protects us," I said.

"Do I? Today I quite feel like it is attempting to spank me."

We were passing the town hall. A small crowd had gathered around a wooden noticeboard. The crowd's worried murmurs and shaking heads, so different from the village's general air of festivity, caused Berta and me to stop.

Everyone was looking, not at a printed announcement, but at three photographs tacked to the board. From a few paces off, the photographs looked like nothing more than black, white, and gray blobs.

Yet something about the haphazard way they'd been pinned gave me the collywobbles.

Hugging Cedric to my chest, I inserted myself into the crowd and looked.

One photograph depicted Patience Yarker, laughing and rosy cheeked, ice-skating in baggy trousers and a fitted jacket. She looked fresh, lovely, and free—and very much as though she was unaware of being photographed.

The second photograph was one Berta and I had seen drying in Fenton's darkroom: Patience and George Goddard in a snowy wood, locked in a passionate kiss.

The third photograph depicted a young woman sleeping peacefully in bed. This one was quite grainy—the room was dim—but there was no mistaking that this, too, was Patience.

My skin prickled, and it wasn't because of the winter air. Because who had a camera?

Fenton. That's who. Fenton Goddard, near-murderer of nursery-maids.

Fenton had been in Patience Yarker's bedroom while she was sleeping, photographing her. And hadn't George told us that Fenton latched on to women in an obsessive fashion?

"Oh my," Berta whispered.

"Ditto," I whispered back. "Come on." I looked around the group of gawkers, which was growing as passersby peeled off to see what the fuss was about. "We should tell Patience about these photographs—surely she'll want them taken down."

"*We* should take them down."

"No." I shook my head. "Sergeant Peletier will accuse us of meddling."

We hurried to the inn. Patience herself was seated behind the front desk in the lobby. She looked up in surprise when Berta and I stopped, both of us agitated and panting, before her. Even Cedric was panting, which was absurd, since I had carried him.

"What's the matter?" Patience asked.

"*You* tell her, Mrs. Woodby," Berta said.

"Miss Yarker," I said, "I'm afraid we have some unsettling news. On the town hall noticeboard, there are . . . three photographs of you."

"Of me?" Patience's eyebrows shot together.

"You'd better go and see," I said. "We would have taken them down ourselves, but we feared Sergeant Peletier would accuse us of meddling again."

"I can't leave the desk unattended. Dad would be so annoyed. We have six check-ins today—"

"We'll mind the desk," I said. "Go on."

"All right. Thank you—I'll be back in a few minutes. If anyone comes to check in, have them wait for me." Patience went away, her cheeks pale and her eyes wide.

18

I went behind the front desk and sat down on the swiveling stool. Cedric snuffled the unoccupied cat cushion at my feet. If he hadn't been wearing a turtleneck sweater, I'm sure his hackles would've risen.

"I shall just go upstairs for my rest," Berta said.

"Not so fast," I said.

"My feet are aching loaves of agony, Mrs. Woodby."

"But we haven't discussed those photographs." I looked left and right. The lobby and stairs were unoccupied. Still, I brought my voice down to a whisper. "Those photographs—are you supposing that Fenton snapped them?"

"Seeing as one of them was identical to one in his darkroom, yes, of course."

"I think so, too. But do you suppose Fenton pinned them to that noticeboard?"

"Anyone could have pinned them, and they could have been pinned up at any time. The question is, what do they *mean*?"

"Isn't it obvious? Fenton's been snapping secret photographs of

Patience, and that means he has some kind of . . . of unwholesome interest in her. I mean, it's downright spooky. He skulks around after her with a camera, watching her smooch his brother, watching her sleep . . . I'm afraid Patience could be in danger."

"That is taking it a bit far."

"Is it? There's a murderer afoot, Berta. We can't be too careful. We've established that Fenton is violent, that he is dangerous, *obsessive*—"

"What do you propose? That we ask Patience if she would like us to be her hired muscle? Please. I *must* rest." Berta went upstairs, looking alarmingly slow-footed and stooped.

She was fed up with gumshoeing. I knew that. But why wasn't she as worried as I was about Fenton?

I swiveled the stool I sat on, back and forth, back and forth. I examined my fingernails. I hummed a Christmas carol or two, and in the middle of "Silent Night," I noticed a corner of what I thought was a magazine, protruding from beneath the reservation book.

A magazine. Just the ticket for while I'm waiting.

I slid aside the reservation book to reveal not a magazine, but a selection of colorful hotel brochures from Catalina Island, California. Waikiki, Hawaii. Havana, Cuba. Swanky hotels. The sort of hotel you wouldn't suppose was in the budget for a young woman employed at an inn in rural Vermont.

Unless, of course, Patience was, say, *planning her honeymoon.*

But whom was she going to marry? George Goddard? Or was it Maynard Coburn? I wasn't even sure if Maynard could afford such luxurious hotels, unless—*yes*—unless he had a windfall.

A windfall, for instance, from Judith Goddard's will. If, as George had suggested, Maynard had managed to get himself named as a beneficiary even before the marriage.

My thoughts spun and mad theories half presented themselves

as I absently polished off the maple sugar candies in my handbag. Cedric drifted to sleep on the cat cushion. No one arrived in the lobby to check in. None of my theories seemed especially plausible.

After several minutes, Patience burst into the lobby in a swirl of wind and snowflakes. Her eyes glittered with fury, and her cheeks were fuchsia. She clutched the photographs in one mitten.

"The nerve of him!" she said, striding over to the desk. She left a trail of snow on the floor. "He was—he was *spying* on me!"

"You mean Fenton?" I asked, standing and stepping away from the stool.

"Yes, of course, Fenton. He . . . he . . ." Patience's voice trailed off and she sank onto the stool. The photographs trembled in her hand.

"I think you should tell the police, Patience—"

"The police!"

"Fenton intruded upon your bedroom when you were asleep. How did he get in there, anyway?"

"We don't keep our doors locked here in Maple Hill. He knows where I live. He must have simply . . . walked in." Patience shivered. "I'll tell you one thing, Mrs. Woodby, I'll be locking my bedroom door from now on."

"Are you sure you won't report Fenton to the police?"

"No." Patience jutted her chin. "I don't want to cause a fuss. The coronation's this evening, and I don't want it to be spoiled by Sergeant Peletier nosing around. Although . . ."

"What is it?"

"It's probably nothing, but, well, Fenton has been really chewed up about George and me being the carnival king and queen—"

"Surely Fenton can't have hoped to be crowned carnival king," I said.

"No! What a thought. Still, he's mad with jealousy."

"Because he's in love with you."

"Ugh. It's not love—well, I suppose *he* thinks it's love."

"And because you and George . . . have reached some sort of understanding?"

Patience looked down—to, it seemed, the corner of the Waikiki brochure poking out from beneath the reservation book. She sighed. "Not yet."

"Did Mrs. Goddard—?"

"*No!*" Patience looked up at me again, her eyebrows drawn. This time, she was angry at *me*. "Everyone's had it up to here with your snooping. Why don't you and Mrs. Lundgren just—just *go home*?"

How I wished that I could.

"Patience," I said, "I don't like to spread gossip, but in this case . . ." In low tones, I relayed to Patience the story George had told us, of how Fenton had once tried to push their nurserymaid out the window.

By the time I had finished, Patience's eyes were wide. "George told you that?"

"Yes."

"He never said anything like that to me, and we . . ."

I leaned forward a bit. "Yes?"

"Well . . ."

Patience and I both regarded the topmost photograph in her hand, the one of George and her in the midst of a winter wonderland smooch.

"Perhaps George didn't wish to upset you," I said.

Patience shook her head. "George would never say anything against his family."

That was funny, because he'd had no qualms about disparaging all of them to Berta and me.

"He's really proud of his family's station, you see," Patience said. "Proud of their wealth. He refuses to say anything, *do* anything, that might bring them down a notch in anyone's eyes." She was still wearing her checked wool coat, and she ran a mitten fleetingly across her belly.

She caught me looking, and glanced away. Then, if I wasn't mistaken, she gulped.

Something was bugging me. I mean, I'd read piles of novellas in which the peasant girl is spurned by the family of her hoity-toity lover. It rarely ends well. And if Patience really *did* have a pea in the pod—George's pea—and Mrs. Goddard had not been sympathetic . . . well, maybe Patience or George or both of them together bumped off Judith Goddard for the sake of their pea.

Not that poor Patience, slumped there on the stool with embarrassing photos in hand and snow melting on her boots, seemed like a killer. But *George* could've done it, easy as pie.

If that were the case, what in the bally bazookas had Patience been arguing about with Maynard Coburn yesterday morning? Could she still be caught between the two men, regardless (or *because*) of a pea? And, could I truly be thinking such shocking things about angel-faced Patience Yarker? Patience was the sort of girl who probably made you feel like Lancelot or something if you were a fellow. Never mind that damsels are never as naïve as they seem. Heck, even Guinevere was probably on the make.

"Patience," I said, "yesterday I happened to witness what appeared to be an argument between you and Mr. Coburn, outside his door—"

"Spying?" Patience smirked as she unbuttoned her coat. "Well, I suppose detectives simply can't help themselves, can they? He borrowed something from the kitchen—a coffee percolator—and Grandma needed it back because of all the extra guests."

I was almost sure she was lying—she hadn't left Maynard's door with a percolator in hand—but I said, "Oh, that makes perfect sense. Now, listen, Patience, please do be careful about Fenton. The thing is, those photographs must have been posted—posted *today*—for a reason."

Her eyes grew round. "What sort of reason?"

"I suspect it's some sort of warning. Or a threat." I picked up sleepy Cedric from the cat cushion. "Please be careful, Patience. If Fenton comes into the lobby—"

"I'll run straight to the back office," she said. "Dad keeps his gun there."

I went upstairs to Berta's room, my man-boots clunking on the carpeted treads. I found her with her stocking feet propped up on a footstool before the electric fire, novel in lap and flask in hand.

I sat down, released Cedric (he went straight to the electric fire), and told her about Patience's reaction to the photographs.

"Oh, and listen to *this*," I said. "She has quite an assortment of full-color brochures for swanky hotels hidden under the reservation book downstairs."

"For her honeymoon," Berta said at once. "I *knew* she was a plotter."

"We know nothing for certain. She could simply enjoy looking at the brochures—fantasizing, I mean."

"She seems more practical than that."

"True." On the other hand, getting into the pudding club without benefit of marriage was just about as *im*practical as it got. "Berta, I fear that Fenton could present a danger to Patience. She told me he thinks he's in love with her, and if the nurserymaid story is true, Fenton's idea of love is dangerous, especially when he grows jealous. He knows about George and Patience, and what's more, she said he's torn up about them being crowned king and queen of the carnival this evening. I figure Fenton posted the photographs today because of the coronation coming up. What if he's planning something? Something violent?"

"It all sounds very *petty*, does it not? Quite like a radio drama."

"People lose their perspective."

"Or, Mrs. Woodby, is it only that *you* have lost *your* perspective?"

"I can't helping thinking Fenton threw Cedric's ball out onto the river yesterday—that he tried to kill *me*."

Berta sighed. "Oh, very well. We will keep our eyes upon Fenton this evening at the carnival. But in the meantime, we *must* rest. It is unwise to continuously expose oneself to the elements, as we have been doing. We will catch our deaths if we are not careful."

19

I don't know, Berta," I said with a shiver. "This is supposed to be festive and yuletide-ish, but doesn't it all seem a little, well, *sinister?*"

It was past six o'clock, the sun long set, and we were walking amid a stream of merrymakers onto the village green. Kerosene lanterns hung from bare tree branches. Everyone—man, woman, and child—was bundled up, so only watering eyes and red noses could be seen. In the center of the green, the ice castle glittered by torchlight. Laughing children crawled in and out of the igloo. Lovers holding hands *ooh*ed and *ahh*ed over fanciful ice sculptures. Snowmen leered from the shadowy margins.

"Sinister?" Berta said. "That is simply your imagination, Mrs. Woodby. Or perhaps you are suffering from a touch of indigestion due to the three slices of pie you enjoyed for dessert?"

"We've got to keep our strength up in this cold. I read that Eskimos eat blubber straight. They say it tastes a bit like butter." I craned my neck, searching for Fenton, except with everyone so bundled up, how would I spot him if he were here? "Oh," I said, my belly lurching. "Now, *that* is decidedly sinister."

We stopped before an ice sculpture of a bear rearing up on its hind legs. It was at least eight feet tall, and something about the snarling curl of the bear's lip made my neck crawl. "I suppose that's good old Slipperyback," I said. "He certainly seems to have captured the local imagination. Golly, look at those claws. You could make shredded wheat with those."

Berta wasn't listening to me. "Ah, there is Patience, over there beside the ice castle," she said. "Goodness, she is in trousers."

I had vaguely assumed Patience, as the Winter Carnival Queen, would be attired in some sort of gown, but instead she wore snow boots, trousers, and a short fur jacket. She had the look of some sort of glamorous flapper adventurer.

She was speaking—shyly, it seemed—with a cluster of fellows. One of them held a camera. Another was wrestling with a notebook and pencil with mittened hands. Newspapermen.

"The fellow with the camera is Mr. Persons," I said to Berta.

"Angling for his scoop on Maynard Coburn, I suppose."

"By speaking with Patience?"

"Well, she is surely familiar with every syllable of local gossip."

A clump of people walked past, obscuring our view of Patience and the newspapermen.

"We've got to keep moving or we'll freeze," I said. "There is a hot cocoa stand—I could use a splash of that."

"We are here to spot Fenton and prevent him from committing nefarious deeds. Or have you given up on that outlandish theory?"

"It's not outlandish, and the hot cocoas will help us to *blend in*."

We threaded through the crowd, which was growing thicker and noisier by the minute.

We passed a tent selling baked goods to benefit the Methodist church. Hester Albans, bundled head to toe in wool, was grimly doling out slices of what I guessed was fruitcake, although it very well could have been lead bricks. The Reverend Mr. Currier was assisting her in a hapless fashion, as though juggling newborn kittens, not passing plates of cake.

We arrived at a second tent. A banner announced in red, holly-festooned lettering,

HOT COCOA 5¢
Support the
Maple Hill Mothers' Temperance League

I gave Berta a nudge. "Say. Rosemary Goddard is helping out with the Mothers' Temperance League. Perhaps that's what her little meetings with the village women are all about."

We got into the line. Rosemary was ladling hot cocoa from a big, steaming tureen into china cups. A delicious, chocolatey-creamy aroma drifted on the biting air.

When Berta and I arrived at the front of the line, Rosemary regarded us through her gleaming eyeglasses.

"Good evening, Mrs. Rogerson," I said cheerily, sliding my nickel into the donation jar. "The Mothers' Temperance League! Is that what all the secrecy was about, slinking around from house to house around the village? Temperance is nothing to be ashamed of."

Rosemary only sniffed in response. The portions of hot cocoa she ladled into our cups were skimpy. "Make certain to return the cups. Next!"

Berta and I carried our cups off to the side, and Berta stealthily unscrewed her gin flask and medicinally spruced up our hot cocoas.

"Do you suppose that's all it was?" I asked Berta. "I mean about Rosemary skulking. The Mothers' Temperance League?"

"No. I am certain she is hiding something. What, I cannot begin to imagine."

"Mrs. Lundgren! How good to see you!" Mr. Pickard, the bow-legged, white mustached co-president of the Maple Hill Alpine Club, parked himself in front of us.

Mr. Strom, the other co-president, popped into view over his shoulder. "Mrs. Lundgren, good evening!" he cried in his resonant baritone. "How well you look! What a charming hat! Did you knit it yourself?"

"I did," Berta said, giving her fleecy blue hat with the earflaps a pat.

"Could I interest you in a turn around the ice-skating pond?" Strom asked her. "We could rent you a pair of skates."

"I was just about to ask Mrs. Lundgren the very same thing," Pickard said through his teeth.

"Were you?" Strom said, rocking on his heels. "Too bad you were so slow about it." He looked to Berta. "What do you say? I'll bet you're an ace on the skates."

I cleared my throat. "Mrs. Lundgren and I were actually here to view the corona—"

"Boring," Strom said.

"But—"

"Won't be starting for a good fifteen, twenty minutes," Pickard said. "Plenty of time for skating." He proffered a plaid wool arm to Berta.

"Just a moment, Mr. Pickard, Mr. Strom," I said.

Berta dropped her arm to her side. She glared at me, but Strom appeared to be relieved. He'd have another shot at cutting Pickard off at the pass.

"I'm simply wondering," I said, "who chooses the carnival king and queen. Is there some sort of vote?"

"Nope," Pickard said. "*We* decide."

"You?"

"The Alpine Club."

"That's rather interesting," I said.

"*Is* it, Mrs. Woodby?" Berta said in an undertone. She clearly couldn't wait to go ice-skating with her double helping of beaus.

"Yes," I said, "because, well, George Goddard isn't even a year-round resident—or, I've got it—I suppose you chose him because, with his gossip-column sort of notoriety, he'll bring extra publicity to the carnival?"

Pickard and Strom exchanged sidelong looks.

"What?" I said. "What is it?"

The two men seemed to come to a silent understanding. Then Strom turned to me. "We chose George Goddard as the carnival king because he asked us to choose him."

"Why would he want that?" Of course I wouldn't say it aloud, but it seemed a rather Podunk honor for a cosmopolitan playboy.

"So that Maynard Coburn *couldn't* be the king," Strom said. "We *had* planned to ask Maynard Coburn, of course, since he's the only celebrity Maple Hill's got."

"But George Goddard has got this *itch* to outdo Maynard at every turn," Pickard said.

Berta said, "I beg your pardon, but why did you agree that George Goddard should be king? Did he—" She delicately cleared her throat. "—offer a financial incentive?"

Once again, Pickard and Strom exchanged looks. Once again, they seemed to come to an unspoken agreement.

"Nothing like that," Strom said, fiddling with his glove.

"Nope," Pickard said. "Nothing too interesting." He looked up into the starry sky. "Nice night, isn't it?"

They weren't going to spill.

"Why did Patience Yarker consent to be the carnival queen?" I asked.

"Why, isn't it obvious?" Pickard said. "She's the prettiest gal in the village, by a long shot. Don't let my great-niece Mary know I said that, or there'll be hell to pay." He chuckled.

"Nah, that's not it," Strom said. "Oh sure, she's pretty as a picture, but so are plenty of other girls—my great-niece Astrid, for one." He said this with a competitive look at Pickard. "Patience is no spring chicken, either—why, she's twenty-three if she's a day. People are starting to wonder why she hasn't wed, truth be told. She'll wind up a spinster."

I thought of the Possible Pea and Samuel Yarker's gun, and figured that the Alpine Club co-presidents might be in for a big surprise.

Strom went on, "Patience has been Winter Carnival Queen for, well, I guess it's nigh on five years now, ever since we started the carnival up again after the war."

"Why is she always the queen?" I asked. "I mean to say, she seems to be a serious, hardworking young woman, not in any way frivolous or attention seeking."

Strom said, "She does it for her father. She'll do anything for that father of hers, bless his soul."

"Because he is . . . ill?" I asked, thinking of Samuel Yarker's cough.

"That's right. Weak lungs. Can't be cured. Been sick for years. And poor Patience, why, I've seen the look on her face, watching him hacking his lungs out. She looks as though her heart is right breaking in two. And that's why she's always carnival queen. It pleases her father. Makes him proud to see his little girl up there with a crown on her head."

"Nope, nope, you got it all wrong." Pickard was shaking his head, eyes closed. He sighed, opened his eyes, and looked at me. "My co-president oftentimes gets the cart a little ahead of the horse—don't mind him. Now, see, Mrs. Woodby, the truth of the matter—and this is something Mr. Strom here has plumb forgotten, but he can't be blamed—did you know, Mrs. Lundgren, that he's four years older than I?—he's forgotten that George Goddard said he wouldn't be the king unless Patience was his queen."

"But why?" I asked.

"To one-up Maynard Coburn, of course," Pickard said. "With George, it's all about Maynard. Men who try to one-up their fellows, well, they're to be pitied, I suppose. Now, Mrs. Lundgren." He proffered his arm again. "I think we still have time for a few turns around the skating pond before the coronation. What do you say?"

"She said she'd go with *me*," Strom said, flushing.

"I will go with both of you," Berta said, hooking her free arm through Strom's.

"What about our investigation?" I whispered through clenched teeth. Had she completely forgotten our aim to keep track of Fenton?

"We will split up," Berta said, looking rosy and glowy eyed. "That will be most efficient. I will find you when the coronation begins, Mrs. Woodby."

"Sure," I said, but I didn't think she'd heard, and the men whisked her away into the crowd.

20

After that, I had nothing to do but lurk and slink with Cedric in my arms, searching for Fenton in the commotion.

I spied Roy Ives. He was bundled in head-to-toe cashmere, his face as red as beet stew. Ammut, the enormous, furry black dog, plodded beside him with his jowls festooned with drool.

In my arms, Cedric curled his lip and let lose a growl.

"Shush, peanut," I whispered. "That dog sheds hairballs larger than you." Louder, I called, "Good evening, Mr. Ives!"

Roy stopped, and looked around. His eyes were filmy and pink-rimmed, his mouth slack.

Drunk.

"How nice to see you," I said, stepping closer. "Are you enjoying the carnival?"

"It's not what I'd term 'enjoyable,' my dear Mrs.—was it Woodson?" Roy's words were ever so faintly slurred.

"Woodby."

"One must walk the dog, and so one may as well take in the bread and circus, as it were." He cast a pitying glance around the throngs of merrymakers. "And, of course, one gathers inspiration for one's work on such occasions."

"You mean for your Christmas cards," I said.

"Mm. Although really, once you've seen one ice-skating pond stuffed with rosy-cheeked brats, you've seen them all. Good evening, Mrs. Woodson." Roy walked on.

"Woodby," I called after him.

He didn't appear to have heard.

Next, I caught sight of Sergeant Peletier striding around on his short, bandy legs, elfin face scrunched against the cold, beady eyes peering hard at everyone, as though he were searching for someone.

For, perhaps, Berta and me?

I ducked out of sight behind an igloo and waited for him to pass—

And bumped right into someone. I swung around. In my arms, Cedric snarled.

Fenton Goddard, thin and stooped, stood with a camera in his gloved hands.

"Goodness!" I cried, recoiling. "What are you doing back here? Taking more photographs?"

"That's none of your business," Fenton said in a raspy voice. He wore a puffy, dark fur coat—mink?—and a fur hat. His face was pinched against the cold, his long, thin nose pink at the tip.

He moved to sidle past me.

"Might I have a word?" I asked brightly, stepping into his path. Cedric writhed and growled in my arms, as though he'd attack Fenton.

"Step aside."

"I'd like to speak with you."

"After you set that bloodthirsty dog of yours after me? After it *bit* me?"

I petted Cedric's ears, trying to calm him. "I suppose you miss your mother awfully, Fenton."

"Not a bit. I'm free."

I lifted my eyebrows. "But everyone has been telling me—"

"Mother was always bossing me about. Mocking me. Belittling me. I wished to go to college, you know, but she made out as though she simply couldn't do without me. So I put aside my plans, and then—and then she got engaged to that—that pompous pretty boy and she cast me aside! Told me she was going to honeymoon in Europe with him for six months, perhaps longer. She was going to leave me behind with *Uncle Roy*." Fenton's eyes were glassy, almost feverish.

"Would being left behind with Uncle Roy truly be so bad?" I asked. "I mean, surely you would've had the run of Goddard Fa—"

"He's a drunk!" Fenton cried.

Cedric yipped.

"And that awful, *revolting* dog of his," Fenton said, bestowing a look of contempt upon Cedric. "Oh, Uncle Roy lives in his cottage now, but he wants the big house. He'd creep in. He'd take over. Before I'd know what was happening, he'd be staggering about the house stinking of wine and wearing his robe in the afternoon."

"You threw the ball out onto the river yesterday, didn't you, Fenton? You tried to kill me."

"You deserve to be killed."

Was that a confession?

"I saw the potassium ferricyanide in your darkroom," I said. "It was cyanide that killed your mother."

"Every darkroom requires potassium ferricyanide. Your little *clue* means nothing."

"You had easy access to the poison."

"Any one of the family could have brought their own supply."

True. I'd try a different tack to rattle him. Rattled suspects slip up. "I saw the photographs you took of Patience, Fenton. I saw them pinned up in front of the town hall. Why did you do it? To frighten her? To humiliate her, or to wreak vengeance?"

"I didn't pin up those photographs," Fenton said. "Someone stole them from my darkroom."

"Who?"

"I don't know."

"When?"

"*I don't know.*" A flash of Fenton's sharp incisors.

Bats had those sorts of teeth, didn't they? And vampires, of course, although I had never seen a vampire at the cinema who wore a fur coat.

"Well, then, I'm not sure I can believe you, Fenton," I said.

"I don't care."

"Do you mean to take more photographs tonight?" I asked, gesturing to the camera slung around his neck.

"I take my camera everywhere. You never know what you might come across." He gave me a nasty little smile.

"And I suppose you intend to photograph Patience Yarker some more?"

"The coronation might make for a good shot, but then again, the light isn't good."

"No, it isn't. Say, are you just a wee bit, well, jealous of your brother George?"

Fenton scoffed. "George is an idiot. He devotes all his time to attempting to break his own neck."

"But Patience loves him."

"She doesn't!"

"I believe she does."

"*No.* She wouldn't. She isn't that—that *stupid.*" Fenton's face drained of color, and his eyes flicked left, right, down, up. He leaned closer and in the torchlight, I saw the red capillaries in his eyes.

Cedric's growling grew louder, and it took all I had to keep him from boinging free.

"George doesn't care for Patience. He's toying with her, simply to boost his own ego. I have proof."

"Go on."

"I saw a letter to George. From a girl. Another girl. A love letter."

"Who is the girl?"

"Someone named Juliet who writes with violet ink."

Poor, poor Patience. Poor, poor little Possible Pea. "Where was the letter?" I asked.

"In his bedroom. On his highboy."

"What were you doing in his room?"

"I—I'm sick of your questions! Leave me alone!" Shoving his hands into the pockets of his fur coat, Fenton slid past me.

I watched him cross the crowded village green, cringing and darting from every person who came within five feet of him. Then he disappeared behind a tree.

It was obvious that Fenton was infatuated with Patience, a sentiment I knew she did not return. He could be a killer, an irrational, jealous, cold-blooded killer.

Which begged the question, what else was he capable of?

The crowd was beginning to congeal around the torchlit ice castle. I allowed myself to be pulled along. The coronation was to be at the castle, so that's where Patience would be, too.

Making certain Patience remained unharmed by Fenton was the main thing.

Strom and Pickard were standing in front of the ice castle now, cheerfully announcing the beginning of Maple Hill's 1923 Winter Carnival, cracking jokes about Jack Frost and jingle bells to the delight of the crowd.

Where was Berta?

I inched closer to the ice castle, accidentally treading upon a few toes in the process. Luckily, everyone was wearing snow boots, so no one complained.

I spotted Maynard Coburn leaning on a tree trunk, arms crossed, in an attitude that looked deliberately casual. His dark-gold faux hair was visible under his hat. He was working his jaw.

Someone was blatting out a fanfare on a trumpet. Then, applause and cheers as George Goddard and Patience Yarker appeared in front of the ice castle, smiling—

There. I saw him. Fenton, over at the farthest edge of the crowd, holding one of the cocoa cups. Just like Maynard, he was watching the proceedings with a frightening intensity.

Pickard began to talk about kings and queens and Maple Hill. Strom was holding up a sparkling crown.

I must get over there and stop Fenton from doing, well, whatever it is he's—

"What I wouldn't give for a sprig of mistletoe right about now," a man said very close to my ear.

I spun around. "Ralph!"

Ralph, in a tipped fedora and an overcoat with a turned-up collar, smiled down at me. "Lola." His warm gray eyes glowed in his gorgeous, weathered face. "I've missed you, kid. Say, did you get a little shorter?"

These dratted flat-heeled man-boots! And me without a speck of lipstick or mascara. "I—"

"Don't get me wrong." Ralph edged closer. "You're prettier than ever."

Cedric dabbled his legs in the air, whimpering with frantic joy.

"What—what are you doing here?" I asked, toasty from my ears to my blistered toes—which, as it happens, suddenly didn't hurt in the least. "Golly, I've missed you, too—has it really only been a few weeks?"

"Yeah, only a couple weeks, but I'll be darned if they didn't feel like centuries."

Then I was in Ralph's strong arms, and he gave me a kiss that was worth waiting two weeks for. Heck, it would've been worth a two-*year* wait. Not that I'd tell that to Ralph, for fear of giving him the go-ahead.

Coming up for air, I asked, "Truly, Ralph—what *are* you doing here? What about your job in Chicago?"

"I wrapped it up and I was on my way back to New York City. At the station, I bought a couple papers, and what do you know, the news of Judith Goddard's murder was splashed on the front pages. 'Maple Hill,' I thought. 'Now, why does that ring a bell?'"

"I told you that I was going to Maple Hill."

"Yeah. And I knew that if there was a murder and you and Mrs. Lundgren were there, well, there was a chance you were mixed up in it—"

He was cut off by a woman's scream.

My blood went cold.

Ralph tensed in my arms.

Oh golly. Fenton. *Patience.*

Ralph gently peeled my hands from his shoulders, and set off running toward the screams.

The crowd was in a tizzy, murmuring and looking around.

Another scream, and a wail of "Help! Oh, *help*!"

I ran after Ralph to the back of the crowd, stumbling, breathing hard, with Cedric bundled like a bread loaf under my arm.

There was the igloo up ahead, from behind which another "Help!" issued. Ralph was dashing around the corner.

I followed—and slammed into Ralph's back. He had stopped hard.

I peered around his arm.

A weeping woman lay crouched beside something. Some*one*.

Fenton.

"He's—" the woman whimpered. "He's—"

"Yeah, I see," Ralph said.

Fenton lay sprawled on the snow behind the igloo, his camera on its twisted strap beside his head, a breeze ruffling his fur coat. An upended cocoa cup lay nearby, pale brown cocoa staining the snow.

And his *face*—wide eyes, gaping mouth . . .

He was dead.

21

I wasn't exactly sure how I'd gotten it all wrong. But I had. Fenton wasn't the villain I'd supposed him to be. Well, all right, if the story about him trying to push the nurserymaid out the window was true, he'd possibly been a villain as a child. But all the rest of it—the mad jealousy of George, the suspicion that he meant to harm Patience—had utterly missed the target.

And now Fenton was dead. Perhaps I was partly to blame.

Ralph knelt beside the body, checking for a pulse. I helped the weeping woman to her feet and led her away, murmuring, "There, there, it's all right."

More people came rushing in around the body like a noisy, babbling surf. There were cries of "Murder!" and "Poison!" and "Where in the blazes are the police?" and "Stay back, Molly, it's no sight for a woman," and then Sergeant Peletier strode onto the scene and urged everyone back, all except a man who crouched beside the body, saying, "I'm a doctor," and then, "Ah, poor fellow, he's dead."

"Yep," Ralph said to the doctor, shaking his head sadly. "Say, what's this he's got in his hand? A note?"

"You," Peletier said softly to me. "You *just so happen* to be at the scene of the crime again, eh?"

I pointed. "There's a note in his hand."

"I'm not through with you, Lola Woodby." Peletier went over, bent over Fenton's corpse, plucked the folded paper from his hand, and slid it into his coat pocket.

"Someone fetch Dr. Best!" Peletier bellowed to no one in particular. "Someone fetch a sheet or a blanket or *something* to cover this poor soul up." He turned to me. "And you—I want you at the station, you and your sidekick. *Immediately.*"

"Sure thing," I said, swallowing hard.

Ralph was on his feet, looking between Peletier and me. Once Peletier began speaking with someone else, Ralph came close to me and said softly, "What's going on here, Lola? You've got the fuzz on your case?"

"Something like that."

Ralph groaned. "Every time. *Every time!*"

I pushed out my lower lip. "Now you're making me feel bad."

Ralph scratched his temple. "Sorry, kid. It's just that . . . *every* time?"

Berta appeared, and hurried over to Ralph and me. "Good evening, Mr. Oliver. What a surprise to see you here, and—" She cast an appalled look at Fenton's corpse, now covered with a red blanket. "—under such dreadful circumstances."

"Sergeant Peletier wants to see us at the station," I said. "Immediately, he said."

"Oh, for heaven's sake," Berta said. "He simply cannot let go of the wrong end of the stick, can he?"

"And—I overheard the doctor saying something about poison."

"Oh dear. Not again."

"The first one was cyanide?" Ralph asked.

"Yes," I said. "I'll fill you in on the details later—we must go, or risk antagonizing Peletier further."

"I'll come with you," Ralph said.

"No." I *did* want him to come with me, but I'd never admit it. I had my own agency to run, and it would make me look like a dumb bunny dilettante to tote a fellow with me. Peletier would probably speak to Ralph over my head and Berta's. That's what men did. "Here," I said to Ralph, thrusting Cedric into his arms. "It would be a great help if you took Cedric—Peletier isn't precisely sending fan mail his way. Would you meet us in the lobby of the Old Mill Inn in an hour or so?"

"If we are not nailed by the police and put under glass, that is," Berta said grimly.

"Sure," Ralph said, sounding slightly muffled because he was scrunching his face against Cedric's enthusiastic licking. "Better yet, I'll book myself a room."

"They're all sold out," I said, "so—"

"Don't worry." Ralph winked. Or perhaps he was simply protecting his eye from Cedric's tongue. "I'll figure out something."

Berta and I set out, weaving through the hushed, gawking crowd. Mr. Persons, the journalist, hovered nearby. I saw him take a stealthy snap of the covered body with his camera, but I doubted it would come out, since the area was lit only by juddering lanterns.

When Berta and I arrived at the police station, Sergeant Peletier was alone. He looked at us accusingly as we entered with a blast of cold air.

At Peletier's desk, he slid a sheet of paper toward us in silence.

A note read in a quavering hand,

I killed Mother. I couldn't bear that she was going to marry that oafish Maynard Coburn and abandon me, yet now I find that I cannot bear to live another day without her. Farewell, cruel world.—Fenton Burke Goddard

"Suicide?" I whispered. "Good golly."

"Cyanide in his hot cocoa. George Goddard confirmed that this is indeed his brother's handwriting, and there was a bottle of potassium ferricyanide—photographic stuff—in Fenton's coat pocket, so that's everything squared away, then," Peletier said gruffly. He seemed embarrassed and relieved. "And there I was, thinking I'd have to get the County Sheriff involved. You're free to leave Maple Hill."

Relief flowed through me, and I saw that Berta's shoulders sagged in relief.

But as we were climbing back into the Speedwagon, I said, "I can't believe it."

"Believe what?" Berta asked.

"That Fenton killed himself."

"Does it not make perfect sense? Think of it. Realizing that his mother would abandon him once she married Maynard Coburn, he did the only thing he could think of—he killed her so that no one could ever, ever take her away. It is likely that George's dalliance with Patience proved to be too painful for him, as well. Perhaps he fostered some insane hope that Patience would become the new woman to which he could attach himself, and yet her taking up with George—with that kiss Fenton himself photographed as proof—dealt the final blow. He could bear it no more."

I started the engine and maneuvered onto the dark road. Ice glistened under the cast of the headlamps. "I can't say that you don't make it all wrap up neatly, Berta, but my gut tells me that Fenton was murdered, too. I spoke to him less than two hours ago. He didn't seem happy, but neither did he appear to have suicide on the brain.

He had been taking photographs—I wonder what of—and he said he *wished* to go to college, but his mother had never allowed it, and that now he felt free. He even told me about some love letters he'd seen in George's bedroom—"

"Indeed!"

"—love letters from some girl named Juliet who writes with violet ink."

A pause. "Could George have overheard your conversation?"

I thought of how Fenton and I had been standing behind the igloo. Anyone could've been just around the igloo's curved walls or, perhaps, inside them.

"Yes, I suppose George *could* have overheard," I said. "But all our other suspects were there tonight, too. Roy Ives. Maynard Coburn—"

"Patience Yarker."

"And Rosemary—who likely served Fenton the cup of cocoa that wound up with poison in it. Anyone could've tipped a little cyanide into Fenton's cocoa cup when he wasn't looking, really. There was such a crowd, and such poor light. . . . The killer is craftier than we supposed. The killer set us up to be suspicious of Fenton with those photographs pinned up at the town hall, don't you see? The killer is attempting to put us—to put everyone—off the scent." Cold fear traced my spine. "And just think about it, Berta. Each suspect we interviewed in one way or another implicated Fenton as being unsettling, unpredictable, or downright dangerous."

"And yet, Sergeant Peletier has absolved us from suspicion."

"But what about the burnt dossier in Roy Ives's fireplace? What about Patience arguing with Maynard Coburn? What about Rosemary slinking around the village like a guilty woman, and George possibly two-timing Patience, and the furry thing you saw in the forest—"

"Calm yourself, Mrs. Woodby. Although . . . I *would* like to know why Mr. Ives burned my dossier. All my hard work, burned to a crisp . . ." Berta sniffed. "Yet none of it matters anymore. Is that not a relief? We are free to go."

"Yes," I said with a sinking stomach. "Free."

Ralph and Cedric weren't in the lobby when we arrived at the inn. Not that I had expected they would be. Ralph had said he'd figure out something, and experience had taught me that he always did.

Funny Papers was lounging behind the front desk, chewing gum with his head propped on his hand, staring glumly into space.

Berta got her key, said good night to me, and went upstairs.

I said to Funny Papers, "Has a man by the name of—"

"Mr. Woodby?" Funny Papers said around his chewing gum.

"I beg your pardon?"

"Your husband. Mr. Woodby. Hauling that little dog of yours around? Ginger hair?"

"The man or the dog?"

"Well, both, actually. I directed Mr. Woodby to the airing cupboard."

"Ah," I said. "Thank you."

My heart thumped as I went up to the third floor, and it wasn't simply on account of the stairs' steepness. Murder and guilt and bewilderment faded into the background. I felt as though Christmas had come early, because, quite unexpectedly, I was to have my gentleman caller all to myself.

Ralph always seemed like a gift. Sometimes when I was still not fully awake in the morning, I would think myself still trapped in my old, unhappy life, without love. Then I would open my eyes wide, remembering Ralph in a delighted flash, and I'd smile.

I wasn't alone. I had love.

On the other hand—phooey. Having packed for Vermont with practicality in mind, I had only the frumpiest nightgowns and warm woolen underthings in my suitcase.

Reaching the airing cupboard, I gently rapped before I opened the door a crack. "Ralph?" I poked my head in. The bare lightbulb made the suspended drying bedsheets glow. Ralph lay on my cot in trousers, shirtless and shoeless, with Cedric curled up beside him. He lowered my copy of *Christmas Romance* magazine and smiled. "Hiya, kid." He sat up.

"Hello." I stepped inside and shut the door behind me, but I didn't take my hands off the doorknob. The sight of Ralph's bare skin and rounded muscles made me inexplicably shy.

Ralph gave the magazine a wiggle. "Gripping read. I just got to the part in 'Meet Me Under the Mistletoe' when the spinster librarian's glasses fly off on the toboggan ride, and the handsome widower with the six kids suddenly realizes what a looker she really is. Say—what's the matter? You're here, which means the cops didn't arrest you, so—"

"Berta and I are free to go."

"Great!"

"That was a suicide note in Fenton's hand. He claimed to have killed his mother. It's all over. . . ."

"Except you don't buy it."

"No, I don't."

"This isn't a paying gig, kid. Leave it alone."

"How can I leave it alone? The murderer is still on the loose, and now no one is going to do a thing about it!"

"So you want to stay up here in Vermont—" Ralph swept a hand around the room. "—sleeping in a closet, in order to crack a case for free?"

"Well, yes."

"That isn't good business, Lola."

"I know."

"You're a saint."

"Not precisely."

"Ah, well, that's a relief." He sent me a mischievous, lopsided smile, tossing the magazine aside. "Say, what're you doing in that coat and hat and—*whew*—those big boots? It's awful warm in here, and anyway, it's time for bed."

I swallowed. "That cot is quite narrow."

"I think it'll do just fine."

I unbuttoned my coat with jittery fingers. What was the matter with me? I was behaving like some sort of dizzy girl on her wedding night, not a woman—a *widow*—of thirty-two.

"How long are you prepared to be Mr. Woodby?" I asked Ralph as I bent over to untie my man-boots.

"I guess I can pull it off for a few days if it means I get to stay with you."

He said this with such tenderness, I glanced up.

His gray eyes were wide and vulnerable, almost as though he were trying to gauge my reaction.

I quickly looked down at my bootlaces again, feeling heat surge in my ears.

You see, Ralph and I had come to an understanding. Discussing the nature of our relations, giving them a definite label, or talking about a future together was off-limits. Taboo. Potentially explosive, actually, given the damaged domesticity in Ralph's past, and the matrimonial pain in my own. Ralph had had a rough-and-tumble childhood in South Boston, followed by a shipbuilding stint in Maine. Then he'd been a soldier in the Great War, which had left him scarred inside and out. My own life had been cushy by comparison, filled with galas and promenades and embarrassing accidents with fruit parfaits. But I *had* been strong-armed by Mother into marrying, at nineteen, a lothario in cashmere socks.

Until just now, I had thought Ralph's and my understanding was chugging along all right.

I arranged my boots carefully beside Ralph's. They weren't much smaller than his. I looked at him. "About this Mr. and Mrs. business, Ralph—"

"Why don't you come a little closer to talk it over?"

I padded closer in my stocking feet, taking care not to look at his chest or his arms or his shoulders.

I knelt beside the cot.

He reached for me, gathered me close. I felt his warmth and smelled his skin, and the immediate sense of homecoming made moisture spring to my eyes. "Lola," he murmured, his lips on my neck, my hot cheekbone, my mouth—

I drew away. "Ralph," I whispered.

His eyes, so close, were drowsy with sleepiness or desire. "Yeah?"

"I feel funny about pretending to be . . . husband and wife."

His voice was low and measured. "Why's that?"

I wasn't sure. But it made something buck with unease, deep inside me. "I don't know. It simply feels odd. To say we're married when we're . . . not."

"We'll make a game of it."

"A game?"

"Sure. Does that make you feel better?"

It did not. Unease kept on bucking.

"C'mere," Ralph murmured. "What is this thing you're wearing? Wool? Let me help you with that. . . ."

I slid my hands down his back. There was no need to speak.

22

Ralph and I went downstairs the next morning quite like a married couple, close enough for our arms to touch. Cedric, whom Ralph had gallantly taken out for his morning promenade while I had been applying my makeup, frolicked at our feet. My feet, by the way, were in my velvet T-straps, because I simply couldn't picture myself attending Judith Goddard's funeral and reception shod like Frankenstein's monster.

I wasn't accustomed to being touching-close to Ralph in public, except for in the anything-goes atmosphere of a speakeasy, or under the flickering silver light of the movie palace. And I *would* have been wallowing in the sense of wifeliness, except I couldn't shake an awful feeling: This was all a game to him. He'd said as much.

Patience Yarker greeted us at the dining room doorway. "Good morning," she said, her big blue eyes glued on Ralph.

"Good morning," I said. "This is my husband, Mr. Woodby."

"Morning," Ralph said easily to Patience.

It was nice that *one* of us was relaxed; Patience nearly dropped the bills of fare she was holding. Ralph has that effect on females (and, indeed, selected males), so I wasn't surprised. However, my craving for johnnycakes doubled in one second flat.

"I suppose you'll be leaving on the afternoon train?" Patience asked. "Since Sergeant Peletier said Fenton . . . *you* know."

Killed himself, she meant.

"We haven't decided," I said. Ah, that smug royal *we* of married couples. "We're having such a marvelous time, we thought we might stay for a bit longer, simply to enjoy the country. Isn't that so, darling?"

Ralph nodded. "I'd like to see that ski jumping contest tomorrow. Maynard Coburn's pretty famous." This was an act. With regards to sports, Ralph only followed the Yankees. He worked hard and didn't have time for all the rest.

Patience Yarker led us to a window table. The dining room was half-full and the festive mood of yesterday had evaporated.

"How are you feeling?" I asked Patience as she arranged a pot of coffee, sugar bowl, and creamer in front of Ralph and me. Ralph had, husbandlike, unfolded the newspaper he'd picked up in the lobby, but I was sure he was listening.

"I'm just fine." Patience smoothed her apron. Truth be told, she looked pale, and lavender shadows ringed her eyes. "Poor Fenton. Somehow, it all seems to make sense now." She shook her head. "The bad business is over, and yet, well, I suppose it'll take time for things to get back to normal around here."

"Will you attend Mrs. Goddard's funeral this morning?" I asked. It was to be at ten o'clock, and it was already after nine.

"I can't. My cousin Sam went to Waterbury to see the dentist—toothache—and Dad is feeling poorly, so I must stay and help out at the inn. I reckon people will be checking out early, with these terrible deaths."

Patience went away, and Berta arrived a moment later. She, too, looked weary and faded.

I poured her a cup of coffee. "Good morning."

"Good morning, Mrs. Woodby. Mr. Oliver. Oh, I cannot wait to leave this godforsaken village this afternoon. We must purchase our train tickets at the depot right after breakfast to ensure we get on the—"

"I think we should stay," I said.

Berta's coffee cup paused en route to her lips. "It is none of our affair! And we are not being paid to investigate. Each day we linger in Vermont, our agency is losing money."

"Money can't be the only reason to investigate," I said.

"It is the *only* reason if one is a professional detective, Mrs. Woodby. Mr. Oliver, please help me talk sense into her."

Ralph lowered his newspaper and said softly, "For the time being, Mrs. Lundgren, I'm *Mr. Woodby.*"

"Ah. Well, Mr. Woodby, your *wife* has latched on to the wild notion that it is our duty to catch the murd—"

"Because the police won't," I whispered hotly. "What about *justice,* Berta? What about finding out the truth? What if . . . what if the killer strikes again? I already feel rotten enough about having got hold of the wrong end of the stick when it came to Fenton. Judith Goddard's funeral is this morning, and after that, her will is to be read. That will could crack this case open like a coconut. This is a wealthy family we're talking about, and one thing I know about wealthy people is that their money is always—*always*—a character in the drama. Rich people's money is supposed to set them free, but the truth is, it's a big lurking creature in the corner. It's always there, and it's always forcing people's hands in one way or the other. Besides, won't you wonder why Roy burned your dossier and what was in Judith's will, if we left so soon?"

"My dossier." Berta's eyes snapped. "And the *will*, yes . . ."

I guessed this meant she was once more rah-rah about our investigation.

"I do hope you have thought of a way to eavesdrop," Berta said.

"Why is that *my* job?" I said.

"Because you are so very resourceful, Mrs. Woodby," Berta said in placating tones. "Isn't she, Mr. Woodby?"

"That's one of the reasons I married her." Ralph's eyes twinkled over the rim of his coffee cup.

Twenty minutes later, the three of us plus Cedric were all bundled up and walking to the church. Since dogs aren't allowed at funerals, I had dumped out most of the contents of my large handbag and coaxed Cedric (wearing a jaunty Norwegian knit) inside so only his head sprouted from the top, fuzzy and bright eyed. I had slipped a tube of lipstick and my skeleton key—just in case—into my dress pocket.

That morning the sky was not blue, but white. Snow was already melting inside my velvet T-straps.

We crossed River Street, and as we neared the general store, the door swung open and Rosemary Rogerson stepped out in a black coat and hat. Seeing Ralph, Berta, and me, she balked. Then she readjusted her grip on the small brown-paper-wrapped parcel in her arms and strode up the sidewalk in the opposite direction.

"Good morning, Mrs. Rogerson," I called.

No answer.

Rosemary reached her cream-colored motorcar and slammed inside. The engine *vroom*ed, she peeled out of her parking spot, and the car rolled away in a fog of exhaust.

"What was she doing in the store?" I said to Berta and Ralph. "The morning after her brother's lurid death—"

"A mere few minutes before her mother's funeral," Berta said.

"—and she's out doing a spot of shopping? I smell a rat. Let's pop in and find out what she purchased—we have a little time."

We pushed into the store.

Inside, the old-timers sat around the potbellied stove, chinning in low tones. They all glanced over.

"Morning," Ralph called. "Nippy out there, isn't it?"

"Good morning," I said with a cheery twiddle of the fingers.

No answer. The old-timers turned back to their conversation.

"I'm just going to go and look at the milk bottles," Berta whispered. "Recall that Titus Staples, who was lifting crates of French wine for Roy Ives in his cellar, also has a peculiar habit of buying the milk bottle in the back corner every day."

I nodded, even though finding a connection between smuggled vino and milk bottles seemed highly implausible to me.

Ralph and I walked up to the counter, the floorboards creaking beneath our feet. The old-timers fell silent to watch. I must admit, I felt miles more confident about confrontations with a muscly Irishman by my side.

"Can I help you?" the shopkeeper asked, eyeing Ralph suspiciously.

"Yes, actually," I said. "We just saw Rosemary Rogerson coming out of the store. Would you mind telling me what she purchased?"

"I *would* mind," the shopkeeper said in a surly voice. "Anything else I can help you out with? 'Cause I sure would like to lend the big-city detectives a hand."

The old-timers snickered.

"No, thanks. We'll just have a browse."

We went toward the icebox at the back, before which was the round shape of Berta, bent at the waist.

The doorbells jingled in the background.

"I have found something," Berta whispered. She was straightening as Ralph and I reached her side, with a glass bottle of milk in her hand. She latched the icebox shut. "Look at this." She turned the milk bottle sideways. On the bottom, in what looked like grease pencil, was written *II 10p*.

"Huh," Ralph said.

"Roman numeral two, ten, *P*?" I whispered with a frown. "What does that mean? Do the other bottles say anything?"

"No. Only this one—which was positioned in the far left corner—"

"Gimme that!" a man growled. Big gloved hands wrenched the bottle of milk away from Berta.

It was greasy-haired, red-hatted Titus Staples.

"Now, see here, buddy," Ralph said, taking a step forward.

I touched his hand. "*It's all right,*" I whispered. "You're a little late today, Mr. Staples," I said more loudly. "Tell me, what does the grease pencil on the bottom mean?"

"Shaddup and mind yer own business," he snarled over his shoulder. He was loping to the counter—the old-timers and the shopkeeper were agog—then slapping his coin on the counter and pushing through the door. The door slammed, the bells tinkled, and I caught a glimpse of Titus through the front display window, striding away to the right.

"I won't have you bugging my customers," the shopkeeper called over to Ralph, Berta, and me.

The old-timers grunted and nodded in agreement.

Ignoring the urge to flee, I returned to the shopkeeper's counter. "I beg your pardon, but where do you get your milk?"

"Sweet Meadow Dairy on Guildhall Road."

"And you mentioned previously that it is delivered fresh every morning?"

"That's right. Just before eight, which is when I open shop." The shopkeeper's face went mean. "How come you want to know?"

Berta was tugging my coat sleeve. "Come along, Mrs. Woodby.

No, no—leave the maple sugar candies alone—good morning, gentlemen."

We left without purchasing anything.

"Why do I have the feeling that the townspeople's torches and pitchforks are ready to come out?" I said to Berta and Ralph once we were outside. We went along the icy sidewalk toward the church.

"There is something fishy about those milk bottles," Berta said.

"That guy was asking for a sock in the jaw," Ralph said.

"What could those grease pencil figures possibly mean?" I said.

"Some sorta code," Ralph said.

"About what?"

"Something Titus wishes to protect," Berta said. "That much is clear. Could it have anything to do with all the wine in Roy's cellar? Is this related to my burnt dossier?"

My breath caught. "Hold it. What if *Rosemary* wrote those figures?"

"Rosemary!" Berta said.

"She did look pretty guilty coming out of there," Ralph said.

Berta said, "I do not know. . . ."

"Or, I suppose the numbers could've been written on the bottle by someone at the dairy," I said. "We should visit this Sweet Meadow Dairy and ask a few questions." We were drawing close to the church. An organ dirge burbled inside. "After the funeral."

A hearse stood outside the Maple Hill Methodist Church, onyx black, long, grim, and suitably luxurious for Judith Goddard's final ride on this earth. Pale silky curtains hung in its windows.

We were late and the church doors were shut. We hurried up the steps.

23

The funeral service was as bleak as any other. In the drafty wooden church, a few dozen mourners huddled in pews while the Reverend Mr. Currier had a go at making Judith Goddard sound like she would be missed. Then it was off to the frozen cemetery, where snowflakes eddied across crusted snow and around tilting headstones. Judith Goddard was laid to rest next to her husband, Elmer. Mr. Currier murmured rites into the wind, and mourners dumped frozen dirt clods onto her casket. *Clunk. Clunk.*

I furtively studied Rosemary, Roy, George, and Maynard. They all looked pinched and miserable. None of them spoke.

After the burial, Ralph, Berta, and I motored in the long, gloomy train of vehicles up to Goddard Farm. Ralph was behind the wheel of the Speedwagon. That's a nice thing about fellows—even if the world were going up in flames, they'd do the driving.

"Goodness," Berta said, peering out at the dozens of trucks and motorcars parked in front of the house. "They are going to run out of cookies."

We followed the slow herd into the house, which was warm—ah, the deliciousness of central heating—and brightly lit with electric lights against the wan winter daylight.

Rosemary, in a shapeless black wool dress, eyes red behind her glasses, was playing hostess. When she saw Berta, Ralph, and me enter the living room, her eyes slitted even as she continued speaking to an elderly couple.

The Christmas tree had been hauled away. Holly no longer bedecked the mantelpiece. The mirrors, even the one on the drinks cabinet, were draped with black cloth.

Someone—Hester Albans? . . . that would explain her absence at the funeral and burial—had set up a buffet service with the usual funereal fare: sliced cold ham, depressing raisin cakes, shortbread cookies, fruitcake, silver urns of coffee. Despite that we were surely at least one hundred miles away from the nearest commercial hothouse, vases of lilies filled the air with their deathly perfume. The two or three dozen guests huddled, murmuring softly.

Everyone, of course, had murder on the brain.

Well, except for me. Murder had been knocked to the third tier of my mind, supplanted by my aim, first, to find George Goddard's bedroom and take a gander at his purported violet-inked love letter, and, second, to somehow eavesdrop on the reading of Judith's will.

Ralph had been snared in conversation with an elderly lady in black crushed velvet, who was cooing to him about lending libraries. He nodded politely, sipping coffee.

I eyed the grand stairs, visible through the open doorways, longingly.

Berta caught me looking. "*Not yet, Mrs. Woodby,*" she whispered, biting into a square of shortbread. "We must confirm George's whereabouts before we attempt to locate his bedroom." Her eyes landed on something across the room. Her shortbread chewing slowed.

Here came the Alpine Club co-presidents, heading for Berta as eagerly as two cows to a salt lick.

I refrained from rolling my eyes.

"Mrs. Lundgren," Strom said in a decorous murmur that didn't match the glitter in his eye. "May I entice you with a cookie?" He held out a piled plate.

"Surely Mrs. Lundgren would prefer something with chocolate, you dunce," Pickard said, pushing his own plate of cookies in front of Strom's.

It was as though a light switch had been flipped inside of Berta. Gone were her weary posture and grimly pressed lips. She laughed gaily and patted her hair.

How could I tear her away from the only thing that made her happy? Even if that thing was two men with ear hair difficulties? I plunked Cedric, still in my handbag, into Berta's arms and slipped away.

I strolled through the splendid downstairs rooms, searching for George. I saw a library with a dark green carpet and tall shelves of books. A lady's parlor wallpapered with turquoise-plumed birds. Lots of crumbs on the floors, dribbled by funeral guests.

Just as I was peeking into what must've been the breakfast room—unoccupied—someone behind me said, "Casing the joint again?"

I spun around, hand pressed to heart. "Golly! You frightened me!"

"What a pity." Maynard Coburn didn't appear pitying. His eyes practically zapped with malice.

"Ripping reception, isn't it?" I said.

I would've been bowled over by how dashing Maynard looked in his black suit, if I hadn't been acutely aware that his wafting, dark-gold hair was a fraud.

"Say, Mr. Coburn, now that we finally have a chance to schmooze, I simply must ask—what were you doing in the early hours of yesterday morning? Stumbling back home after a motorcar crash after a spot of bootlegging, by any chance?"

For a fraction of a second, Maynard's mouth pulled tight in what was, unmistakably, fear. But in a flash, he rearranged his expression into contempt. "A word of advice, Mrs. Woodby—you're out of your depth. Go back to finding lost puppies in New York before you get yourself mixed up in something ugly."

"Is that a threat?" *Gosh, was that a tacit confession of bootlegging?*

"Think of it as a friendly warning." Maynard's eyes were as friendly as a Nile crocodile's. "I am glad I've bumped into you, however."

"Oh?"

"I want that film."

I batted my eyelashes. "What film?"

"You and that Swedish meatball burst into my rooms, and I clearly saw that she had a camera. She took a picture of me in a . . . a rather awkward . . ."

"State of undress?" I suggested.

Maynard smoothed a hand over his toupee. "*I. Want. That. Film.*"

"Sounds like it's one hot commodity," I said, arching an eyebrow.

"How *dare* you . . . are you attempting to—to blackmail me?"

"Heavens no."

Maynard didn't seem to believe me, because he'd pulled a leather wallet from inside his jacket. He glanced over his shoulder and leaned in. "How much? One hundred dollars? Two?"

"Mind if I ask why you're so upset about having an artificial haircut?"

"It'll ruin my reputation."

"Surely not."

"Do you think the magazine editors and admen will give me so much as a mention if I don't keep up appearances?"

"Since it's question-and-answer time," I said, "I saw you just before the coronation of the Winter Carnival King and Queen yesterday evening. You didn't look particularly joyous."

Maynard's hand pinched his wallet hard. "What are you getting at?"

"I understand there is a strong sense of, shall we say, sporting competition between George Goddard and you. Are you squigged off about George and Patience's . . . understanding?" I was bluffing; I had only suspicions of such an understanding, based upon the Possible Pea, and the swanky hotel brochures Patience had hidden under the inn's reservation book.

"What understanding? George and Patience? Not in a million." Maynard opened his wallet and thrust a few one-hundred-dollar bills in my direction.

"No, thank you," I said, edging past him.

"We're not through—where do you think you're going?"

"Straight to the coffee cake," I said over my shoulder.

Whew. Fellows. And they say we ladies are vain.

A few ticks later, I spied George in the billiards room, hunched over his cue. A lit cigarette dangled from his lips. Mr. Persons, the sportswriter, hovered nearby with an open notebook.

Who had let *him* in?

I loitered just outside the open door. The men hadn't noticed me yet.

". . . and you can quote me on that," George was saying.

"Righto." Persons scribbled in his notebook, tongue bitten between his front teeth. "*Maynard Coburn's jump . . . over Maple Hill . . . will prove . . . he's . . . past it.* Clever, Mr. Goddard, very clever. Readers love a play on words. Say, I wanted to ask you if you think Maynard Coburn is mixed up in all this murder ballyhoo. I mean, two murders? Sheesh."

Crack went the balls, and they rolled and ricocheted in colorful blurs. None of them fell into a pocket.

"I told you, Clint—"

"Clive."

"—Clive—my brother wasn't murdered. He killed himself. Left a suicide note and everything. Fenton killed Mother because she was going to leave him behind on her long honeymoon when she married Maynard. Fenton was a mama's boy, you see."

"But then, why didn't he kill Maynard instead of his mother?"

George shrugged. "Maybe he meant to, and that cyanide of his wound up in the wrong drink."

"Inneresting. Can I quote you on that?"

"Go right ahead." George caught sight of me, and straightened. "Well, well, if it isn't our perpetual uninvited guest. What's the matter? New York City doesn't want you back?" He picked up a glass of some amber liquid and sipped, eyeing me over the rim. "What do you want? I've only got a few minutes before I must trot off to the library like a good boy and listen to the lawyer read Mother's will."

Ah. The Big Moment was to occur in the library, then. Should I grab my coat, go outside, and try to listen to the will-reading from below the library window? No, I wouldn't hear a word. Maybe I could loiter at the keyhole. . . .

"Care for a game of billiards?" George asked me.

"Only if you were hoping to knock out some of these walls."

"That bad, huh?"

"I don't get along well with any sport that involves balls, heights, or speed."

"What's left?"

"The back float. Listen, Mr. Goddard, are you truly going ahead with the ski jumping contest tomorrow under the, um, circumstances?"

"Course he is," Mr. Persons said with a scowl. "Hey, you trying to mess up my story?"

George puffed his cigarette and ostentatiously set his drink on a sideboard. "I'm finally rid of my own mother, and I don't need some female detective to mother-hen me," he said. "I mean to enjoy my freedom."

"I believe it," I said. I watched George closely as I added, "Although, there might be a village lass or two who'd be disappointed to hear that."

George's eyes narrowed. Mr. Persons's pencil froze in midair.

"What did you say?" George asked.

"Come now, Mr. Goddard," I said cheerily. "Everyone saw that photograph. *You* know, the one of Patience Yarker and you having a kiss and a cuddle in the woods?"

"Dammit," George said, suddenly sounding drunk. "I've had it with your prying! I want you out of here!" He pointed a wavering finger toward the door.

"Say," Mr. Persons said to me, "you don't know where I could get my hands on a copy of that photograph, do you?"

"Oh, close your head!" George snapped.

I decided that my work in the billiards room was done. "Toodles!" I said, and legged it for the door.

Back in the living room, Berta was laughing at something either Strom or Pickard had said. And here was Ralph beside me, chewing a gingersnap. "How's tricks?" he said.

"George is in the billiards room, so for the moment, I'm free to search upstairs. I don't think I'll be able to tear Berta away from her beaus. Would you come with me?"

"To the ends of the earth, kid." Ralph smiled, and popped the last bite of gingersnap into his mouth.

How I wished he wouldn't joke about things like that.

I led Ralph toward the kitchen and the back stairs Berta and I had used a few days earlier. As we went, I softly explained how I'd learned that Judith's will was to be read in the library in only a few minutes. "I suppose I have no choice but to listen in at the keyhole," I whispered, "but I won't have much privacy with so many people in the house."

"That'd be pretty risky," Ralph whispered back. "You might have to rely on questioning the family members about the will afterwards."

"But they're a bunch of liars."

"Just watch 'em hard. See if they scratch their ears or rub their lips or shift their eyes around. It's like playing poker, kid."

"But I'm rotten at poker."

Ralph chuckled. "That's only 'cause you burst into a big, beautiful smile whenever you're dealt a good hand. That doesn't mean you can't read other people."

"I can't read *you*," I said. Rats. Why had that popped out?

A pause. Then, in a slightly less jovial tone, "You sure about that?"

24

The first room into which Ralph and I looked seemed wholly unoccupied, without even bed linens on the four-poster. The second door led to a lavatory that was, alas, occupied by a gent arranging his suspenders.

"I *beg* your pardon!" he cried.

"Whoops!" I said. "Looking for the—er—linen closet!" I slammed the door.

Ralph was shaking his head and grinning. I held my laughter in with my palm.

The next door was locked.

Ralph whispered, "Do you want me to—?"

"I'll handle this, darling," I whispered back. I pulled my skeleton key from my pocket, fit it into the keyhole, applied a little finesse, and—*click*—the lock tumbled.

"Gorgeous," Ralph whispered.

I pushed the door open. Ralph looked up and down the corridor, and we darted inside.

The curtains were drawn so the room was dim. I smelled cigarettes and made out clothing—men's clothing—draped over chairbacks and lumped on the carpet.

"Jackpot," I whispered. "This is surely George's room, and Fenton said something about a highboy—and there it is."

Boy, did I ever feel slick. I practically strutted across the room.

The highboy's top was cluttered with the usual rich man's paraphernalia—cuff links, eau de cologne bottles, silver hairbrush and comb set, nail scissors—

"There are no letters here," I said. "Was Fenton lying?"

"Nope." Ralph crouched. "Look." A brass wastebin sat on the floor. From the bottom of the wastebin, beneath a discarded newspaper and an empty Lucky Strike box, he pulled out a crumpled page, stood, and passed it to me.

I uncrumpled it. Blush stationery, floral letterhead, and the name Juliet Vanderlyn with a Cleveland address. Scrawled violet ink. The note was dated December 15.

Ralph and I silently read:

My Darlingest Georgiepoo,

I'm dashing off this note on my way out the door to the big Christmas dance at the Smythes' place. Gosh I miss you, snoogums, and I wish you could see me in my new Florrie Westwood gown! It's positively scrummy and goes just swell with the new motorcar Daddy bought me!

I want to ask you, sweetums, just as soon as the season dies down a smidge and you have time to noodle it over, would you give the idea of wedding bells for us a good long thinkie winkie? I know Daddy won't be pleased one bit if you keep coming around without making your intentions known, as the old folks say, and I don't need to remind you, poopsie woopsie, that Daddy simply adores *Harry Shute!*

Counting the days until I see you on New Year's Eve at the Chesters' party! Until then, darling, I'll dream of your Eskimo kisses.

—Your ickle Jules-Bean

The signature was punctuated by a smudged red lipstick kiss.

"Golly," I said. "Debutantes these days drive a hard bargain."

"A girl on the side," Ralph said. "'Cause didn't you say this Georgiepoo guy and the innkeeper's daughter—?"

"Yes, but it's not clear *which* girl is on the side. There could be even *more* girls. Or—what if George was desperate to get at his inheritance in order to beat this Harry Shute number to the altar with Juliet? George is awfully competitive, so—"

Ralph glanced at the door. "I hate to say it, but time's about up, kid. You found what you were looking for, didn't you?"

"Yes." I crumpled the letter and tossed it back into the wastebin.

On the way to the door, I tripped on something, stumbled, and looked to see what had caught my toe. It was a brass vent set into the floor.

"This house has got central heating!" I whispered excitedly.

"Uh-huh?" Ralph had cracked the door and was peering out.

"We didn't think of a good way to hide in the library to overhear the reading of the will, which—" I glanced at my wristwatch. "—should be almost under way. But if this house has central heating, that means there will be vents like this all over the place. What if there's a vent in the *library* ceiling? You know, where the will is being read?"

Ralph's face lit with understanding. "Got it. Where's the library?"

"In the other wing of the house."

We went out of George's room, I relocked it with my skeleton key, and we hurried along the upper hallways.

I would have liked to locate Rosemary's room and look around for that secret notebook of hers, but there was no time.

We arrived at the east wing's central corridor.

"The library overlooks the side of the house," I whispered, "so I'll bet this room here sits above it." I tried the doorknob, and it gave.

We entered a nursery, with shelves filled with dusty-looking dolls and toy bears, an exquisitely painted rocking horse, and shelves of storybooks.

"I hear voices," I whispered.

"There." Ralph pointed. "There's a floor vent over by the window seat."

We tiptoed over. Ralph crouched and I knelt beside the vent. There were most certainly voices below, although I couldn't make out any distinct words.

"There's a lever," Ralph whispered. "You do the honors."

I eased over the lever that opened the vent slats all the way. Instantly, the voices were louder and I could see, through the gridwork of brass and a blur of dust bunnies, a dark green carpet far below.

The *library* had a dark green carpet.

I gave Ralph a thumbs-up and a smile.

Silently, he reached over, slid a hand behind my neck, and pulled me in for a kiss.

Time stopped. I melted. How could I have said I couldn't read this man? Of course I could. With my eyes closed.

". . . skip to the good part." This was George, speaking too loudly and slurring slightly.

I pulled away from Ralph, flushing. I strained my ears.

George went on, "No one cares about Mother's goddamn rubies and pearls."

"*Some* of us do." This was Rosemary, tearful and sharp. "Some of us care about heritage and tradition and family heirlooms, and that ring was supposed to be *mine.* It has been passed from mother to daughter on the Ives side of the family for a century—don't pour yourself another drink, George! You've had quite enough—"

"To hell with you and your temperance league ninnies!"

Rosemary burst into noisy sobs. "Doesn't anyone care that Mother and Fenton are *dead*?"

There was the sound of clinking crystal.

Uncle Roy spoke next. "A glass of that Bordeaux, too, if you please, George, my boy. There's an open bottle behind the whiskey."

I supposed this was it for Roy. He might very well be out on his ear once the will was read.

There was a great deal at stake for all three of them, actually.

"Why did Judith have to go and get herself poisoned?" Roy said. "So selfish of her. Now we're left to deal with the consequences. And Fenton, too. Although he was always a hideously selfish creature. Had a few screws loose—"

"Fenton wasn't murdered," George said in a droning voice, as though he'd reminded Roy of this several times already. "There was a suicide note."

"That wasn't his handwriting!" Rosemary cried.

"Don't be hysterical, Rosemary. You're getting your eyeglasses all smeary. Of course it was."

"I am uncertain about Fenton's handwriting," Roy said, "but I for one wouldn't have thought Fenton had the guts to kill himself."

"It was suicide, dammit!" George roared. "Why do you two wish to believe this is about anything more than Fenton's being a weak-minded, vengeful, jealous, and *violent* mama's boy?"

Rosemary said, "I think a better question would be, why don't *you*, George?"

This was the second time in the span of thirty minutes that I'd heard George insist that Fenton killed Mrs. Goddard and then did himself in. Did he truly believe that? Or did he have more nefarious reasons to campaign on that claim?

An "*Ahem-hem*" made the family fall silent.

"Now, then," said a man with a voice as dry as melba toast. "I will commence to read the Last Will and Testament of Judith Desdemona Ives Goddard. *Ahem-hem.* 'The estate in its entirety is to be split equally between my two sons, George Goddard and Fenton Goddard—' "

"What?" Rosemary gasped.

"It's an outrage!" Roy cried.

For my part, you could've knocked me down with a false eyelash. Because if George and Fenton were the sole heirs—and Fenton had been blipped off—George was looking fouler by the second.

And . . . he was *laughing*. Great, big, raspy laughs and, if I wasn't mistaken, a spot of knee-slapping as well.

"I fail to see the humor in this," Rosemary snapped. "Mr. Ackroyd"—I assumed this was the lawyer's name—"what will become of Fenton's half of the estate?"

"Well, that, of course, is the interesting part—from a legal perspective, I mean to say. Fenton did not have a will, and there is some legal precedent in the state of Ohio to conclude that his half of Judith Goddard's estate, as well as the remainder of his money in trust, shall pass in equal shares to you, Mrs. Rogerson, and George."

"Outrageous!" Roy cried. "She didn't leave me a thin dime? Why, at the very least, I have a claim to that caretaker's cottage, you know. I've lived there for years. Surely there is some way we might—let me see that will with my own eyes. Could it be a—a counterfeit?"

"Oh no," the lawyer said. "This will has been locked in the safe-deposit box belonging to my firm for more than one year, after Mrs. Goddard revised it in September of 1922."

"How about that, sis?" George said in a needling tone. "I've got three-quarters of the pie. I guess this means I get to call all the shots about what happens to the estate now, doesn't it? Not that you'd know how to manage, anyway. I mean, you can't even figure out how to *bake* a pie—"

"Oh, stop it, *stop* it, you horrible beast!" Rosemary screamed. There were stampeding footsteps, and then a door slammed.

Ralph, getting smoothly to his feet, whispered to me, "She could be coming upstairs. Let's skate." He helped me up and we hurried out of the nursery.

Reaching the living room via the back stairs without any run-ins, I spotted Berta, still flanked by the ski club co-presidents. Pickard was glaring at Strom as Strom said something that made Berta laugh.

I tugged her sleeve. She was still holding Cedric in my handbag. He was asleep, but he woke and perked his ears at me in greeting. "Sorry to cut the rodeo short," I whispered, "but it's time for our exit."

"Woodby," Ralph said loudly, holding out a hand to Pickard. "Ralph Woodby."

Pickard shook his hand. "Pleased to meet you, Woodby. I'm Daniel Pickard, and this big old cadaver here—" He slapped Strom hard on the back. "—is Peer Strom."

"You must forgive my friend," Strom said, shaking Ralph's hand. "He skipped school the day we learned about good manners. You're Mrs. Woodby's husband, then. Funny, she didn't strike me as the sort to have a husband."

"Oh, she's not," Ralph said, giving me a wink. "But here we are, all the same."

"You in the detective line of work, too?"

"Nope. I leave that to the good old ball and chain. I'm in the baking business myself."

"Baking?" Pickard repeated. "You sure don't look like a baker. Matter of fact, you have the look of a sportsman. Tell me, Mr. Woodby, do you ski?"

As the men talked, Berta prodded me and whispered, "What about the *will*, Mrs. Woodby?"

"Success," I said out of the corner of my mouth. "I know everything."

Pickard and Strom traded quick looks. Even though Ralph was saying something, they'd overheard.

Rats.

Berta turned to the men. "It was a delight to see you both again, but I am afraid I must take my leave."

"But—" Strom said.

Pickard said, "—you haven't finished your cookies."

Ralph, Berta, and I were already walking toward the door.

After a stop at the coat closet to gather up our things, we stole out of Goddard Farm and stuffed ourselves into the Speedwagon's cab.

25

The shopkeeper at the general store said Sweet Meadow Dairy is on the highway toward Waterbury," I said as Ralph maneuvered the Speedwagon down the slick road. "On a road called—what was it? Oh yes—Guildhall Road. He said we couldn't miss it. Let's go there next."

"Okay," Ralph said.

"What did you learn about Judith's will?" Berta asked me. "Is it truly still necessary to pursue the mystery of those marked milk bottles?"

"Maybe not. I mean to say, I can't imagine how the two deaths could possibly be related to milk bottles. But on the other hand, I *must* see this bottle business to the end. It's just so very *odd*."

I filled Berta in on the details of Judith Goddard's will. It didn't take long. The will had been, just like the woman, brisk and brutal. "In a nutshell," I said, "George appears to have the best murder motive in the world."

"*If* he had any idea of what the will said in advance, that is."

"Yes. And since Maynard Coburn wasn't even mentioned in the will—it hadn't been altered for more than a year, long before Judith and Maynard were an item—he couldn't have expected to gain anything financially from her death. I think we might be able to eliminate him as a suspect."

"I would not go *that* far, Mrs. Woodby. Maynard could have motives that are not financial. We still have not gotten to the bottom of the nature of his relations with Patience Yarker, for instance, and there is still the faint possibility that he runs rum down from the border."

"You didn't mention that part," Ralph said.

"It's a long shot," I said. "Based on a tip from an unreliable source—a seedy sportswriter." I filled in the details for Ralph.

Next, I told Berta about the letter from Juliet Vanderlyn in George's wastebin. "As suspected, he's a scoundrel."

"Poor Patience," Berta said with a sigh.

"You know," Ralph said, "I'm just here to lend a hand, but aren't you jumping to conclusions about this Patience girl? I mean, she doesn't *look* like she's in the club."

"Not yet, anyway," I said.

"These things take time," Berta said.

"And, well," Ralph went on, "she wouldn't be the first female to pretend that kind of thing to get what she wanted."

"What an awful thing to say!" I cried.

"Mr. Oliver, how *could* you?" Berta said.

Ralph hunched over the steering wheel, pressed his lips tight, and kept mum for the remainder of the drive.

After we had motored alongside the frozen river for four or five miles, a farm came into view off to the side. There was a trim farmhouse, a red hay barn, and another long, low, white barn that looked like the sort of place you'd stash a few dozen cows. The steep fields around the farm were white with snow, terminating in forest.

"Look—here's a road sign," I said. A hand-lettered, black-and-white sign read GUILDHALL ROAD.

Ralph drove up the narrow road, following tire ruts in the snow. He parked in front of the farmhouse, behind a Willys-Overland pickup. A curly-haired young man in dungarees, a thick blue wool sweater, and snow boots came out onto the porch. He carried a pipe, his frozen breath mushrooming around him.

Berta lowered her window.

The man came up. "You folks lost?" he asked.

"No," Berta said. "We are looking for Sweet Meadow Dairy."

"That's me."

"Oh, good."

"You wanting to buy some milk or butter?"

"As lovely as that sounds, no," Berta said. She passed over one of our agency cards. "We are private detectives, looking into the Goddard deaths—"

"Terrible business."

"Indeed. I wonder if you could answer a few questions."

"Don't see why not." The man gave his pipe a bemused puff. "May as well enjoy the fresh air while I might." He squinted up at the white sky. "Storm's comin'."

Berta told him how she'd happened to see mysterious grease pencil markings on one—and only one—bottle at the Maple Hill general store that morning. "Do you make such marks on your milk bottles, Mr.—?"

"Tunkett. No, I don't mark up my bottles. Why would I do a fool thing like that?"

Tunkett seemed relaxed and honest. If he was telling the truth—and I thought he was—that meant someone else was marking those milk bottles, *after* they were delivered to the general store.

"What time do you deliver the milk?" Berta asked.

"Eight o'clock in the morning, right after Green—he's the

shopkeeper—opens the place up. I bring a crate of a dozen in through the back, like clockwork. Then I pick up the crate from the day before and any empty bottles, and I'm on my way."

Leaning forward to be seen around Berta, I said, "Do you know a man by the name of Titus Staples, by any chance?"

"Titus? Oh, sure. I know Titus—well, I mean to say, I know *of* him. Can't say I've ever spoken two words to the fellow. He's something in the way of a recluse, you know."

"Where does he live?" I asked.

"I wouldn't go paying calls on Titus, ma'am," Tunkett said. "He's, well, he's not too sociable."

"It's terribly important that we speak with him."

"Suit yourself, but don't forget, folks, you're in the country now." Tunkett was eyeing Ralph, as though attempting to size up his bear-and-bootlegger-wrestling prowess.

"Oh, we know," Berta said archly. "It is *ever* so much safer than New York City."

Tunkett rattled off directions to Titus Staples's place, which entailed going back through Maple Hill, going a mile more, and then turning onto Concord Road. "When you see an abandoned sugar shack," he said, "you'll know you're there."

"Pardon me, but what is a sugar shack?" I asked.

"Building for boiling up maple sap for syrup."

"Ah," I said. "Thank you very much for the directions."

"Sure. And you folks'd best get yourselves inside in an hour or so, or you risk getting stranded. We're in for some weather."

"Well?" I said as Ralph steered the Speedwagon away from the farm. "Shall we pay a call upon Titus Staples and ask him about those milk bottles?" I looked back and forth between Ralph and Berta.

"Why not?" Ralph said.

"I do not know," Berta said. "He could be dangerous. He was vicious about wrenching the bottle from my hands."

He *had* been, and the thought of confronting him made my skin prickle. "When has danger ever stopped you?" I asked.

"I am fatigued, Mrs. Woodby. I feel brittle and so very *cold*."

She had looked plenty warm in the company of Pickard and Strom, but I kept that observation to myself.

"Berta," I said, "how would you like it if Ralph and I visited Titus Staples without you?"

"I would like that very much," Berta said. Her relief was palpable. "I could take your canine if you like."

"Dandy."

Ralph and I let Berta and Cedric out in front of the Old Mill Inn and continued on our way.

"Is Mrs. Lundgren okay?" Ralph asked me.

"Honestly, I'm not sure. She's . . . tired. Of everything. Just between you and me, I wouldn't be surprised if she . . ." I looked out the window, at the smear of bare branches and interminable white.

"What?"

"Well, she always has suitors, wherever she goes, and she's never taken anyone seriously. There's Jimmy, of course—"

"The Ant?" Ralph said roughly. He wasn't fond of gangster types.

"Yes, and as odd as it seems, she has preferred him above all others. But now, well . . . I'm afraid she is done with adventure. I think she wants to settle down."

"Huh," Ralph said, keeping his eyes on the road.

We motored steadily along River Road, leaving Maple Hill behind. The road followed the frozen white river, and on either side of us, hills rose up, covered in grayish-brown puffs of dormant trees. Ice streaked high granite outcroppings. The sky sank heavier with each passing minute, and I tasted the dusty, metallic air that foretold snow. However, only a few aimless flakes floated across the windshield.

I cuddled close to Ralph. I could feel his heat and his life even through our combined layers of wool and fur. I asked myself if it really mattered if he thought the idea of marriage was a joke, if we could simply *be,* together like this, from time to time. I could store happiness up, like a cactus stores water. Then I could survive without promises of forever.

Presently, a road branched off to the left.

Ralph braked slowly so as not to skid.

I peered up the road, which followed a tight ravine before twisting out of sight into the trees.

"Do you suppose this is the Concord Road the dairy farmer mentioned?" I asked. Why was my voice so quivery? "It isn't marked."

"We've gone about a mile—and he said the turnoff was a mile out of town—and I haven't seen any other roads." Ralph turned up the road, but promptly braked again. "Tire tracks."

"So there are. Two sets. Wait for a moment."

I climbed out of the truck, went over to the tire tracks, and bent to inspect them. Then I got back into the truck. "They appear to be from the same vehicle."

"Someone came and went, then."

"You mean *Titus* came and went."

"Maybe."

"Well, if he isn't home, then perhaps we ought to turn back."

The truck was still idling. Ralph dipped his face to look into my eyes. "Kid, if this is giving you the jumps, then sure, we can turn ba—"

"The jumps?" I laughed, sounding distressingly like a cockatoo. "Silly darling, of course I haven't got the jumps. Please." I swept a hand in the direction of the windshield. "Proceed."

"I'll keep you safe, you know," Ralph said, motoring carefully up the road. "You don't need to be scared when you're with me."

26

The woods pressed in. We rounded a bend, and then another, gaining a little elevation, and then the road opened out onto a snowy meadow fringed with feathery bare trees. A lone grayish building stood at the edge of the trees, with a metal chimney and small windows.

"That must be the abandoned sugar shack the farmer mentioned," I said. "But where is Titus's house? Or do you suppose he *lives* in that shack? It appears a little . . . drafty."

Ralph was studying our surroundings with keen eyes. "The vehicle tracks go all the way to the side of the shack, in front of that door, see, and then circle back this way. I don't know if Titus lives in this joint or not, but that's where our mystery vehicle went."

We rolled closer to the shack. There were no signs of life, and when Ralph parked a few yards from the shack and switched off the engine, the silence around us spread, cushiony and vast.

"I'll take a look," Ralph said, opening his door. The hinges groaned.

"I'm coming, too." I scrambled out after him, and he held out a hand for me as I hopped to the ground.

We went toward the shack's door.

"Footprints!" I whispered, pointing to the ground. "*Lots* of them."

"They look like they're all from the same person," Ralph said. "Someone who made two or three trips back and forth from his vehicle."

My eyes swept the line of trees behind the shack. The woods were serene, and the maple trees were too slender to conceal a human being. And yet, couldn't a person be crouched behind one of those big humps that were perhaps snowy rock walls or boulders?

My eyes drifted up the treed slope and—oh golly—there was a ramshackle little cabin up there on a sort of outcropping, with smoke pluming from its crooked chimney and sullying the sky. I supposed we'd missed it because of the way it was burrowed into the landscape, more like a rodent's nest than a human habitation.

"Um, Ralph?" I croaked.

"Yeah?" His hand was on the sugar shack's door handle.

"There is Titus's house."

He followed my pointed finger.

"There's smoke," I said.

"Uh-huh."

"Which would suggest he's at home."

"It would."

"He wouldn't be too pleased about us snooping in his sugar shack."

"Likely not, no."

"Then we'd better dash, because *here he comes*!"

A lanky form was hastening down the slope through the trees, his red hat vivid against the brown-and-white landscape.

Ralph and I ran to the Speedwagon.

"Hey!" Titus shouted, his voice muffled by the snow. "Stop!"

I scrambled up into the cab, and Ralph leapt in after me and slammed the door. The engine gurgled to life, and we lurched into Drive.

"Oh golly!" I said, craning my head to keep my eyes on Titus. Ralph turned the truck. "Hurry! He's running now—he has a rifle—"

BLAM!

"That was his rifle," I whispered. "Are we hit?"

"Don't think so." Ralph pressed harder on the gas. "Soon as we round that first bend up there, we'll be out range of—

BLAM—ding!

"He hit the bumper!" I shouted. "The absolute nerve!" I cast an angry glance into the rearview mirror. I saw Titus, a tiny, hunched figure with a rifle braced against his shoulder—

Then we were swooshing around the bend. Safe.

I couldn't seem to unclench my hands from the edge of the dashboard. "I suppose it's pretty obvious that Titus Staples is hiding something in that sugar shack of his, otherwise he wouldn't be going around shooting at—at innocent people who are only having a quick peek! Whatever he's hiding in there, well, to begin with, it must have to do with that secret code written on the bottoms of those milk bottles he collects every morning, and further, well, don't you think it must have something to do with Maynard Coburn? Or Rosemary or Roy? Or maybe all three of them? Because Maynard might be a bootlegger, but Titus was also helping Roy with wine crates in his cellar and Roy *did* burn our dossier—and then there was the way Rosemary skulked out of the general store bright and early this morn—"

"You're babbling, Lola," Ralph said, concentrating on the road. The snow was coming down more heavily now. "You've got the jitters."

"Of course I've got the jitters! Someone fired a gun at us! He's loony! What are we going to do? We can't tell Sergeant Peletier, because he'll want to know why we're still in town to begin with, and—"

"Lola. Honey. Calm down. We're all in one piece, right? You oughta be happy."

"Happy?" I yelped.

"Well, sure." Ralph was smiling. "'Cause now you know Titus is likely guarding something shady in his sugar shack back there, so all you've got to do is figure out what, and maybe—don't hold me to it—just maybe you'll have your killer."

When Ralph and I walked into the lobby of the Old Mill Inn a little later, Patience Yarker sat behind the front desk, small, pale, and despondent in a black dress and a flowery woolen shawl. "Oh, hello," she said, more to Ralph than to me. "It's really starting to come down out there, isn't it?"

"Sure is," Ralph said, dusting snowflakes off his coat sleeve.

"Just come back from the funeral reception?" Patience asked.

"We attended the reception, yes," I said as Ralph and I approached the desk.

"I suppose Hester Albans put out a lot of that icky fruitcake of hers?"

Ralph smiled. "I ate about three slices."

Patience cast her eyes down. Her eyelashes were childishly thick. "What about . . . the will?"

Ralph and I traded a glance. On the one hand, we had eavesdropped on the will reading, so we didn't have the right to broadcast the news. On the other hand, it would be illuminating to see Patience's reaction to George's newfound fortune.

I glanced around. No one else was in the lobby or on the stairs. The doors to the sitting room opened off the lobby, but I didn't see anyone in there except for a tabby cat curled on a sofa. "It isn't public knowledge yet," I said softly, "but it seems that George has come into the lot."

Patience's lips parted. "George? *Only* George?"

"Per Mrs. Goddard's will, the estate was to be split between the two sons," I said, "but since Fenton has passed over into the great beyond, three-quarters of the lot fell into George's lap. The rest goes to Rosemary."

"But that means . . ." Patience's eyes were once again cast down, and I was reminded of the colorful hotel brochures that had been hidden beneath her reservation book. "The house," she murmured, as though to herself. "The land."

Was it my imagination, or did she look a little starry eyed? And—*oho*—there went her hand, sliding over her still-flat belly.

"I suppose Rosemary is steamed?" Patience said, looking up.

She'd caught me watching her hand on her belly. Her hand fell away, and she bit her underlip.

Patience knew I knew. About the Possible Pea, I mean, except now it seemed that the Pea's existence had been confirmed. Oh dear. Unwed mothers always have a rotten row to hoe, and in a village like this . . . what would become of her? Of the two of them?

I said, "Oh yes, Rosemary is steamed. And Roy, too."

"I wonder where he'll live now," Patience said.

"You suppose George won't allow him to stay on in the cottage?"

"What?" Patience looked a little misty. "Oh. Perhaps he will. George has a heart of gold, you know." She looked at Ralph. "Men with hearts of gold are awfully hard to find."

That settled it for me: George Goddard had sired that Pea. I figured this was no time to mention Juliet Vanderlyn—a.k.a. Ickle Jules-Bean—to the poor girl.

Ralph and I went up to our airing cupboard to change, since his socks and trouser cuffs were soaking wet, and so were my velvet pumps and woolen stockings. I had after-jitters from Titus and his rifle, and I dropped my hairbrush when I tried to smooth down my bob. It clattered on the floorboards.

"Rats," I muttered, picking it up.

Ralph, who was (unfortunately for my composure) in shirtsleeves and suspenders, came over and took my shoulders. "Say, you're a little shaky, aren't you?" he murmured.

"I'll never get used to being shot at, I'm afraid."

"No one gets used to it, unless they're jingle-brained." His warm hands slid down my back. "Lucky for you, I know a real good remedy for the shakes."

"Oh?" In fact, he was making me shake even more.

"Yeah."

When we went downstairs for a late lunch, the dining room was empty except for Berta at the table in front of the fire.

She looked up from a novel as Ralph and I approached. A teapot in a cozy stood on the table.

"You look like you're feeling better," I said, pulling out a chair. Cedric was curled up on the seat, sleepy and warm. I picked him up, sat, and arranged him on my lap. *Ahh.* Warm puppy. Better than a hot-water bottle.

"I feel much better, thank you," Berta said, closing her book. *Bedlam in Berlin* by George B. Jones, Jr. "Did you have any luck speaking with Titus Staples?"

Ralph's and my eyes met.

"Not precisely, no," I said.

Ralph and I sketched out our adventure at Titus's sugar shack. Outside, snow fell in big, slow flakes. Triangles of white piled in the corners of the windowpanes.

"That is dreadful," Berta said when we had finished. "A gun!"

"Dreadful, yes," I said, "but as Ralph pointed out, if Titus is guarding something in that sugar shack, and if we think it may be somehow connected to the murders, well, now we have a clear path going forward."

"Ah. Discover what is in the sugar shack," Berta said with a knowing nod. "In a stealthy fashion, preferably under cover of darkness."

"That's it," I said. "It'll be a cinch."

Ralph, I could tell, was suppressing a chuckle.

I scowled at him.

"What?" he said. "I admire your gumption."

Berta glanced to the windows. "I am afraid we will not be able to do much more in the way of sleuthing today, though. The snow has become terribly heavy. It would not be safe to drive."

"You look relieved," I said.

"So do you."

All right. That was fair.

"If we can't get to the sugar shack tonight," I said, "perhaps the next best thing would be to stake out the general store tomorrow morning, before that person has a chance to write on the milk bottle. If we see who is doing *that*, we may not need to go back to that sugar shack at all."

Patience Yarker was gliding toward us, carrying an envelope. She set it beside Berta's teacup. "Telephone message for you, Mrs. Lundgren. Now—" She looked at Ralph. "—may I take your lunch orders? Grandma says there's still ham-and-pea soup and bread rolls, and plenty of apple pie."

While Ralph and I ordered, Berta opened the envelope and read the message. Her face took on the distinctive rosy smugness it always did when she was reminded of one of her conquests.

Patience went to the kitchen.

"Is it from one of the Alpine Club co-presidents?" I asked Berta.

"Both co-presidents, actually. They request our presence at the club's lodge this evening."

"For what purpose?" I asked.

"Roast venison and a game of checkers."

"Is that what they're calling it these days?" Ralph said with a grin.

"Mr. *Oliver*!" Berta said.

"What time?" I glanced out at the ever-thickening curtains of falling snow.

"They write that they will come to the inn at five o'clock to collect us."

"Are you certain Ralph and I are invited?" I asked. "I'm not sure either Pickard or Strom has completely focused his eyes on me yet."

"The note is addressed to 'Mr. Woodby and the ladies of the Discreet Retrieval Agency,'" Berta said.

"I get it," I said to Ralph. "We're the chaperones."

"They are only attempting to be hospitable," Berta said.

"You sure about that?" Ralph said.

"As sure as eggs are eggs," Berta said stiffly.

"Huh," Ralph said, "'cause I remember pretty vividly how they overheard Lola telling you how she heard what was in Judith Goddard's will."

"What are you suggesting?" Berta asked.

"They looked pretty interested in the will is all," Ralph said. "Which isn't to say, Mrs. Lundgren, that they weren't also pretty keen on feeding you cookies."

Berta appeared to be placated. "Do you intend to accompany me this evening, or not?"

Ralph and I looked out the windows. Then we looked at each other.

"Could be a hoot," Ralph said.

"All right," I said, "but I'm not sure about roast venison." I turned to Berta. "We'll go—if for no other reason than to keep you out of mischief."

27

At five o'clock sharp, a geriatric Model T depot hack emerged from the pelting snowflakes and rolled to a stop in front of the inn. Ralph, Berta, and I had been waiting and watching from the sitting room windows, and we went outside.

"Just look at that motorcar," I said, walking arm in arm with Ralph. "No sides—only a windshield. We'll freeze!"

"It is only a few miles," Berta said, walking eagerly to the curb.

Pickard was behind the hack's wheel, and Strom stepped out. "Evening!" he said. "Glad you could come! All the club boys'll be glad! We tire of each other's company sometimes." He helped Berta into the second row of seats and got in beside her.

Pickard glared over his shoulder, only his slitted eyes visible between his hat and scarf. Now he was all alone up front.

Ralph and I climbed into the third row, dusted snow off the seats, and sat. Cedric was inside my coat with only his head protruding. I had no desire to learn if dogs are able to contract pneumonia.

We rumbled forward into the falling dusk. Snowflakes swirled dizzily and stinging wind gusted through the unprotected hack. The village had a hunkered-down look to it.

"Where is the Alpine Club Lodge?" Berta asked Strom loudly, to be heard over the wind and the engine.

Strom took the opportunity to scoot closer to her. "Oh, only a mile out of town, halfway up Moose Mountain—that's the mountain the ski hill's on. We've got ourselves some nice trails up there for snowshoeing and mountaineering. Last summer we cleared trees from a strip—it's not far from the ski jump—so we can even do a little alpine skiing."

Pickard, hunched over the steering wheel, called over his shoulder, "*Some* of us cleared trees, anyway. Other fellows stood around and yapped."

"Oh, I am so glad alpine skiing is growing more popular here in America," Berta said. "Such an exciting sport!"

"Yup," Strom said. "Say, would you like to have a go? In the daylight, I mean. All this fresh snow'll be a treat to ski on tomorrow. Smooth as custard."

"Perhaps," Berta said.

After a mile of slow, uphill driving, Pickard parked the truck in a flat spot and switched off the engine. We all got out. Several empty vehicles—trucks and hacks mostly—stood gathering snow around us. It was only a little after five o'clock, but it was almost completely dark. What light remained in the atmosphere created a faint, directionless gray glow. Now that the sound of the engine was gone, the whistling of the wind seemed louder still.

"We walk the rest of the way," Pickard said. Snow was collecting on his mustache. "Too slick for driving." He led the way up a steep forest path. The wind smelled fresh and wild and piney.

I looked hard into the darkness beyond the falling snow, searching for Titus Staples and, perhaps just a teensy bit, for bearlike black fur. I was glad to be walking close to Ralph.

We emerged in a clearing to find ourselves facing a building with glowing yellow windows. Snow pillowed up on the roof and icicles saw-toothed the deep eaves. A white-and-green sign above the door read MAPLE HILL ALPINE CLUB LODGE. The shadowy mountain jutted behind it.

Inside, it was warm and smoky, and it smelled of sap, spilled liquor, and roasting onions and meat. A fire danced in a massive granite fireplace, logs stacked high beside it. Several men in sweaters and wool pants were drinking, smoking pipes, and playing cards and checkers. Most of them appeared to be over fifty years old. When they saw us enter, they roared in greeting, many of them lifting glasses as though in toast. "The lady detectives are here!" "There's a husband, too, Ignatius." "Well, let him in if he's good at checkers!" "Women! Finally a few women." "Could you think of something besides women for a change, Morton?" "Someone fetch 'em drinks! Why, they look frozen stiff."

Ralph, smiling with his eyes, said softly to me, "Looks like *I'm* the chaperone for both you and Mrs. Lundgren."

We removed our coats, hats, scarves, gloves, and mittens, and hung them on rough-hewn pegs just inside the door. Ralph followed Pickard and Strom toward the fire.

"*Psst,*" I whispered to Berta. "Look."

She looked.

Several rifles were leaning, muzzle up, in the corner by the door.

"Aren't you worried?" I whispered.

"Mrs. Woodby, where do you suppose they got the roast venison? From a can?" Berta swanned away into the crowd of appreciative men.

I eyed the guns. They were hunting rifles, not, say, tommy guns. Still, bean-shooters give me the willies. I always expect them to start banging of their own accord.

I joined Ralph near the fire, glasses of whiskey were pushed into our hands, and someone started playing the accordion. Cedric took up a spot next to the fire and laid his chin in his paws.

"To your health, kid," Ralph said, clinking his glass against mine.

"And to yours." I sipped. "This is really good."

"Yeah, it is," Ralph said. "Doesn't taste like it was made in someone's woodshed. I wonder where they get it."

"You're thinking of that crashed touring car."

"Sure am."

"Let's ask someone."

"All right, but be subtle—"

"I'm always subtle!"

"Be roundabout—you're always a little impatient, and so you ask these point-blank questions."

"No, I don't," I said, pouting.

"We don't want anyone thinking we're undercover Customs agents. That'll make them clam up in a second."

A weathered man came over to Ralph and me and introduced himself as Ezekiel Morton. "Glad you could make it up on this rotten night. It's always nice to see new faces. Pickard and Strom are both over the moon that your friend Mrs. Lundgren agreed to come. Just between me and you, they're goners."

We looked over at Berta, enthroned on a rocking chair and laughing. Pickard was pouring whiskey into her upheld glass. Strom appeared to be telling a witty story.

"This is simply scrummy whiskey, Mr. Morton," I said, taking a sip. "Where do you get it?"

Whoops. I supposed *that* was a point-blank question. I avoided Ralph's eye.

"Where do we get it?" Morton grinned. "That's an Alpine Club secret, my dear."

"It tastes like Canadian whiskey," I said, trying to sound conversational.

"Well, we're within spitting distance of Canada, aren't we?"

Morton wasn't going to crack. I'd try another angle.

I said, "Is Maynard Coburn a member of this club?"

"Coburn? Sure. But he never comes up here to the lodge."

I thought of Maynard walking home at three thirty in the morning, either blotto or stunned from a motorcar crash. "Never?"

"Nope."

Berta's ladylike laughter cut through the hubbub, and we glanced over at her. Now Pickard was telling a funny story and Strom, positioned so Berta couldn't see his face, was giving Pickard the stink-eye.

"I sure hope Strom and Pickard have good intentions," Ralph said to Morton. "I'm fond of Mrs. Lundgren."

"Well, course they do. They're both wanting a wife badly. Pickard's never been wed—not for want of trying—and Strom's been a widower for five years. Not that they don't want to outdo each other almost as badly as they want a wife." Morton chuckled. "Folks' reasons for marriage are usually a lot more problematical than just a couple I-love-yous. But I'm sure you two know that, being wed yourselves. Although, come to think of it, you look like newlyweds, sitting so close."

"That's right," Ralph said easily. "Married last June."

"Big wedding?"

"Oh yes," I said.

Ralph simultaneously said, "Nope. City Hall."

"Yes, well," I said quickly, "it *seemed* big since there are always so many people rushing around City Hall. In New York, you see."

Morton was inspecting my man-boots. "Usually newlywed gals like to spruce themselves up for their new husbands."

"Oh, she *is* spruced up." Ralph squeezed my hand. "Prettiest girl in the world."

"It's just that I have rather large feet," I said. "I can't help it."

"She got 'em from her dad," Ralph said.

"You aren't wearing wedding rings," Morton said.

I looked at Ralph. "*You* tell him why, darling."

"We left 'em at home," Ralph said. "For safekeeping."

"Now, listen, it doesn't matter to *me* if you're not really married," Morton said, waggling a bushy eyebrow. "I'm no prude. You young folks have got modern ideas, and that's all right with me."

"Since we're being so very open," I said in a cheery tone, "would you tell me why Pickard and Strom are so interested in the contents of Judith Goddard's will?"

"What do you mean?" Morton scratched his beard and cast his eyes away.

"That's why we were invited here this evening, isn't it?" I said. "They overheard me telling Mrs. Lundgren I'd learned how the estate was divvied up, and they invited us to learn more."

I fully expected Morton to deny any knowledge of this. But instead, he sighed and said, "All right, all right. It's not only the co-presidents who are interested in that will. It's all of us in the club. We're itching to know who got what."

"You're hoping Judith Goddard left the club something in her will?" I asked.

"No, nothing like that. It's . . . say, who *did* get what in that will?"

"I'll tell you," I said, "if you tell me why you want to know."

Ralph hid his smile with his whiskey glass.

"All right," Morton said. "The thing is, the club doesn't have much land—only ten acres, which isn't much when you're wanting to ski and snowshoe all day long. For years, we've been trespassing on the Goddard land—they own everything on three sides of the club's own land, for miles and miles around. All those wild hills stretching north and east? That's Goddard land."

"How did you wind up with a patch carved out of their land?" Ralph asked.

"Elmer Goddard sold it to us. He was a good fellow. But after he died, Judith refused to part with any more land once we'd saved up the money to buy it. I don't like to speak ill of the dead, but she was greedy."

"I think I understand," I said. "You're hoping that whoever inherited the estate will sell more land to the Alpine Club."

Morton nodded, and leaned in. "So. Who is it?"

"George," I said. "Well, three-quarters of the estate goes to George, and the rest is Rosemary's."

"George! Well." Morton was grinning. "That's just great."

"You're thinking George will sell you some land?" Ralph asked.

"Yep. He's an outdoorsman, you see. A skier. What's more, he doesn't have any silly notions in his head like Rosemary does, about keeping great tracts of land in the family like some kinda high-muckety-muck English gentry. He'll be reasonable. We'll ask him straightaway. Ah, that's just grand."

Another fellow came bustling over, carrying a steaming, fragrant plate of food, which he passed to me. "Ladies first—oh—and here's your fork."

"Thank you," I said.

A few minutes later, everyone was eating. The roast potatoes and venison tasted delicious. I dampened my guilty thoughts of Prancer and Dancer with a second glass of whiskey.

I was feeding Cedric a last morsel of meat when one of the men cried, "What in tarnation's that? Boys, something's out there!"

Everyone spun around.

The man who had spoken was bounding to a window. He cupped his hands around his face and peered out.

He reared back. "Grab your guns, boys! It's that confounded bear." He strode toward the front door and the rifles leaning in the corner.

"Stay inside," Ralph said to me, getting to his feet.

I set aside my plate and stood. "I'm coming, too." I placed Cedric on my chair and told him to stay.

There was a flurry of footfalls and coats being flung on and rifles being hoisted. Pickard was helping Berta into her coat.

Strom said to Pickard, "My papa always said never mess with guns when you're drunk."

"You're drunk, too," Pickard snapped.

The man called Ignatius said, "Heck, we're *all* drunk. Come on. We're wasting time. This could be our chance to nail Slipperyback!"

"Lola," Ralph said to me, shrugging on his coat. "You really oughta stay ba—"

"No." I put on my own coat and grabbed my hat. "This is pertinent to my investigation."

"That's why *I'm* going. I'll report back to—"

I sailed past Ralph, following the stream of a dozen armed, drunken men into the night.

28

"There!" one of the men shouted, his voice shrunken by the wind. "Fur! Disappearing into that thicket up the slope! Confound that critter! Let's get 'im!"

The men swarmed uphill. A man with a kerosene lantern led the way, with Berta, Strom, and Pickard somewhere in the middle, and Ralph and me trailing at the rear. The forest yawned blackly. Snowflakes stung my cheeks, and I had to lift my feet high to clear the deep snow.

Did I want to see a bear? No, I did not. Which made me feel like a lousy detective, because shouldn't detectives always wish to confront the terrible truth?

"Footprints!" the man with the lantern shouted. "Only a pair. Oho, it's Slipperyback, all right, walkin' upright. C'mon! Hurry up! Cock your rifles, boys!"

"I cannot believe," I said breathlessly to Ralph, "that a bear would bother to walk upright when it could go on all fours."

"Who knows?" Ralph said, giving me a hand over a fallen log. "Maybe it escaped from the circus."

"This is no joke, Ralph. There's something out there."

"I don't believe in monsters, Lola, and besides, you're safe with me."

We slogged upward after the men, following the swinging orb of the lantern.

A few moments later, Berta cried out, her voice frail in the stormy night.

"That was Berta!" I said to Ralph, picking up my pace. "She sounds hurt!"

I pushed through the men, who had come to a standstill, to see Berta flat on her back, half-absorbed by snow, and Pickard kneeling over her.

"Mrs. Lundgren," he was saying. "Where does it hurt?"

"My ankle," Berta said, her voice small and tight. "I have twisted my ankle. The branches hit my face and I lost my balance—*oh.* I do not believe I will be able to walk any farther."

"Durn you!" Pickard snarled up at Strom. "You let those tree branches whip into her face! Didn't anyone ever tell you that a gentleman always holds the branches for a lady behind him? Come on, Mrs. Lundgren, let me help you up before all this snow starts melting on you."

"Uh . . . what about Slipperyback?" one of the men said.

This was met with jeers and shouts and murmurs of things like, "Lady's been hurt, man!" "Can't you think of anything but hunting, Johns?" "We'll have to nab that bear later. Got to tend to the lady!"

With Strom looking sheepishly on, Pickard slid an arm around Berta and attempted to hoist her upright. She cried out again and sagged in his arms. Her weight made him crumple like a paper doll, but with a grunt, he straightened. Then, bowlegs sagging, he swooped Berta into his arms after the fashion of a romantic cinema hero.

"Let us through," he grunted.

We all parted to let Pickard pass, and he started down the snowy slope. He cast a swift glance over his shoulder, straight at Strom. He bared his teeth in triumph.

Strom glowered.

"Let's take a look at those footprints," Ralph murmured to me.

"But Berta is hurt."

"You don't want to miss your chance."

"Oh, all right."

Ralph asked the man with the lantern to illuminate the footprints for us.

"Sure," the man said.

The rest of the men were straggling, deflated, down the slope, their rifles drooping in their arms.

With the snow pelting down and the wind swaying the fir branches above us, the man with the lantern stooped to show us the prints.

They were man-sized, and they had been made by someone or—*gulp*—something walking upright on two legs, not four.

"Here's a good print—look at the shape of 'em," the man said, pointing a gloved finger at one of the prints. "No bootheel marks. They're triangular like a bear's pad. And see the claw marks?"

I swallowed. Five long, teardrop-shaped claw marks were clearly pressed into the snow.

"Well, I'll be," Ralph murmured.

"It sounds as though you've seen prints like these before," I said to the man with the lantern.

"I have, though not since I was a boy. But folks up in these parts have been seeing glimpses of Slipperyback—or maybe his ancestors—for centuries."

"No one has ever caught more than a glimpse of him?" I asked, looking up the slope where the tracks merged into the darkness.

I thought I heard the faint snap of a branch.

Run! my muscles shouted.

I stood my ground.

"Nope. He's wily like that. But *someday* . . . Seen enough?"

Ralph looked at me.

"Yes," I said. "Except for one more thing. What's at the top of this slope here?"

"You mean, where's Slipperyback headed?"

"Yes."

"Well, it's Goddard land up there—"

"Yes, I know."

"—and it's the ridge running north to south. There are caves up there, too. I wouldn't be surprised if he's got a den in one of those. You wouldn't catch *me* venturing near those caves—no, sir."

We started down the slope, the man with the lantern leading the way.

"Wait a minute," I whispered to Ralph as we went. "I've just remembered something. Mr. Currier, the minister, told Berta and me that he ran into Maynard Coburn up on a ridge last summer. Mountaineering, you know. What if Maynard was really scoping it out or, I don't know, searching for Slipperyback, or . . ." My voice trailed off, and a violent shiver shook me from head to toe.

"Come on." Ralph curled his arm around me. "Let's get back inside before this snowstorm blows us away."

Back inside the lodge, the party spirit was extinguished. Berta reclined on a chair with one boot propped in Pickard's hands. She wore a grimace of pain.

"Berta, are you all right?" I asked, hovering over her.

"No. I suspect it is a sprain. *Mrs. Woodby.*" Berta beckoned me closer and lowered her voice to a whisper. "Promise me you will stake out the general store in the morning and get to the bottom of who is marking those milk bottles. I may not be able to go, but it will drive me potty if I never find out."

"I promise," I whispered back.

"I think you oughta have your ankle looked at by Dr. Best," Pickard said. "He's got an office at his house."

"I'll drive her," Strom said quickly.

"No, Strom," Pickard said, "I think *you've* done quite enough."

I meant to wait up for Berta's return from the doctor's office that night. But the airing cupboard was too warm, Ralph's arms were so comforting, and Cedric's snoring so sweet. The snowstorm rattled and swished on the windowpanes, and I fell into a dreamless sleep.

"They say it's always coldest just before dawn," I said to Ralph the next morning, "and this morning is proof. It's colder than a Frigidaire out here!"

"Mmph," Ralph said into his turned-up collar.

We crunched across River Street toward the general store, where we meant to catch the milk-bottle marker in the act. I had stashed Cedric in Berta's room—she was still sleeping—in order to be nimble. Five pounds of dog tends to gum the game.

Only one set of tire tracks marred the street's thick, snowy quilt. Pale pink saturated the eastern sky behind mountain silhouettes. Smoke drifted from chimneys, but not a soul was out and about. I enviously imagined everyone curled up in feather beds. And somewhere, probably not very far away, a killer was abed, too. At Goddard Farm, or the Old Mill Inn, or within a snug clapboard cottage.

Or, perhaps, the killer wasn't abed at all, but lacing on their snow boots in preparation for a day of villainy—beginning with a grease-penciling excursion to the general store.

Ralph tried the store's door handle. "Locked," he said into his scarf.

A figure appeared behind the glass of the door—Green, the shopkeeper. His eyebrows shot up when he saw us, and he unlocked and opened the door with a clatter and a bell-jingle.

"You're bright and early," he said gruffly. "You can come in, but the stove's not lit yet. Almost as cold inside as out."

"Thanks," Ralph said, and he and I filed inside.

"What're you needing at this hour?" Green asked with his back to us. He crouched in front of the potbellied stove and opened its little door.

"Milk," I said. "Fresh milk."

"Farmer Tunkett just left his crate round back." Green was arranging kindling inside the stove. "Soon as I get this fire going, I'll put it out in the icebox."

"Dandy," I said. Since Green's back was turned, I gave Ralph a thumbs-up sign with my mittened hand. Actually, my mittened hands were more or less fixed in the thumbs-up position.

Ralph and I pretended to be engrossed in a bin of penny candies, and then a display of wool long johns, as we waited for Green to put out the milk bottles. Once we heard the distinctive glassy rattle of the bottles going into the icebox, we went over.

"There you go," Green said, picking up the empty wooden crate. "Fresh milk." He disappeared into the private realm at the back of the store.

Ralph and I eagerly examined every one of those milk bottles. They were icy to the touch, all with lightning-style metal and porcelain stoppers.

"No grease pencil," I whispered.

"Nope," Ralph whispered back. "So now we wait."

"How are we to explain to Green why we're hanging about?"

"If he asks questions, we'll say we're going back to New York this afternoon and we're picking up Vermont country gewgaws for our friends back home."

"Spiffy idea." I made for the maple sugar candy display.

Ralph and I loitered. We gradually piled up quite a lot of little things to purchase at Green's counter: boxes of candies, bottles of the local maple syrup, handmade pot holders, birch baskets. I hadn't done any Christmas shopping yet, so I felt that I was virtuously killing two birds with one stone. Meanwhile, the woodstove was starting to emanate warmth, and Green had unfolded a newspaper. He kept an eye on Ralph and me over the top edge, but he didn't ask any questions.

Customers trickled in. We didn't recognize the first several, but we watched all the same to see if they went to the icebox. The first person to visit the icebox was a small girl of about six with pigtails sprouting from below a fleecy hat. After she paid for her milk and left—she had to stand on tiptoe to give Green her quarter—I went to the icebox. I felt absurd, of course, but while Ralph distracted Green up at the counter, I checked the bottoms of the remaining eleven milk bottles.

No grease pencil.

I went to peruse the crank-operated apple peelers.

Ralph and I had been in the store for more than half an hour when it was suddenly rather crowded. The old-timers had taken up their chairs around the potbellied stove. A woman inspected the shelf of canned foods. Mr. Pickard bustled in, purchased some magazines and newspapers, and left. Two small children were counting out their pennies for peppermint sticks. Mr. Strom came in, piled his arms high with purchases, and left. And then . . . Rosemary Rogerson came in, bundled in black wool.

Ralph was up at the counter again, talking to Green. He hadn't noticed Rosemary's arrival, and I thought it would be indiscreet to alert him. I'd keep tabs on her myself.

I was behind a shoulder-high shelf, and Rosemary didn't appear to have noticed me yet. I was wearing a hat, and I slouched so that only my eyes would be visible should she turn around.

Rosemary went straight to the high shelf holding jars of spices, yeast, coffee, and tea. She appeared to be searching for something in particular—her head moved left to right along the shelves. This went on for a minute or two. She appeared to find what she was looking for, and pulled a jar from a high shelf. Then she repeated the process, and pulled another jar. She carried both jars to the counter. When she saw that it was Ralph standing there talking to Green, her pace faltered. Then she lifted her chin and barreled over.

"Excuse me," I heard her say to Ralph in a cold voice.

Ralph stepped aside.

Green measured out portions of whatever was in the jars into tiny paper sacks. Rosemary paid and left.

Perhaps she had come to mark the milk bottles, but seeing Ralph and me there, she had changed her plans.

And—it occurred to me that I hadn't looked in the direction of the icebox in about five minutes. I hurried to the icebox. I reached for the bottle in the rear corner, the one that Titus always purchased. I turned it over.

Grease pencil on the bottom of the bottle said *II 6p.*

No.

With shaking hands, I replaced the bottle, shut the icebox, and walked swiftly to the front door.

"Lola?" Ralph said as I passed him.

There was no time to answer. I shoved open the front door, blasted by cold air, and looked up and down the sidewalk.

There was Rosemary, hurrying toward her parked motorcar far up the street. And . . . here came Titus Staples, greasy black hair straggling from beneath his red cap.

I dodged back inside the store.

Ralph was right there. "What's up?" he whispered.

"The bottle has been marked—and Titus Staples is coming to get it! I want to go after Rosemary—would you stay here to see what Titus does? Thank you, darling." I went on tiptoe, kissed Ralph's cheek, and darted outside.

29

I passed Titus Staples just outside the general store, and although he didn't even look at me, I couldn't help shrinking away, remembering the *BLAM!* of his rifle.

I bobbled up the sidewalk in knee-deep snow after Rosemary.

She was thumping into the driver's seat of her cream-colored motorcar, shutting the door—

I broke into a clumsy run.

—she was turning over her engine—

I slipped and scrambled over a snowbank and into the street in front of her motorcar. "Mrs. Rogerson!" I shouted.

She wrestled with her steering wheel and tried to drive around me. But her motorcar wasn't agile in the snow, and I easily blocked her path.

"Mrs. Rogerson!" I shouted over the warble of her engine. "Might I have a word?"

I wasn't certain if she could hear me, but her face behind the windshield flushed with fury. She switched off the engine, threw open her door, and came at me with her handbag swinging from one arm and her teeth gritted.

"How dare you block my way, you—you wicked creature!" she cried.

"What were you doing in the general store?" I asked. "What are you hiding?"

"Hiding?" Rosemary scoffed. "I'm not hiding anything. *You*, on the other hand—"

"Did you mark a milk bottle with grease pencil?"

"*Grease pencil?* You're mad."

"What did you purchase?"

"It is none of your affair, but—nutmeg and cloves."

"Why are you still here in Maple Hill?"

"To bury my brother Fenton, you fool! Now, you listen to me. Leave Maple Hill. Leave *today*, or you'll be sorry." Rosemary's glasses gleamed, and I couldn't see her eyes. "Two people are dead. *Murdered.* You must face facts. You're out of your depth."

"What are you suggesting, Mrs. Rogerson? That you intend to murder me if I don't obey your instructions?"

"Oh, I don't need to murder you." A smile stretched Rosemary's sallow cheeks. "I have *this*." She reached into her handbag and fished out a handful of glossy photographic prints. "That's right. Have a nice, hard look. I motored over to the camera shop in Waterbury yesterday to have these developed. I think this one's my favorite." She held up a photograph of Berta and me hunched over the open breadbox at Goddard Farm. "Mother's ruby ring still hasn't turned up, you know. That ring is *mine*! It was passed down from mother to daughter on that side of my family for generations, and now it's simply gone, and George has gotten practically everything else. It's not fair!"

"I figured *you* took the ring," I said.

"Oh, shut up. Now, *this* one—" Rosemary shuffled the photographs. "—comes in a close second in terms of favorites." The photograph depicted Berta and me in Goddard Farm's butler's pantry, among the gleaming silver. It must have been taken our first evening there, when we were trying to decide whether or not to skedaddle after Judith's death. "Last but not least, there's this one." Rosemary shifted the third photograph to the top.

Exceptionally wide-looking likenesses of Berta and me stood in Goddard Farm's kitchen. Berta was holding up a silver teaspoon as though assessing its value. It would've been taken when we put together a coffee tray for hungover Aunt Daphne.

"Did you *spy* on us?" I asked Rosemary.

"Don't be stupid. Fenton did. I developed the roll of film that was in his camera when he died."

"What else was on that roll? Whom did he photograph at the carnival that night? He could've—"

"That is none of your affair." Rosemary stuffed the photographs back into her handbag. "I can make these photographs turn up at the police station whenever I please. Sergeant Peletier is awfully eager to arrest you and your sidekick. All he's looking for is an excuse. I'll tell him lots of jewelry and silver and things have gone missing at the house—not just the ruby ring. It'll all be utterly clear what you've done. Unless, of course, you and that grifter granny accomplice of yours do as I say and leave Maple Hill on this afternoon's train. Do I make myself perfectly clear?"

"Oh yes," I said. "Quite. One bitty question, though—*why* are you so desperate for us to leave town?"

Without answering, Rosemary swung around, slammed herself back into her motorcar, started the engine, and rolled away in a haze of foul-smelling exhaust.

"Lola." Ralph was standing on the other side of the snowbank. "You okay?"

I nodded. I climbed atop the snowbank, and Ralph put his hands on my waist and helped me hop down.

"What happened with Titus?" I asked.

"He went straight to the icebox, took the marked milk bottle, paid for it—didn't say a word—and left. Whoever marked the bottle had to have come through that door leading out the back of the store. I had my eye on the front door the whole time I was up at the counter talking to Green. I went and had a look around the back of the store. There are a couple doors back there—delivery doors, you know—and they weren't even locked." Ralph shook his head. "We messed up, Lola. The person who marked the milk bottle—today, at least—they came in through the back."

"And *Rosemary*." I scowled. "What if she went in there simply to distract us? What if she's working with someone? Because the timing . . ."

"Yeah."

I told Ralph about Rosemary's incriminating photographs, and her threats.

"You and Berta were correct," I said. "We shouldn't have stayed up here. We should've gone home when we had the chance."

"We still have a chance, Lola. Heck, everyone's just dying for you to leave."

"That's just it, though. If everyone wants to get rid of me, that means I'm close to cracking this case. I'm not running off just because the kitchen has gotten hot."

"Things could get dangerous."

"I'll manage."

"You're really something, you know that, kid?" Ralph's lips twitched.

"I've heard rumors."

He laughed. "I can't do without you, you know."

What did *that* mean? And why had he laughed? I said airily, "Food, shelter, water, Lola. The bare necessities."

"You got it." He bent and kissed me, our lips cold and dry, our frozen breath escaping in little puffs. My heart, however, felt like a melting marshmallow.

We went back into the store and purchased the little things we'd selected during our stake-out. Oh, I had been outsmarted, but at least my Christmas shopping was complete. If, that is, I managed to spend Christmas at home rather than in the clink.

Back at the inn, Ralph and I went up to Berta's room to find her in an armchair with pillows mounded around her. She was alone except for Cedric, who was basking in front of the electric fire.

"How is your ankle?" I asked, sitting in the other armchair. Ralph leaned on the wall and folded his arms.

"The village doctor—Dr. Best—pronounced it sprained, and with a name like that, why, who am I to question him?" Berta picked up an open box of chocolates from the table beside her and held it out. "Cherry cordial?"

I selected one. Ralph said no, thanks.

"Now I see why Mr. Strom and Mr. Pickard were buying up the general store this morning," I said, looking around the room. There were stacks of newspapers and magazines, boxes of chocolates, tins of cookies, and a potted orchid. "Orchids in December?"

Berta patted her bun. "Mr. Strom feels terribly guilty—he believes, quite rightly, that he was to blame for my injury—and he seems to have gotten his hopes up about getting an answer from me regarding—" Her eyes flicked to Ralph and back. "*—a question.*"

"A question?" I repeated.

"Yes. He posed it to me last night in Dr. Best's examination room.

Of course, Mr. Pickard posed an identical question only half an hour ago, when he brought his gifts."

I swallowed cherry cordial, and the sugar seemed to burn my throat. "Oh," I said. This could mean only one thing. Marriage proposals. Would Berta really up and leave our agency—and me, and Cedric, and New York—to live with a crusty-yet-devoted old fellow in the yonder of Vermont? She would certainly attain the domestic stability she apparently yearned for. "And have you come to any conclusions regarding your answer?"

"Not yet, no. But enough of that." Berta leaned forward. "Tell me what happened this morning at the general store."

Ralph and I told her.

"Outsmarted! And Rosemary, attempting to extort us?" Berta's face was furious. "What could it all mean?"

Ralph said, "About the markings Lola saw, let's see . . . the roman numeral two—that must mean something's happening for the second time, or it means there's two of something, like, oh, I dunno, two people, or two vehicles."

"And the six?" Berta said.

"Well, the fact that it's not a roman numeral, like the two, makes me believe the two and the six mean different things. As for the *p*, well, if we were in England it would mean 'pence,' but—"

"*Time.*" My breath caught. "Six P.M. That must be what the *p* indicates. Six o'clock. This evening. We must see what Titus Staples does at six this evening!"

"I wonder if you'll catch Rosemary red-handed," Berta said. "Or perhaps it will be Maynard, or even George. It'll be bootleg, of course." She selected another cherry cordial.

"Bootleg," I said. "You're probably right." I stuffed another cordial into my own mouth.

"You're looking a little green about this, Lola," Ralph said. "You don't have to go, you know. Fact is, it would be safer if I went it alo—"

"Absolutely not," Berta said. "This is *our* investigation. Mrs. Woodby must go."

"I want to go, Ralph," I said. I pushed all my trembly, bunny-rabbit fear to the back of my mind. "How do you suppose we might stake out the sugar shack without being seen? All this fresh snow . . . the tire marks, you know."

"We'll have to walk in."

"Ugh."

"Or ski," Berta said.

"Ugh!"

Ralph thought about it. Then he broke into a grin that crinkled the corners of his eyes. "Ever tried snowshoes?"

I folded my arms. "No."

"Aw, c'mon, Lola. Say yes." Ralph's gray eyes twinkled. "Just say yes."

Pickard and Strom arrived after that, both eager to help Berta to the ski jumping hill for the big contest. They planned to motor her the short distance in Pickard's depot hack and install her on a portable stool so that she could view the contest in comfort.

"Are you two coming to the contest?" Strom asked Ralph and me.

"Oh, I don't know," I said. I had a mind to rest up for my evening of snowshoeing into the icebound wilderness. "Sporting events aren't really my cup of tea."

Strom and Pickard looked shocked.

"It could be a gas," Ralph said.

"In addition, it may be interesting to observe George Goddard's behavior now that he has inherited a fortune," Berta said, giving me a meaningful look. "Perhaps have a few words with him?"

I got the message: Despite all the cloak-and-dagger business with the milk bottles, and despite Rosemary's threats, George was still our most obvious suspect. He had inherited the lion's share of the

Goddard estate as the result of the two deaths, and he alone insisted that Fenton had committed suicide.

"All right," I said. "We'll meet you there."

An hour later, Ralph and I, having eaten breakfast and dressed ourselves warmly, descended the stairs in the lobby. Patience Yarker was just sitting down at the stool behind the front desk.

"Good morning," I said to her, pausing. "Will you attend the ski jumping contest, or must you work?"

"I beg your pardon?" Patience's eyes were glassy and her cheeks red. "Oh! The contest?" She touched a hand to her chin. "No. Dad's abed and my cousin's gone to Waterbury, so I've got to stay and mind the desk."

I stared at her hand. Something was glittering there, a gemstone the same rich pinky-red as a pomegranate. A ruby.

The ruby.

Ralph had noticed it, too.

"Patience," I said slowly, "where did you get that ring?"

She tucked the ring out of sight under her other hand, on her lap. "Oh! I—well, I haven't told Dad yet, so I shouldn't—"

"George?" I asked softly. My pulse thrummed. "Did George Goddard ask you to marry him?" *Those swanky hotel brochures.* Those were for her honeymoon with George!

"Yes." Patience's blue eyes sparkled. "*Yes.* We're to be married! It's—I'm so relieved—" Her hand fluttered to her belly, and the ring glittered darkly. "—so *happy,* I mean to say. Now everything's going to be all right."

"Congratulations," Ralph said.

"Don't tell Dad," Patience whispered, "okay? I want to tell him myself—when he's feeling a little better."

"Mum's the word," I whispered back.

30

Ralph and I walked through the village toward the ski jump hill, following a straggling stream of others on their way there, too. Cedric was burrowed inside my coat, only his head protruding between two buttons. I couldn't blame him. The cold was making my nostrils stick together.

My mind fizzed with theories.

"Suddenly, it all makes sense," I said softly to Ralph. "Think about it. Judith Goddard was by all accounts a snob, so she wouldn't have approved of George marrying the innkeeper's daughter. The fact of George and Patience's little Pea would have made things even worse. Judith might've threatened to cut George out of her will, or—or *something.* By getting rid of his mother and Fenton—with whom he would've had to share half his inheritance—George paved the way for himself and Patience and their Pea to live happily—and wealthily—ever after."

"But what about Titus Staples and the milk-bottle business?" Ralph asked. "What about how your dossier was burned in Roy's fireplace? What about George's other girlfriend in Cleveland? Then there are the sightings of this so-called bear that strolls around on two legs—and didn't you say Patience had some kinda passionate argument with Maynard Co—?"

"Okay, well, *almost* all of it makes sense!"

"I'm not trying to rain on your parade, kid. I'm just here to help."

I spread my arms wide. "Must every itsy-bitsy little detail add up? Can't there be a few rough edges and extra pieces? This is *life*. Life is untidy."

"Okay, okay."

Ralph didn't say more, but in the back of my mind, I fretted. *Were* there too many misfit pieces? What was I forgetting or failing to spot?

We walked in silence, passing the village green—the igloo, ice sculptures, and ice castle eerily abandoned—the shut-up maple syrup factory, the town hall with its empty message board.

Ralph said, "You know, if you tell Rosemary that Patience has the ruby ring, maybe she won't hand those incriminating photographs over to the police. 'Cause it seems to me that Rosemary's chief concern is getting hold of that ring."

"But then I'll be breaking my promise to Patience," I said. "I can't do that. I'll have to take my chances—and surely Rosemary won't be watching the ski jumping contest. I'll tell Berta what's happened, and try to speak with George after the contest, and decide what to do after that."

A crowd of a few hundred milled at the bottom of the ski hill. The frozen breath of hundreds billowed in the air, and hundreds of boots packed the ground to an ice slick. Bundled-up newspapermen brandished cameras, jostling for front-row positions around the bottom of the slope. Mr. Persons was right up at the front.

The sky was still blue, but although it was not yet noon, the sun skimmed the southern hills. The balsam firs on either side of the ski slope looked black. Stray snowflakes meandered through the air. And call me a jitterbug, but the jump's wooden scaffolding looked especially precarious.

"Ladies and gentlemen!" Pickard's voice squawked through a red megaphone. "Welcome to Maple Hill and the Alpine Club's Annual Winter Carnival Ski Jump Contest!"

"Quite a mouthful," I said, arriving at Berta's side. She sat on a portable stool with wool blankets heaped on her lap.

"Hello, Mrs. Woodby," she said. "Mr. Woodby."

I leaned close to her ear. "There's been an astonishing development," I whispered. "Patience is engaged to George—and she's got the ruby ring!"

"Could we discuss this after the contest, Mrs. Woodby?"

"Of course."

Well. That sealed it: Berta no longer cared about our investigation. The knowledge made me feel bereft. At least I still had Cedric, even if hauling him around under my coat like an infant was making my lumbar ache. And at least I still had Ralph—even if he didn't like my detecting theories and even if he joked about the idea of marrying me. I peeked his impossibly handsome profile. He caught me looking, and winked.

It was unfair, so cosmically *unfair,* that one twitch of his eyelid should make me weak in the knees.

"What exactly is the point of ski jumping?" I asked Berta.

She clucked her tongue. "The skier launches from the top of the jump, gains momentum, swoops up the jump, and sails through the air and down the hill, landing, one hopes, upon both skis."

"Yes, I know, but how shall we know who's the winner? Is it a race?"

Berta pointed to a black line I hadn't noticed in the snow near the bottom of the hill. Strom stood beside it, hands on his hips. "The contestants—there are five—will take turns, both aiming to land at that line or beyond it. The line is thirty yards down from the jump. The man who lands the farthest down the hill is the winner."

"Ladies and gentlemen!" Pickard cried through his megaphone. "As our first contestant, I give you the one, the only, the world-famous three-time Chamonix third-place champion, Maynard Coburn!"

Wild cheering. And there, up on the scaffolding, was Maynard. He positioned himself at the very top of the run. He rolled his shoulders. He bent his knees.

The crowd held its breath.

Maynard slid down the jump, faster, faster, gaining speed—then up into the air he flipped, and he was sailing, spinning his arms as though trying to swim through the air—

"He would do much better if he leaned forward over his skis," Berta muttered.

—and then—*plunk*—Maynard landed a few feet past the black line.

The crowd cheered. Photographers shoved each other for the best angles. Maynard swirled to a stop and waved, beaming, at the crowd.

"Can our second contestant, George Goddard, top that, folks?" Pickard boomed through his megaphone. "CAN HE TOP THAT?"

The crowd roared.

Down, down the white swoop of the ramp George went, then up the curve at the end—there was an extra little bump at the top—and he was sailing high into the air.

Except one of his skis had come off and it was twirling through the air, and George's arms waved frantically—

"Oh no," Berta said with a gasp. "No!"

Screams and shocked murmurs from the crowd—

George was sailing down over the snowy hill, not like a bird, but like a flapping rag doll—

Ralph was already running toward the spot where George would land.

—and George hit the hill with a sickening impact, tumbled in an impossible tangle of limbs and skis, and at last skidded to a stop, his spine cockeyed.

The crowd cried out.

I stood there, frozen with shock, my mouth open, snowflakes falling onto my tongue and melting.

Berta, murmuring what I vaguely understood were Swedish prayers, hobbled forward with a pushing crowd. I stumbled forward, too, but by the time I had wedged myself through the frantic throng, Ralph and two other men were kneeling around George's mangled body. All three were shaking their heads.

"Telephone the police!" one of the kneeling men shouted.

"Telephone the morgue is more like it!" someone shouted back.

"Everyone stand back!" This was Sergeant Peletier. "I'm the police!"

Peletier took charge, commanding the crowd to disband, barking orders here and there. Some of the crowd was already leaving the slope, especially those with children.

Berta was beside me. "I refuse to believe that was an accident, Mrs. Woodby," she said softly.

"I agree. Three deaths in the same family? That's too much of a coincidence."

"As the famed novelist George B. Jones, Jr., wrote, 'Coincidences are for suckers.'"

"So poetic."

"I did not hear you complaining about Mr. Jones's prose when you were devouring *Honolulu Heist* on the train."

"Wait a moment," I said. "The *ski.* George crashed because his ski fell off. Come on, let's try to find it before Peletier does. It flew off to that side." I pointed. "Close to the top."

"I do not think I can make it up there on my sprained ankle—"

"Of course not. Stay here. If I find it, I'll bring it down to show you."

I trudged up the steep slope, Cedric peeking from my coat. The farther I went, the more the sounds of the crowds were muffled by wind and snow.

I had been dead wrong. *Again.*

I slogged through the snow to a narrow dark shape in the shadow of the jump. George's ski was covered with a film of snowflakes. I picked it up and hiked back down the hill. No one seemed to notice what I had done. The remaining people were still crowded around poor George's body.

"The ski doesn't look broken," I said, reaching Berta.

"Look again." Berta took the ski from me and positioned it upright. In its middle was a tangle of leather straps and buckles.

"I don't know what I'm looking at," I said.

"These are the bindings, Mrs. Woodby, with which the ski boot is affixed to the ski—this is a Huitfeldt-style binding, but without the Hoyer-Ellefsen toggle that is growing in popularity. The binding mechanism is quite simple. The skier simply stands on the ski, positioning the boot between the two metal brackets protruding from the front of the binding, tightens the three buckles, and away they go."

"But—" I frowned. "—you said *two* metal brackets? There's only one."

"Precisely. Look." Berta poked a piece of metal dangling from one of the leather straps. "Someone filed this bracket down. It must have snapped apart from the impact when George hit the crest of the jump, freeing his boot from the ski. . . ." She shuddered. "Oh, how diabolical."

"How could the killer have been sure one filed bracket would've been enough to polish off George?" I said. "What if he'd only, say, broken a leg?"

"Then perhaps the killer would have tried to do him in another way," Berta said. "The killer took a risk, and the risk paid off."

"I hate to say it," I said, "but we must show this ski to the police."

"Yes."

When Berta and I drew near the group, George's body was covered with a wool blanket. Peletier, the policeman Clarence, Mr. Persons, Ralph, and a small crowd were listening to a ranting old man.

"I saw a thing!" the man babbled. "A—a horrible, dark thing, with fur and—and—it was running away from the bottom of the jump. Mr. Goddard's skis were leaning on the stairs, see, leaning there when that thing went bounding away!"

"Now, now, Mr. Peters," Peletier said. "Tell me, how much have you had to drink today?" He cast a knowing smirk around the ring of onlookers as if to say, *You can't trust the town boozehound.*

"I know what I saw!" Peters exclaimed, but a note of shrill doubt had crept into his voice. "A shape! A great, black shape! It was Slipperyback!"

The crowd gasped, all except Peletier, who shook his head, and Ralph, who was walking toward Berta and me.

Seemingly emboldened by the crowd's response, Peters went on more avidly still, "He's stirred up these days—doesn't like all these outsiders traipsing around in his territory, I reckon."

"Excuse me, Mr. Peters," I called out, stepping forward.

"What're *you* meddling in this for?" Peletier asked me with narrowed eyes. "Why are you still in Maple Hill? And is that Mr. Goddard's ski you're holding?"

I held out the ski. "Yes. Here, take it. I think you will find that one of the, um—" What had Berta called them? Oh yes. "—the bindings—you know, the little metal bits that hold all those straps on—was filed down, with the purpose of having it break when Mr. Goddard launched off the jump."

"Filed down by Slipperyback!" Peters shouted. "Oh, Lord have mercy on us all! Slipperyback's pranks are going too far! He'll kill us! He'll—he'll murder us in our beds! He'll—"

"Come along, Mr. Peters," a man said, taking him by the arm and steering him away. "We'll get you a nice hot cup of coffee, all right? Sheesh, you oughta stay off the juice. Slipperyback? What next? Count Dracula?" They crunched away, and the rest of the crowd began to disperse, too.

Ralph was by my side.

Peletier prodded his mitten and me. "Happy now? Stirring up superstitious rumors? Why don't you go back to the city, where you belong?"

"Have you no interest at all in the fact that Mr. Goddard's ski was intentionally damaged?" I asked.

"This is your final warning, you three." He addressed Berta, Ralph, and me. "You keep your noses out of this, or there'll be hell to pay."

31

Ralph and I started the walk toward the inn. We had seen Berta off in Pickard's depot hack. I had taken Cedric from under my coat so he could walk and, hopefully, pay his taxes.

"Pickard promised to look after Mrs. Lundgren," Ralph said. "He seems like a decent fellow."

"I suppose you gathered that he and Strom both asked for her hand in marriage."

"Yep. She sure has a way with fellows—and say, they haven't even tasted her baking yet."

"She once told me that Jimmy the Ant had proposed to her on numerous occasions, but she turned him down. But Strom and Pickard are different. They aren't criminals. They own houses—Strom even owns a farm. And Berta . . . Berta is tired."

"Yeah. I can see that."

"If she marries, I won't have a partner," I said. "What shall I do?"

"I can't make cinnamon rolls," Ralph said, "but if you don't mind that, well, you could be *my* partner."

"Don't tease, darling. Not when there's just been another murder. What comes next?" Clammy, gray despair was settling over me. "Oh golly, poor Patience and her Pea! And George dead, just when everything seemed to be coming up roses for her! What will become of her now?"

"Her family'll take care of her."

"I hope so. An unwed mother in a tiny village like this . . . And what'll *we* do next?"

"Well, I don't suppose I could convince you to give up the case—"

"No."

"—but we had a plan, right?"

"Staking out Titus's sugar shack?" In the shadow of death, the plan sounded limp and improbable. I mean, could that snow-covered sugar shack truly hold all the answers?

"That's right," Ralph said. "Staking out the sugar shack. I asked Strom if he could lend us a couple of pairs of snowshoes, and he said sure, we could help ourselves from what we find up at the lodge. Said he could meet us up there at four thirty. He said if we went straight up Moose Mountain from the lodge, we'd find a track along the ridge, and then when we see a sign nailed to a tree, head down the ridge on the other side and we'd be on Titus Staples's land."

My scalp crawled. "The ridge? But, Ralph, that's Goddard land up there. That's where the upright-walking bear thing went last night."

"Yeah, I know. What a coincidence, huh?"

I swallowed. "Berta says coincidences are for suckers."

"Exactly."

Ralph, Cedric, and I ate an enormous lunch at Peggy's Restaurant. When we returned to the inn, Funny Papers was sitting behind the front desk.

Ralph and I exchanged a look.

"How is Patience?" I asked Funny Papers. "Has she heard—?"

"She's hysterical," Funny Papers said. "She's with Grandma."

"Did you know about—?"

"The engagement? Yeah. I mean, Patience told us just now." Funny Papers stuck out his chin. "And she's keeping that ruby ring if it's the last thing I do."

"I think she deserves to keep it," I said.

My heart was breaking for Patience. My only consolation was that she hadn't seemed to be in love with George. She'd only been desperate to provide a father for Pea. Maybe the ruby ring was valuable enough to help her start fresh somewhere else, somewhere where she could pretend to be a widow.

Ralph and I took a nap with all the grim determination of soldiers preparing for battle. At four fifteen, after I had taken Cedric for a quick stroll and left him in Berta's care, Ralph and I set forth. He drove the Speedwagon in silence up to the ski club lodge. Strom was there to greet us at the door, and he, knowing we were detectives, didn't ask questions as he fitted us with snowshoes.

I take that back—he asked prying questions about Berta, trying to figure out if she'd said yes to Pickard or not. He also asked if we had a flask of water—Ralph did—and a gun. Ralph did. I also had the Eastman Kodak Brownie hung around my neck, underneath my fur coat.

Ralph and I took the snowshoe trek up Moose Mountain slowly. Very slowly. I'm not sure there is any other way to take a snowshoe trek. It's a bit like having cookie pans strapped to one's feet, and all the high stepping made my leg muscles read me the riot act.

It was somewhere near five o'clock when we finally reached the top of the bare, snowy ridge.

"We're making good time," Ralph said. His breath floated sideways.

"Don't lie." I gazed at the frozen, sprawling world around us. Moonlit hills, black and white and silver, mounded up and rolled away. The western horizon glowed a pale yellow where the sun had melted. The lights of Maple Hill twinkled in a valley alongside the white sash of river. And up here, a trail snaked northward along the ridge, disappearing around a bend.

"Strom said we take this ridge trail north a quarter mile, and then drop down the other side. That'll take us to Titus's place. Water?" Ralph had drawn a metal water bottle from inside his coat. He unscrewed the cap and passed it over.

I drank deeply, and then drank some more. Ralph drank, too, capped and replaced the bottle, and then we were plodding northward on along the ridge.

We had gone that quarter mile, as per Strom's directions, when Ralph slowed his pace. He stopped. "*Son of a gun,*" he muttered.

I stopped, too. "What is it?"

"Tracks." He pointed to the ground. "And they look fresh. See? They haven't frozen around the edges yet, and it's cold enough up here for that to happen pretty quick."

"Tracks?" I stooped to see. *Oh, thank goodness.* They were grooved ski prints—two overlapping sets. Not, say, the clawed prints of a jumbo bear walking around on two legs.

"Someone's up here," I said stupidly.

"Yeah. Two people." Ralph dug into his coat pocket, pulled out a wristwatch, and squinted at it in the faint moonlight. "Five fifteen." He stuck the watch back in his pocket and looked at me. "What do you say?"

"About following the ski tracks?"

"Uh-huh. You're calling the shots, kid. It's your case."

Cold was leaking through the seams of my clothing. My legs felt as stiff as a couple of pirate's peg legs, and my heart was shriveling with fear. But I thought of how this was Goddard land up here—that a skier was on Goddard land, at night. Why? I thought of how the Reverend Mr. Currier had said he encountered Maynard Coburn up on this very ridge last summer, and how Roy's dog Ammut ran free in these woods. I thought of Judith, Fenton, and George, all dead now, and how ownership of their land—*this* land—had passed through each of their hands in the past few days.

"We have time," I said. "Let's follow the tracks."

The ski tracks followed the ridge trail without digression for I wasn't sure how far. We went ten minutes, then fifteen. I worried that we would be late to spy on Titus's sugar shack at six o'clock, but I was increasingly determined to tail those ski tracks to their end.

Although we had joined the trail on an open, treeless ridge, the terrain gradually changed. Fir trees loomed in from both sides, blocking some of the light. There were rocky formations up here, too, glistening with icy architecture. I glimpsed shadowy splotches and seams under iced rocky protrusions that could've been the mouths of caves.

Caves big enough for even rather large bears to hide.

"The ski tracks turn here," Ralph whispered.

We followed the grooves off the main trail a few yards, circled around a large boulder—

Two skis and two poles were leaning against the backside of the boulder.

"Look!" I whispered, pointing. The snow was packed down, as though something had happened. A single, wide track—wide as a body—went off into the shadows. "That looks like someone was *dragged* over—" I fell silent; Ralph had put a finger to his lips.

"*Listen,*" he whispered.

I heard the wind in the fir boughs, the skitter of tiny grains of ice across the top crust of the snow. I listened to the blood pounding against my eardrums.

And . . . crunching. Stealthy crunching. Coming closer.

Oh sweet baby bejeezus.

Ralph was drawing his pistol. "Your camera," he said so softly, the breeze whipped his words away.

Right. My camera.

I fumbled with my coat buttons—

The crunching was just on the other side of that boulder now.

—I pulled out the Brownie with shaking mittened hands.

Rats. *Mittens.* You can't operate a camera wearing mittens!—

Crunch. Crunch.

—I tore my mittens off with my teeth. Ralph aimed his pistol toward the side of the boulder. I aimed the Brownie, positioned my freezing fingertip on the button—

Something big, dark, and furry burst out from behind the boulder.

—I snapped a photograph and, at the same time, I screamed.

"Stand down!" Ralph shouted.

The thing—oh, that awful dark fur! Those erratic motions!—pounced on Ralph and took him down into the snow.

"Ralph!" I shouted, jumping onto the back of the thing.

Its back was hard and angular, and it was making an oddly familiar rattling sound.

Quite like booze bottles in a wooden crate, actually.

Ralph and the thing were locked in a wrestling match, twisting and pummeling each other. I was thrown off into the snow. I staggered to my feet—snowshoes still strapped on—and went back at the writhing thing, still on top of the cursing, grunting Ralph.

But instead of leaping on the thing again, I took hold of a loose-looking flap of its fur—

And yanked it off.

There was a wooden crate under there, all right, strapped like an oversized knapsack to the back of Titus Staples.

Ralph, though still underneath Titus, managed to sock him in the nose. I heard a splatting crunch. Blood spurted. Titus grunted and slugged Ralph in the jaw.

"Ralph!" I cried again.

Titus was reaching a gangly arm out, pulling a thick stick from the snow.

"My . . . gun . . . Lola," Ralph said. "Flew . . . into . . . the sno—"

Thunk.

Ralph sagged back into the snow. Titus had clubbed him over the head with his stick.

"You monster!" I screamed.

Titus, his face expressionless, got to his feet, panting and unsteady. Again, he hefted the stick in his hand.

I staggered sideways and tripped on my own snowshoes. I fell back, back, like a child flopping down to make a snow angel.

The last thing I saw was Titus looming up over me, his big stick raised against the moonsheened sky.

32

Ralph," I whispered. My throat was painfully dry and my voice sounded far away, as though it belonged to someone else. Louder, I called out, "Ralph?"

I was curled on my side. My head hurt like the dickens. There was something numbingly tight around my ankles and wrists, and I could feel that my snowshoes were still buckled to my boots.

With great effort, I cracked my eyelids. There was a bright ball of light somewhere nearby. A small, steady hissing. The air smelled of dirt and kerosene and stale liquor.

"Your mascara's running," a man—not Ralph—said. "I'm surprised you could get your eyes open at all."

My eyes flew wide. I struggled to a seated position, despite the snowshoes and—*rats*—my rope-bound wrists. "Maynard?"

Maynard Coburn sat nearby, leaning on some kind of curved dark wall. His legs were outstretched and bound with rope at the ankles. His wrists were bound, too, hands in his lap. He wore a coat and boots and thick pants.

"Where's Ralph?" I said, my voice curling upward in panic.

"Don't get hysterical. He's right over there." Maynard tipped his head.

I twisted around. Ralph lay on his back nearby, eyes shut, ankles and wrists tied. Blood trickled from his temple but he was breathing—yes, thank God, *breathing.*

Tears filled my eyes, and I spun to face Maynard. "What's happening?"

Maynard snorted. "What's happening? Isn't it obvious? Look around, princess."

I looked.

The ball of light, the hissing noise—that was a kerosene lantern set on the floor a few yards away. We were inside a cave with moist, curved granite walls, the size of a room in a house. Wooden crates, dozens and dozens of them, were stacked around the cave's perimeter. I knew it was booze; I could smell it.

"*That's* how it's done," I said, half to myself. "Titus disguises himself as Slipperyback whenever he's hauling whiskey crates. He drapes the huge bearskin over the crate on his back, perhaps to scare anyone he might happen to run into. That's why the ski club fellows say they've been glimpsing more of Slipperyback lately. They've been glimpsing *Titus.* Titus must have been creeping around wearing his bearskin and—what?—special bear-paw-shaped molds on his feet?—just to scare everyone, too. To keep people from venturing up to the ridge, and to keep people distracted from the truth."

"Someone puts in an order, see," Maynard said, "for however many crates of hooch they want. Titus carries crates down to the transfer point at the sugar shack. Someone picks up the crates and takes them away. But who the heck's putting in the orders and picking up the crates?"

"Ralph and I meant to stake out the sugar shack tonight and find out," I said. "We've missed our chance, because now that Titus knows we're onto the operation, the whole thing will stall. But we were right about the milk bottles. . . ."

"The *milk bottles*?" Maynard said. "What on earth are you prattling about?"

He didn't know about the milk bottles, then, and I didn't feel like filling him in. The gink.

"All this time," Maynard said, "I was looking for bootleggers on the roads—'cause we knew a whole lot of hooch was coming through Maple Hill. We traced it back from Boston and Hartford and Albany. I never thought to look up here in the caves. They must be bringing it along the ridge clear from Canada before the snow falls, and stockpiling it in these caves."

"What do you mean, all this time you've been looking for—? And, 'we'? I don't understand."

"I thought you'd have figured it out by now. Didn't you mention bootleggers when you were trying to give me the shakedown at the funeral the other day?" Maynard snorted. "Women detectives."

"Figured out what?"

"That I'm a Fed."

A Fed? Maynard Coburn was a *Fed*?

"What do you think I live up here in Vermont for?" he said.

"To ski?" I said lamely.

"Anyone in their right mind would move to Switzerland or Austria if all they wanted to do was ski. No. I was offered a job with Customs right after the war. Chasing down bootleggers from the border, see. Turns out, I'm pretty damn good at it, and it's steady pay. The skiing gig isn't. Funny thing is, you can be on magazine covers and in the papers and still not have any dough."

"Which is why you meant to marry Judith Goddard."

"One of the reasons. She was a knockout, too, and . . ."

"And it felt pleasant to anger George by marrying his mother?"

"Sure did."

"Now they're both dead."

"Yeah. I feel bad about . . . about the games I played. With both of them. I mean, they were both just spoiled-rotten rich people, but they didn't deserve to be murdered."

"Which you didn't do."

Maynard scoffed. "Of course not. Why would I? Judith was my ticket to the good life."

As much as I disliked Maynard, I believed him on this point. He was selfish and arrogant, yes, but he had no motive for having rubbed out the three Goddards. "Then who?"

"Someone who's got a stake in this smuggling scheme, of course. Someone who was willing to kill to protect it."

Which narrowed it down to the two surviving Goddards in the mix: Rosemary and Roy.

And suddenly, I knew exactly why Fenton had had to die.

Fenton had followed Titus up here. He had photographed him doing his dirty work. And when the killer found out—the killer must have ventured down into Fenton's darkroom—they realized he *knew too much*.

It's a frightening thought, knowing that one could be bumped off simply for being a good observer or, as in Fenton's case, a good observer and documenter. Not that Fenton was utterly innocent, since he'd taken those intrusive photographs of Patience Yarker. But he hadn't deserved to die.

And Judith and George, well, they must have been somehow involved in the smuggling operation, or perhaps they, like Fenton, had simply seen too much.

My eyes had been resting upon Ralph's unconscious face, but now I realized Maynard was standing up and tossing pieces of rope aside. "There." He folded a pocketknife and stashed it in his coat pocket as he strode toward the door.

"Wait!" I shouted. "Aren't you going to untie *us*?"

He stopped, and turned. The kerosene light threw his eye sockets into shadow. "Why would I do that?"

I swallowed. "Um. Because you're a . . . gentleman?"

He tipped his head and laughed. "Aren't gentlemen really only obliged to help *ladies*?"

"Ralph is hurt!" I cried. "He's unconscious and bleeding! You can't just—just *leave* us up here!"

"You managed to get yourselves up here. I'm sure you can get yourselves down. It's really no concern of mine."

"You're a beast!"

"I'm in a hurry." Maynard turned again.

"Wait!" *The film in the Brownie.* The camera was by some miracle still stashed against my bosom, under my half-buttoned coat. "Oh, but it *is* your concern," I called. "Unless, of course, you don't mind the whole world seeing you without the doormat you wear upon your head."

Maynard's shoulders tensed. Slowly, he turned. "Are you *blackmailing—*?"

"Untold numbers of tawdry publications would surely *adore* publishing a photograph of the almost-famous Maynard Coburn with his scalp, as it were, in the altogether."

"There will be no piece about my hair!" Maynard shouted so loudly, it echoed off the cave walls.

Ralph stirred.

"Cut the ropes *and* tell me what you were doing up here on the ridge tonight, and I'll give you the film," I said.

"Where is the film?" Maynard asked, his voice now low and smooth.

"In a safe place."

"Why should I trust that you'll turn it over?"

"Have you any choice?"

"Well, yes, actually, I have. I could simply abandon you and your husband here to your fates, while I return to your room at the inn and locate your roll of film."

"Knock yourself out. I think you'll be sorely disappointed. You see, the film is still inside the camera, and the camera, I'm afraid, is at this moment upon my person."

Maynard looked me up and down incredulously. In all my warm layers, I probably resembled a tuber.

"Cut Ralph and me free," I said, "and then, upon my honor, I'll hand over the film."

Maynard sighed, took out his pocketknife, and set about sawing ropes. Moments later, Ralph—still unconscious—and I were both free.

"Now, hand over that film," Maynard said, folding up his pocketknife again.

I undid my remaining coat buttons, opened up the Brownie, removed the film, and passed it over.

Wordlessly, Maynard slipped it into his pocket and was gone.

That was it, then. The case was closed—or, rather, it would be just as soon as Maynard Coburn alerted his Fed cronies to the location of the bootleg cave and the smuggling route.

Maynard had crabbed the act. Because if *he* cracked the smuggling case, he'd also expose the murderer, and that would mean the Discreet Retrieval Agency's efforts were all for naught. He'd get the credit. That hardly seemed fair, but at that precise moment, fairness wasn't paramount in my mind.

My snowshoes dragging, I crawled closer to Ralph. His gloved fingers were moving a little, but his eyelids quivered without opening.

"Ralph," I whispered, stroking the hair from his forehead.

A bump the size of a hen's egg had risen where Titus had clobbered him, just under his hairline. There was an open, blood-wet wound on the bump, and dried blood caked his eyebrow.

My voice thickened. "Please wake up, darling. *Please*."

Ralph's eyes opened, their bright agate gray heart-stopping even in these horrid circumstances. "Lola," he mumbled. "Sweetheart. You look like an angel."

"What, in *this* hat?"

Ralph smiled weakly. "Marry me."

"Still teasing me with that?" I whispered with a lump in my throat.

"I'm not kidding. Let's be a family. You, me, and the pooch."

My heart felt as though it were blooming wide open, tender, fresh. *Vulnerable*. Eek.

"We can't get married, Ralph," I whispered. "I mean, just look at us! Our jobs—our *lives*—are just crazy. That's no way to be a family."

"That's what I thought," Ralph said. "Before. But I realized that the craziness, Lola, the craziness is exactly *why* we need each other. Why we oughta be a family."

"But like . . . *this*? Now?"

"Okay. We don't have to talk about it just now." Ralph eyes flicked away. They widened. "Are those crates of bootleg? Is this a cave?"

"Yes."

Ralph's proposals *weren't* teasing, I realized that now . . . but oughtn't we be someplace more romantic than a smelly bootlegger's cave when he officially popped the question?

"Hell." Ralph winced. "My *head*." He was sitting up.

"We've got to get out of here before Titus returns. Do you think you can walk?"

"I'll give it a shot."

We set out on our snowshoes toward the Alpine Club Lodge. On either side of the ridge trail, the pointed fir trees with their white shawls looked so lovely, like giant Christmas trees in the moonlight. And yet the night felt hostile.

We could've died. Titus could've killed us, or we could've perished from cold or thirst if Maynard had left us tied up in that low-slung cave, where no one would find us but hungry animals.

We trudged along the ridge, down the switchbacking slope toward the lodge. In breathless spurts, I told Ralph what I'd learned from Maynard, and how Maynard intended to take all the credit for getting to the bottom of both the smuggling and the murders.

All the while, my eyes flicked left, right, forward, over the shoulder, searching for Titus.

We didn't see him, nor did we see any sign of Maynard. And at last, there was the lodge down below, windows glowing cheerily, its chimney piping smoke. We went inside to give the snowshoes back to Strom.

"Mrs. Lundgren gave me her final answer this evening," he said.

My belly twisted. "Oh?"

"Turned me down flat! Guess that means she'll be Mrs. Pickard soon." He snorted. "That just sounds stupid, doesn't it? Berta Pickard? Too many *a*'s in there. Sounds like you're opening wide for the dentist."

"Um," I said.

Strom peered at Ralph's head. "You'd best pay a call on Dr. Best and have that looked at. That's a nasty bump."

But Ralph didn't wish to see Dr. Best; he wished only to drink a lot of water and go to sleep. It sounded pretty good to me, so I got behind the wheel of the Speedwagon and aimed it toward the Old Mill Inn.

33

Forty-five minutes later, Ralph was fast asleep on the army cot in our airing cupboard. Berta was likely canoodling with her new fiancé, Mr. Pickard, but she'd want to know that the case was—as far as *we* were concerned, anyway—closed. Besides, I couldn't sleep, despite the weariness in my bones, and I wanted Cedric.

I donned a warm, dry dress and went down to the second floor. I rapped on Berta's door.

Instantly, I heard thumps inside—yes, as though she was hopping on one foot—and the door swung open.

"Mrs. Woodby! I have been on pins and needles waiting for you to return! Thank goodness you are all right!"

I looked past her. No Pickard. Only Cedric, lounging paws-up on her bed. He regarded me with idle curiosity.

I said, "No . . . beau?"

Berta made an impatient noise. "Oh, come in, come in. We're letting out all the heat."

I stepped in, and Berta shut the door. "It's really warm in here," I said. "Won't that melt your chocolates?"

"No, because I have already eaten them all."

"Won't it wilt your orchid?"

"I could not take a potted plant back to New York on the train. Just think of the hassle and fuss."

"Back to New York?"

"Mrs. Woodby, you did not think I was going to stay in the snowy wilderness forever, did you?"

"But Mr. Strom said you turned him down."

"Precisely. And I turned down Mr. Pickard as well. One day of sitting in pampered idleness led me to conclude that becoming a Maple Hill housewife would be a terrible, terrible mistake. Why, I would be bored silly."

I smiled for the first time in what felt like ages. "Then we—you and me and Ralph and Cedric—we'll all go home tomorrow. That's Christmas Eve, you know. We'll be home for Christmas!"

Berta's forehead crinkled. "But what of our investigation?"

I sighed. "It's curtains, I'm afraid."

I couldn't help feeling bad that the chocolate was all eaten up as I told Berta the tale of Titus-as-Slipperyback, the hooch-filled cave, and Maynard Coburn, federal agent and all-around arrogant louse. I could've done with a cherry cordial or two.

Berta's expression grew increasingly thunderous. "No," she said once I had finished. "We cannot allow Maynard—oh, to think I admired that man once!—to cut us off at the pass." She stood abruptly, winced, and shifted her weight to her good ankle.

"You shouldn't be—"

"Come with me." She hobbled over to a chair, over which her coat was slung. She picked it up and put it on.

"Where are we going?"

"To tell the police what you saw up there in the caves. Even if Maynard Coburn and Customs are onto the smuggling operation, if Peletier takes your story seriously, perhaps he will go up to the cave first. Then we will beat Maynard Coburn. *We* will get credit for solving the case."

"It's tempting, Berta, but Sergeant Peletier isn't likely to believe anything we say. He has never made a secret that he loathes us."

"We *must* try."

"All right—but mark my words, it'll take more than the lurid tales of two exhausted women to pry those men away from hot cocoa at the electric hearth on a night like this."

I motored us to the police station. The closer we got, the more hope buoyed my heart. Peletier would take me seriously—why wouldn't he? I'd be insane to make up stories about crates of tiddly in caves—and then they'd go up there and, well, figure something out. Something that gave Berta and me all the credit.

Gosh, I couldn't *wait* to see Maynard Coburn gnashing his teeth in frustration.

I parked the Speedwagon and we went into the station. I was already stiff and sore from the snowshoeing expedition. Tomorrow, I would be like an unoiled suit of armor.

"By gum," Sergeant Peletier said. He sat at a desk, boots propped up, the orange glow of an electric fire pulsating beside him. "Looks like Santa Claus came early today, Clarence." He slid his feet off the desk, and they hit the floor with a thud.

Clarence, holding a steaming mug of something, let out a low whistle.

Peletier's desk was strewn with lots of untidy papers, a plate of half-eaten fruitcake, and a few black-and-white photographs.

There were quite a lot of photographs floating about Maple Hill, so I wasn't sure why seeing those in particular—which I couldn't even make out from this distance—sent a surge of bitter fear through my veins.

"I never thought for a second that you'd turn yourselves in," Peletier said, standing. "I'd pegged you as the kind to run."

"I beg your pardon?" Berta said.

"Turn ourselves in?" I said. "What do you mean?"

"But I shouldn't complain, should I?" Peletier was advancing slowly toward us. "No one wants a scene. Not this close to Christmas. Hey, if you play your cards right, maybe someone will cough up bail for you two, and you won't be spending baby Jesus's birthday in the slammer. Clarence, why don't you show Mrs. Lundgren and Mrs. Woodby the little surprise we found this afternoon?"

"Sure, boss." Clarence set down his mug and picked up—*oh no*—the photographs. He waddled over and held them out.

They were, of course, the damning photographs Rosemary had shown me that morning. The one with Berta inspecting the silver teaspoon was on top.

"Unflattering, isn't it?" Peletier said with a humorless chuckle. "In more than one way."

"Precisely what are we to make of your photographs?" Berta asked coldly.

"You don't need to make anything of them," Peletier said. "That's up to a judge and jury. But they were enough to make up *my* mind."

"Did Rosemary Rogerson give the photographs to you?" I asked. It seemed like some sort of unfunny joke, really, that the photograph of Maynard Coburn applying his toupee would have gotten me out of one vat of soup, only to have these photographs plunge us into another.

"Found 'em in an envelope," Clarence said through a mouthful of fruitcake, "slid under the station door."

"Can't you see someone's trying to frame us?" I cried. "That *Rosemary Rogerson* is trying to frame us?"

"A frame-up job?" Peletier said. "Oldest story in the book, lady."

I took a deep breath. We were getting sidetracked. "Would it interest you to know that we discovered an alcohol-smuggling cave up on the ridge?"

Peletier and Clarence burst out laughing. "Nice try!" Peletier wheezed, slapping his thigh. "Ha-ha-ha! How'd you get up on the ridge? Reindeer sleigh? Ha-ha-ha!"

"I saw Slipperyback!" I blurted.

Both men went quiet. Then, meeting each other's eyes, they burst into fresh gales of laughter. "That's—a—hoot!" Clarence managed between guffaws.

"I snapped a photograph!" I cried. "But, um . . . Maynard Coburn stole the film."

"You really reckon we'll buy that? This isn't New York City, girls. We got brains up here in Vermont. Ha-ha-ha!"

It all sounded outlandish. I couldn't deny that.

My weary mind rummaged around for a new plan. Berta's and my arrest was imminent. I felt it in my bones. These boys would be slapping the cuffs on us just as soon as they laughed themselves out.

Berta said loudly, to be heard over the men's chortling, "Would it interest you to know that the cave in question sits on the Goddard family's land? That we strongly suspect the smuggling caves are somehow related to the three deaths in that family? No? Then you are very foolish men." Her Swedish accent had thickened with anger.

The men fell silent. Clarence wiped a tear from his eye.

Peletier's eyes narrowed. "What was that you said about foolish men?"

I trod on Berta's toe to stop her.

No dice. "My partner, Mrs. Woodby, has discovered criminal

activity that lies, presumably, within your jurisdiction, but you are doing nothing but laughing like two hyenas. Thus, you. Are. *Fools!*"

Peletier's face turned an unappealing shade of magenta. "That's funny, because the joke's on you, Mrs. Lundgren. You're under arr—"

"Oh!" I yelped. "I've just remembered something in the truck! A clue!" I bugged my eyes at Berta. "Come on. Let's go get the—um—the clue!"

"Not so fast," Peletier snarled. "Mrs. Lundgren, you're under arr—"

"Go," Berta murmured to me. "Quickly. I will take care of myself. There are still *the milk bottles to be considered,* Mrs. Woodby."

"But—"

"Go!"

I went. I trotted right out of that police station, Peletier and Clarence shouting after me. I slipped and slid across the snow, threw myself behind the wheel of the Speedwagon, and got the engine growling just as Peletier burst from the door, shouting and shaking his fist.

I gave him a twiddly-fingered goodbye and gassed the truck onto the road.

I drove as quickly as I dared, given that I was quivering with nerves. I kept glancing into the rearview mirror, expecting to see headlamps bearing down, but I reached the center of Maple Hill without seeing any.

I wondered if Berta had figured out a way to stall the cops. Cookies in her handbag, perhaps. She often had some stashed in there, much in the way mailmen carry dog biscuits to keep the hounds at bay.

Okay. Okay. Think, Lola, think. Berta had been arrested. Now I was on the run, but to what end? Maynard Coburn was already in the process of beating us to the punch. Perhaps I ought to turn around and turn myself i—

Wait. The milk bottles. Maynard Coburn knew nothing about the milk bottles. And that meant I had—possibly—one last chance to nab the killer before he did.

Before I was arrested.

An idea thunderbolted at me—and, boy, was it a doozy.

I circled to the back of the inn and parked.

Above the garage, Maynard's windows were dark. Where was he? Still gliding on his skis through the deep dark woods?

I switched off the engine and got out. I'd go inside the back way. The police would come looking for me at the inn. Of course they would. They'd expect me to cower there, or at least make a grab for my suitcase. But I had to see Ralph, let him know what was happening. He was sleeping off a bad head injury, of course, but maybe he could also help me figure out what to do next. Where to hide.

The inn's kitchen windows shone out onto the snowy ground. I heard the muted clatter of dishes, caught the mingled aromas of spices and sizzling fat. I went to the kitchen door and peeked through the lace-curtained window.

Ralph was sitting at the kitchen table, forking food into his mouth. He must have been too hungry to sleep. He appeared bleary and pale. Grandma Yarker was hovering over him. The table was cluttered with bowls and canisters, as though Grandma Yarker were in the middle of baking something.

I heard Cedric yap somewhere. He could always sense my presence.

Rats. Grandma Yarker was a stick in the spokes. She was a local. She'd squeal to Peletier, easy.

The churn of an engine had manifested in the distance, growing incrementally louder. It would be a motorcar carrying Peletier, Clarence, or both.

With my gloved index finger, I got to work digging and scraping at the frost on the nearest kitchen window. When I was done, it said—backwards, so Ralph could easily read it from inside—*YES.*

Then I bolted. I dodged behind the garage just as headlamps shot out from around the corner of the inn, illuminating the snow behind me.

I couldn't have been seen, but they'd be able to find my footprints if they looked.

I circled the inn's garage, and then I hurried along the sidewalk, kicking through snow, leaning into the stinging wind. My big boots were soaked. All the shops on River Street were dark. The wooden houses looked smug and unwelcoming with their shuttered windows and curling smoke.

I reached the Methodist church. Its windows were dark, its spire disappearing into the purple-black sky. Next door, however, the minister's house was all lit up and, unlike the other houses in the village, it seemed . . . safe.

Surely Mr. Currier wouldn't give me up to the police.

I pushed through his gate, went up the scraped walk, took a deep breath, and hit the door knocker.

34

Mr. Currier let me in, wide eyed, and led me straight to his parlor. There, I explained to him that Berta had probably been arrested and I was on the lam ("Good gracious!" he exclaimed), that we were innocent of any wrongdoing ("Of course"), and that I needed a place to stay for the night so that I could take one last crack at catching the killer.

"Well, it is of course most irregular for a lady to stay under an unmarried minister's roof," Currier said with a cough. "On the other hand, I have a comfortable spare room that Miss Albans always keeps ready for guests, and, well, if it is in the name of bringing a murderer to justice . . . Very well."

"Thank you," I said.

"Would you like a cup of tea, Mrs. Woodby? Something to eat? There is a nice fresh fruitcake in the—"

"Only tea, thanks," I said quickly.

A few minutes later, Currier carried a tea tray in and set it on the table before the fire. The tray held a teapot, two teacups on saucers, a little jug of cream painted with holly berries, a bowl of sugar lumps, and a half-full jug of Rogerson's Brand Maple Syrup.

Oh, Vermont.

"Mrs. Woodby, would you care for some, ah, *maple syrup* in your tea?" Currier asked, fussing with a teacup and saucer. "Strictly for medicinal purposes, of course."

"Medicinal maple syrup? You Vermonters certainly have some peculiar customs. I'll take my tea with cream only, thank you."

"But it's—" Currier cleared his throat. "Mrs. Woodby, you must understand that it is *medicinal* syrup. For your nerves—for, I beg your pardon if this seems too forward, you are joggling your foot."

I looked at my foot, which was indeed vibrating. "So I am. But I don't think maple syrup is going to help."

Currier raked a lock of hair from his forehead. "Mrs. Woodby, it is whiskey."

I blinked. I stared at the jug of maple syrup. "Why do you keep your whiskey in a maple syrup jug?"

"That is the way Miss Albans brings it to me."

"Hester Albans is your . . . tiddly supplier?"

"Yes—but you must understand that I consume it for strictly medicinal purposes."

"Doesn't everyone? By the way, I *will* have a splash. Does Hester always bring your, um, medicine in maple syrup jugs?"

"Yes." Currier was looking a little pinched. Embarrassed, I supposed.

I leaned forward tensely. "Hester works year-round at Rogerson's Maple Syrup Factory, I understand. Shipping crates of syrup down to Rogerson's Stores in Cleveland. Is she really shipping *whiskey*?"

Currier swallowed, his pale Adam's apple jostling. "No, no. Miss Albans told me that some of the crates—only a very few—contain whiskey, something she discovered quite by accident."

"But where does the whiskey come from? Who puts it into the syrup bottles?"

"Well, Mrs. Woodby, based upon what you have conveyed to me this evening about the smuggling caves on Goddard land, I think you know *precisely* from whence it comes."

My mind was leaping like a deer to conclusions.

Rosemary Rogerson. The smuggler—the killer—was surely Rosemary, perhaps working in conjunction with her husband, the grocery store tycoon. As a result of the three deaths, Rosemary was now sole heir to the Goddard estate. She had gained complete control over the Goddard land, with its smuggling route and caves, control that might've been threatened if her mother or brothers had discovered her scheme, or if they decided to sell off the land.

And Rosemary's sneaking around in the village . . . were those secretive housewives in on her smuggling scheme, too, even as they cozily baked pies?

"What do you intend to do in the morning?" Currier asked.

"I'm going to trap the killer—trap *Rosemary.* Force her hand. Make her talk in front of witnesses. Perhaps even in front of the police, if I can manage it. She must be brought to justice. Would . . . would *you* be a witness, Mr. Currier? People always believe clergymen."

"I will," Currier said. "I am anxious for our pleasant little village to return to normal. Now, you really must get some sleep, Mrs. Woodby. You have had a most shocking day."

I woke at dawn after a lot of sweaty, tossy-turny business. I probably would've felt more rested if I hadn't even tried to sleep. My neck felt like a piece of scrap metal. My eyes were puffed.

Because I'd slept in my clothes—I had refused a loan of Currier's striped pajamas—getting dressed consisted of lacing up my man-boots and trying to plaster down my flyaway bob in the bathroom mirror.

Currier was awake and dressed in his small kitchen when I entered, making coffee. "Good morning," he said.

"Good morning. Have you pen and paper I could use?"

"Yes, of course. In my study."

"Thanks."

I went to Currier's study and, surrounded by religious treatises, got busy penning threatening little notes. After a few crumpled-up tries, I felt as though I had struck the proper tone:

The jig is up. We know who you are and we figured out your game—where the stuff comes from, how it's transferred, where it's going—and you're going to share in the profits, or we'll sing to the fuzz. Meet us to negotiate a deal at the maple syrup factory at nine o'clock sharp this morning, or you'll be sorry.

That would, hopefully, do the trick.

I put on my coat. I folded the note small and placed it in my pocket.

"Don't you require coffee, Mrs. Woodby?" Currier asked, poking his head out of the kitchen.

"When I return. It's almost eight o'clock. Back in a jiffy. Oh—and you do have a telephone, don't you?"

"Yes, but—"

I went out the front door. I was nervous, but a sense of focused determination had settled over me. Rosemary Rogerson wouldn't know what hit her. *Ha.*

I hurried along the sidewalk, keeping my head low. A pale peach sunrise was seeping across white rooftops and snowy streets.

The general store was only two blocks away, and Green was just unlocking the door when I arrived.

"Morning," he said gruffly. "Say, didn't I hear something about the police wanting to talk with you?"

"Oh, that?" I gave a cocktail-party laugh. "All a silly mix-up. Tell me, Mr. Green, has the morning milk arrived yet?"

"Just set it out." He shook his head. "You and your milk."

I passed him, walking swiftly toward the icebox. When I got there, I peeked over my shoulder. Green was rearranging his window display, his back turned.

I took the folded note from my pocket and opened the icebox. I wedged the note snugly under the lightning stopper's wire clamp on the milk bottle in the back corner. I grabbed another bottle of milk, straightened, and shut the icebox. I took the milk to the counter and paid.

Green watched me go with slitted eyes.

Now for the next bit.

I returned to Currier's house without being seen—or, rather, without noticing anyone's seeing me. People might've been peering from behind curtains.

When Currier let me back into his house, he looked a little queasy.

"What's the matter?" I asked, removing my snow-caked boots.

"Nothing, only . . . Mrs. Woodby, perhaps this plan of yours is a little . . . foolhardy. Perhaps you should turn the matter entirely over to the police." His eyes were wide. "You could be endangering yourself!"

"I'm used to danger. Where's your telephone?"

Currier sighed, and led me to a telephone.

I passed him the bottle of milk.

"I'll go and make a fresh pot of coffee," he said, and disappeared into the back of the house.

I dialed 0 and asked the exchange girl for the Maple Hill police station.

Three rings.

"Peletier," came the grunted reply.

Thank goodness he was there already. Or had he spent the night at the station, guarding Berta? "Hello, Sergeant Peletier, this is Lola Woodby."

"Woodby!"

"That's right."

"You're under arrest!"

"I think you'll find that phrase doesn't work very well over the telephone. Listen here, Sergeant Peletier, I've figured out who killed the Goddards, and I am going to trap them at Rogerson's Maple Syrup Factory at nine o'clock—"

"Of all the harebrained—"

"I know it's quite a risk telephoning you about this—"

"You bet it is! Green from the general store telephoned a few minutes ago and said—"

"—but I thought it only right to let you in on the plan. After, if the killer makes a confession, it would be well and good for you to be there with the bracelets."

"Oh, I'll have the bracelets, all right."

"Please, Sergeant Peletier. I only ask you not to arrest me until you hear what the killer says first." I hung up the earpiece.

Jeez. Talk about a girl raising the stakes on herself.

35

At twenty minutes till nine o'clock, I walked alone to the Rogerson's Brand Maple Syrup Factory. I was early, very early, for my appointment with Rosemary-the-killer, and that was precisely the point. I wished to familiarize myself with the interior of the factory before she arrived. Mr. Currier was to arrive a bit later and sneak in through a door, which I would unlock. And the police, well, I hoped they would show up, too, but not until after Rosemary was singing like a soprano at the Metropolitan Opera.

I tried the main door and it was, unsurprisingly, locked. I circled the building and found another, more secluded door. Also locked. I had my skeleton key in my coat pocket, but—ah—here was a sash window with an unfastened latch. With a lot of acrobatic wiggling, I got it open and squeezed through. I dropped onto the cold wooden floor, got up, and dusted myself off. I closed the window and looked around.

Only a little light leaked in through the high windows. Tall crates cast deep shadows on the floorboards. Over on the far side, the boiling and bottling equipment gleamed dim and metallic.

Plenty of places for someone to hide. My scalp crawled.

I went to the main door and unlocked it for Mr. Currier and the police.

Now. Where to position myself for Rosemary's arrival?

"You're early," came a woman's voice from behind a stack of crates.

The tiny hairs sprang up on my arms and neck. *That didn't sound like Rosemary.*

Slowly, I circled around the crates. My breath caught. *"Roy?"*

A mote-swirled shaft lit up Roy Ives, in cotton pajama pants stuffed into untied snow boots and that wine-stained olive green brocade robe. His ruddy, bristly face was slack with terror. His eyes were wide and watery.

One of his arms was twisted awkwardly behind his back, and there was a figure behind him, hidden in shadow. Roy shifted, and the shaft of sunlight picked out a golden glimmer of hair.

"Patience Yarker," I said. My voice sounded muffled and small in the cavernous wooden space.

"You sound surprised," Patience said. "I suppose you were expecting Rosemary? No answer? I'll take that as a yes. You played into my hands, Mrs. Woodby. You gobbled up every last clue I left out for you. It's all right to admit you didn't know it was me. No one expects a dithering lady gumshoe who wears mascara in the snow to be especially bright."

"All right, Patience, I am surprised it's you." I worked to keep my voice steady. "But I figured out everything else. All of it." My brain was shouting and dashing madly about, like a ship full of sailors rerouting an ocean liner. *Patience Yarker. This makes sense . . . give us a moment!*

"Oh, really," Patience said, deadpan. "You figured out everything."

"Yes. You're a bootleg smuggler. Someone brings crates of whiskey down from Canada along that ridge—someone who works for you—and delivers it to the cave. Or is there more than one cave? They deliver it in the warmer months, when it's safe to traverse the ridge. The caves are a sort of storage locker for all your whiskey. You pay Titus Staples to bring it down, one crate at a time, to his sugar shack, where you pick it up and take it here, to the maple syrup factory, where you decant it into maple syrup bottles, ready to be shipped far and wide to, I suppose, your contacts in the cities. Say, what do you do with the empty whiskey bottles?"

"Sink them to the bottom of the river."

"That can't be good for the fish."

Patience snorted. "You've got a soft heart, Mrs. Woodby. Soft as caramel. Just you watch—it's going to be your downfall."

Roy swayed a little. It dawned on me that he was drunk. Was he the reason it smelled so sharply of alcohol in here?

I said to Patience, "You killed Judith Goddard, and then Fenton, because they had figured out your scheme. It was in danger of being exposed. When you saw Fenton's photograph of Titus Staples, you realized Fenton had been up on the ridge, perhaps even seen what was in the cave. Mrs. Goddard saw Fenton's photographs first, didn't she? Then she said something to you, let on she knew about the smuggling—"

"She lorded it over me. Like a cat toying with a mouse."

"So you got rid of her, with the intention all along to kill Fenton shortly after, making him look like a suicide and shifting the blame for his mother's poisoning. Fenton was your sacrificial lamb."

"It should've been clean as a whistle." Patience sounded sulky.

"But it wasn't," I said. "Because then you found out that *George* knew about the smuggling, too—or, wait, I've got it—you found out that he meant to sell some of his land off, maybe to the Alpine Club. Selling the land would mean selling your smuggling route, so you had to kill him, too. You were never engaged to marry George, were you? And you aren't with child, either. That was all a sham to make you look like a victim, to put me off the scent—to put everyone off the scent. I suppose you knew Fenton was spying upon you when he took that photograph of you kissing George. Was that to put everyone off the scent, too? I must hand it to you, Patience, you're an ace at planning ahead. But where was it going to end? Did you intend to bump off the entire village to protect your criminal enterprise?"

Roy spewed a mucousy little cough.

"You're disgusting," Patience snapped.

Coughs.

"And . . . and your motive for all this is greed," I said, "or not outright greed, I suppose, since you are devoted to your father even if you're willing to lay waste to the rest of mankind. He's ill, chronically ill, with a lung ailment. He needs to move to a warmer climate, and you, knowing the hotel trade inside out, planned to take every dime you'd made in your smuggling scheme to buy a hotel in some warm place. Hawaii, perhaps, or California, or Bermuda. Why did I imagine for a second that those hotel brochures were for your honeymoon?"

Patience bared small, white teeth. "Because you noticed me touching my belly occasionally. My what an active imagination you have."

"We felt sorry for you," I said hotly. "Berta and I. We thought you were in a terrible predicament, dizzy in love with George and carrying his pea in your pod and—"

"Then my plan worked."

"And you, Mr. Ives." I regarded Roy. "Why did you burn that dossier for Patience? She stole it from Mrs. Lundgren's room, of course. Why did you tack up those photographs in front of the town hall? Clever of you, Patience, by the way, to have embarrassing pictures of yourself pinned up to direct suspicion elsewhere."

"I don't know," Roy said, his voice cracking.

"You *do* know why, you old fool!" Patience turned to me. "He'll do anything for wine."

"His French wine," I said. "You bring that down from Canada, too?"

"It's a small price to pay to have a puppet," Patience said. "Even a frightened puppet. Then again, I find fear makes people awfully pliable."

"Fear," I said. "Yes. That's one of your favorite tricks, isn't it? You tried to scare me away by throwing my dog's ball out on the ice. When that didn't work, you put the ball in my suitcase. And all along, you've been frightening everyone with that Slipperyback nonsense. You had your minion Titus Staples dress up in a bearskin and wear something on his boots that made bearlike prints in the snow—*so* inventive. You must've had him prowling around Goddard Farm the night you poisoned Judith, just so someone might chance to see him out the window, and you had him prowling around the ski jump when George was killed. You like to stir the pot, Patience. Keep everyone confused."

"It isn't difficult," she said in a nasty voice. "Some villages have one idiot, but Maple Hill has dozens."

I rushed on. "Stealing that dossier was your first error, Patience. You must have been prowling through Berta's things, and you saw it, and panicked. But the missing dossier is what kept us in town. If we'd gone home to New York, you would've gotten away with murder."

Patience's lips pinched.

"And your second error was allowing me to see you argue with Maynard Coburn. What were you arguing about? Had he hinted to you that he was a Fed on your tail? You crashed that stolen car, didn't you?"

"Enough talk," Patience said. "Let's get started."

"Get what started?" I asked blankly.

"Why do you suppose I brought Roy along? For decoration?" Patience gave an upward yank to Roy's already twisted arm.

He yelped, and his mouth remained open.

Patience's voice was brisk. "I'm going to kill you and Roy. Everyone will think Roy killed you—or perhaps the other way around—in a final confrontation about the murders. Roy shall take the blame—I've got it all worked out, I'll plant a few clues in his house for that fool Peletier to find—and Dad and I shall be on the next train out of this dump. I *was* going to wait another year or two, to save up more money, but it's obviously time to cut and run. I've already packed our trunks—that ruby ring is going to fetch a pretty sum—I'm so glad I pinched it from the breadbox as an afterthought. We're going to Hawaii, by way of Los Angeles. We'll change our names. Once I figure out how to buy some fake passports, we might keep going, to Fiji or Bali or Ceylon. Now. Step over here—come on. Snap to it."

I had stupidly supposed that Patience was using both hands to keep Roy's arm twisted like that behind his back. But now I saw that in one of her hands, she held a gun . . . and now she was aiming it at my heart.

Where are the police? Where is Mr. Currier?

I tried to swallow, but my dry throat couldn't swing it. "Isn't this a bit extreme?" I said. "A little melodramatic?"

"Stand over here," Patience said, waving the gun.

I saw now why the odor of alcohol was so strong: puddles of whiskey shone on the floor.

"I've got matches in my pocket," Patience said. "It'll be delicious to watch this damned factory go up on a ball of fire. The hours I've spent in here, bored out of my skull."

The gun was still aimed at my heart, but I would not bally well go down without a fight. So I did the only thing I could think of: I made a mad dash, straight for Patience and Roy.

The gun popped.

Roy screamed.

I rammed into both of them and toppled them in a writhing mound.

Patience swore and kicked.

Roy whimpered.

There was Patience's gun—she was struggling to lift it, even though her arm was pinned under Roy—it was quaveringly moving toward my face, her trigger finger slowly squeezing—

I jerked my own arm free and batted the gun.

It spun through the air and clattered several feet away.

"You bitch!" Patience snarled breathlessly.

I was struggling to my feet—"Roy," I cried, "keep her down!"—tottering to the gun, picking it up—

"Freeze!" a man shouted as a door crashed open. "Police! Put your hands up!"

I burst out laughing and crying at once. "Hello, Sergeant Peletier. You've come just in the nick of time."

You can bet your snow boots that we—Ralph, Berta, Cedric, and I—were on the train out of Maple Hill that afternoon. We just barely made it, the day having been eaten up in giving our statements to Sergeant Peletier and Clarence. Patience Yarker had been arrested for triple homicide and was sitting, sulking and ranting by turns, in the station's jail cell. The county sheriff had been summoned. Things weren't looking too peachy for Patience.

"We didn't make any money on this case," I said, feeling guilty as I snuggled myself a little deeper into my plush crimson train seat. At the Waterbury depot, we had booked a first-class parlor car on the Montreal–New London line. After all, we were on the cusp of Christmas.

"You'll make it into plenty of papers, though," Ralph said. "Starting with a write-up by Clive Persons in the *Cleveland Courier*."

"Which amounts to gratis advertisement for our agency," Berta said, sipping tea that had been festively supplemented with the contents of her flask.

I sipped my own festively supplemented tea. I was feeling *extraordinarily* supplemented, and we'd had a lavish meal in the dining car, too, topped off by extra dessert. After all, I had missed breakfast, and we had all missed lunch—and there had been nothing to eat at the police station but fruitcake. It was also Christmas Eve, and the dining car had been serving chocolate layer cake.

"I would've done it all for no publicity whatsoever," I said, "just to see the look on Maynard Coburn's face when our train was pulling out of the Maple Hill depot."

Ralph chuckled. "He looked like his self-esteem had taken a slug or two."

Maynard Coburn had been in his motorcar, stopped at the train crossing. I saw him from the train window, and he saw me, and his face had been livid.

"I suppose Maynard is just heartless enough to be a good Customs agent," I said.

"There were so very many heartless people in Maple Hill," Berta said. "To think I believed for a moment that it was a charming village."

"Any place is a mixed bag," Ralph said. "No place is perfect. Say, did you ever figure out what Rosemary Rogerson was up to, sneaking around the village with that notebook?"

"I did," Berta said. "She finally copped to it today when she saw me locked away in a jail cell—overcome with guilt, you see. She is writing a companion volume to her first two books, which is to be titled *Mrs. Rogerson's New England Cookbook.* The trouble is, she cannot cook. She is compiling recipes and helpful hints from the village women, with the goal, I understand, of passing it all off as her own to the publisher."

"What a cheat!" I said.

"Mm," Berta said, lifting her book, *Bedlam in Berlin,* and beginning to read. "Yet another reason to stick to reading fiction."

A little later, Berta was gently snoring with the book open on her lap, so I thought it wouldn't be terribly indiscreet to lean over and kiss Ralph.

"Did you see the message I wrote in the kitchen window last night?" I murmured against his cheek. I suddenly felt shy.

"I did," Ralph murmured back. "I've got something for you. It's just a stand-in, till we find something better." He pulled away a little and dug into his jacket pocket. He produced a scrap of red satin ribbon. "Lola, will you marry me?"

"Yes," I said, my throat bubbling up with laughter or sobs or both. I stuck out my left hand, fingers stretched. "Yes."

He tied a little bow on my ring finger with that bit of ribbon, and it was the prettiest ring I had ever seen.

"Oh—and Merry Christmas, kid." Ralph leaned closer again.

Our train chugged and whistled across the snowy dark landscape toward home.